He fingered the cool steel of the gun

Leroy Ponce always relaxed this way, and it was important for him to be at ease. Relaxed people went unnoticed.

Sitting in the courtroom, he watched and waited. Then he saw her. Rosalind Hart was the prosecutor on the case.

The false hairpiece and beard he wore itched, but he made no move to scratch. He looked down quickly and stayed perfectly still as the bailiff's eyes drifted in his direction. Those were the rules— never make eye contact and don't move.

The bailiff led in a jury panel and the judge read the indictment. A perceptible murmur rose at the mention of the defendant's name.

He still didn't know who his client, or quarry, was. But it was a lucky turn of fate that he'd met up with Ms. Hart again. When his assignment was over, he would settle an old score with her. He would think up something good for her while he waited for word from his employer. His fingers were beginning to perspire as they stroked the gun. He wanted the word to come soon. He wanted it to be *kill*.

ABOUT THE AUTHOR

M. J. Rodgers believes there is a special magic to the romantic mystery because it blends the most powerful of human needs: love and justice. M.J. was recently named one of the Best Romantic Mystery writers by *Romantic Times* magazine.

Books by M. J. Rodgers

HARLEQUIN INTRIGUE
102—FOR LOVE OR MONEY
128—A TASTE OF DEATH
140—BLOODSTONE
157—DEAD RINGER
176—BONES OF CONTENTION
185—RISKY BUSINESS

Don't miss any of our special offers. Write to us at the following address for information on our newest releases.

Harlequin Reader Service
P.O. Box 1397, Buffalo, NY 14240
Canadian address: P.O. Box 603,
Fort Erie, Ont. L2A 5X3

All the Evidence

M.J. Rodgers

Harlequin Books

TORONTO • NEW YORK • LONDON
AMSTERDAM • PARIS • SYDNEY • HAMBURG
STOCKHOLM • ATHENS • TOKYO • MILAN
MADRID • WARSAW • BUDAPEST • AUCKLAND

For Jerdan, whose love comes eloquently
wrapped in the million and one thoughtful things
he does for me each day

Harlequin Intrigue edition published November 1992

ISBN 0-373-22202-5

ALL THE EVIDENCE

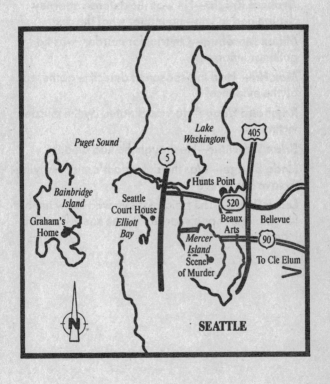

CAST OF CHARACTERS

Rosalind Hart—She was prosecuting the most sensational—and *deadliest*—case of her career.

Graham Knight—He was the defense attorney determined to win—no matter what the cost.

Milton Morebug—On trial for murder, was he guilty or innocent?

Max Hill—Had this seasoned detective gathered all the evidence?

Raymond Hogg—He was cheated by the murder victim.

Brian Wreckter—He thought he had an alibi.

Linda Dodge—Was the defendant's mistress lying to save her lover?

Leroy Ponce—The paid assassin who knew neither his employer nor his target. But he knew Rosalind Hart....

Chapter One

"I didn't kill Warren Beaver. I swear it."

Milton Morebug choked out his denial as though strong, invisible fingers clutched his throat.

Attorney Graham Knight studied his prospective client closely. Morebug was a short, bald, bony-looking man of fifty. All the sallow flesh around his crescent nose, cheeks, mouth and jaw sagged. Deep-set yellow-green eyes bobbed up and down beneath a prominent ridge of bushy gray eyebrows, reminding Graham of olives trying desperately to stay afloat in a stale gin fizz. Without a doubt, Milton Morebug's face looked like that of a guilty man.

Except Graham didn't look for guilt in faces. Graham looked for guilt in hands. Morebug's were open and steady on the arms of his ornately carved and laminated nineteenth-century rosewood armchair.

From the moment Graham had driven up to the security gates at Morebug's expensive Hunt's Point home on Lake Washington, he'd been filled with mixed emotions. On the one hand, he liked the idea of defending the man accused of Beaver's murder, but on the other, he was reminded that wealthy men often considered themselves above the law. Did Morebug?

Graham's fingers strummed rhythmically on the floral arms of a duplicate rosewood chair across from Morebug. He would have to learn more about this man before he made a decision. "Do you know who did kill Warren Beaver?" he asked.

Morebug cleared his throat noisily. He reached for a ready glass of Scotch sitting on a matching rosewood table and after studying the golden fluid for a moment took a swig. "No."

Graham stretched his long legs before him, feeling the heels of his shoes sink into the thick, red oriental carpet that topped the gleaming hardwood floor. He imagined himself a juror seeing Morebug sitting in the defendant's chair or on the witness stand. Nothing about the man was engaging. His lack of hair and chin didn't meet society's preconceived ideas of a strong character. Women of any age wouldn't find him attractive, and his supercilious air would no doubt automatically turn off a man.

Graham didn't like acknowledging the always present prejudices of a jury, but not to face them would be foolish. And what he faced now was that if he took this case, he would be representing a man who neither looked nor sounded believable.

Graham reached for the glass of brandy Morebug's silent, dark and faultlessly groomed wife had given him before vanishing. She had conveyed annoyance that her husband had been charged with murder, as though it was upsetting her daily schedule. Her desire to be elsewhere did not impress Graham.

But his surroundings did. Like the beautiful rosewood parlor suite, the rest of the room could have been a nineteenth-century display from the Smithsonian Institute. Graceful tapestries draped every wall. Elegant china pieces gleamed peacefully in dust-free display cases. Graham had found that a man who surrounded himself with beauty generally yearned for it in his soul.

Graham turned to his host. "Your previous lawyer got you released on a hundred-thousand-dollar bail. That's far less than what would be required for most wealthy men up against murder one charges."

Morebug frowned. "So?"

"So I've read through the testimony from the preliminary hearing. As far as I can see, Sanders and his co-counsel were doing a competent job. Why did you fire them?"

Morebug's olive eyes deepened. "Sanders and his flunky didn't believe I was innocent. I won't pay a lawyer to defend me who doesn't believe in my innocence."

Graham continued to watch Morebug's hands. One was steady around his glass. The other lay open and relaxed on the arm of his chair. "Your trial begins on Monday. Why did you wait until now to dismiss them?"

Morebug flicked a finger at the thick briefcase sitting beside Graham. "It's all there in those court documents that I messengered you yesterday morning. The prosecutor offered a deal two days ago. Second-degree murder if I pleaded guilty. Said I'd get fifteen years and be eligible for parole in eight. Sanders told me to take it."

Graham watched Morebug closely. "So that's when you found out that Sanders believed you were guilty?"

Morebug punctuated the vehemence in his voice with another swig of brandy. "Mealymouthed jerk said it was better than getting hanged for first-degree."

True, Graham thought. If one was guilty. And there was some hard evidence pointing to Morebug's guilt. If he took this case, he'd be representing the underdog. As far as he was concerned, that was another point in Morebug's favor.

Graham was back to strumming his fingers as he thought of the possibilities. "Did you instruct Sanders to reject the prosecutor's offer before firing him?"

Morebug ground his teeth. "No. I told him to get out, he was fired. Fool told me I'd be sorry. Said the only reason the prosecutor was even offering the deal was because Judson Fry, the deputy prosecutor on the case, had had a heart attack and the prosecutor was going to have to bring in an unprepared replacement on the scheduled trial date next Monday. Said I'd gotten lucky."

Graham was silent for several minutes as his fingers strummed a tune on the arms of his chair, his thoughts supplying a steady drumbeat.

Morebug's impatience finally overcame him. "Well, Knight? What do you think?"

Graham looked over at Morebug as he came out of his thoughts, a new gleam in his eyes. "I think, Mr. Morebug, that Sanders was right about your being lucky."

Morebug's eyes focused on Graham's with something like hope. "You mean you're going to represent me?"

"Yes."

"Because you believe I'm innocent?"

Graham leaned forward in a quick movement, coming within a foot of Morebug's face, looking straight into the bobbing green eyes. "Yes. I believe you're innocent. I won't defend a murderer."

Milton Morebug leaned back in his chair and exhaled heavily. "That's what they said about you. That's why I wanted you, Knight. You've got to prove I didn't do it."

Graham leaned back with a confident smile. "I don't have to prove you didn't do it. Under the law, you're presumed innocent. The prosecution has the burden of proof. My job will be to point out to the jury that the prosecutor's evidence of your guilt isn't really evidence at all."

Morebug inhaled deeply, holding on to the breath as though he was almost afraid to let it out. "Sanders said the prosecution has a strong case."

Graham picked up his glass of brandy and took a sip. "Sanders was right. I've read through the transcript of the preliminary hearing. But we have two very definite advantages."

Morebug raised hopeful eyes. "And they are?"

Graham used his fingers to count off his points. "First and foremost, you're innocent. That means all the circumstantial evidence gathered against you has been given the wrong interpretation. What I have to do is make it clear to the jury that the evidence has other, logical interpretations.

"Second, the county prosecutor has to assign a new deputy prosecutor to the case. Deputy prosecutors are not just standing by, Mr. Morebug. The prosecutor will have to pick someone with a full caseload—someone who probably won't even be given your case until the last minute."

Milton Morebug shook his head. "How can that help?"

Graham leaned back leisurely and wrapped his fingers around his own small snifter of brandy. "More than likely the prosecutor's office is waiting for your reply to the deal before it assigns your case to someone new. You see, if you take their offer, they won't have to waste one of their more competent litigators on your case. As your new attorney, I'm going to wait until Friday morning to inform them that you reject the deal."

Morebug still look perplexed. "And?"

"Look at it this way, Mr. Morebug. If you were an overworked deputy prosecutor, would you spend your evenings and weekend reviewing a case just dumped on you when you anticipated getting a postponement?"

Morebug licked his thin lips. "I think I'm beginning to understand. You mean the new deputy prosecutor won't be prepared on Monday?"

Graham took another small sip of the excellent brandy and replaced the glass on the table. "Exactly. But what's more important, we will be. And it won't be expected. And that's where our advantage comes in."

"But we've only got an advantage if the new deputy prosecutor doesn't get a postponement, isn't that right?"

Graham smiled. "That's right. And he won't. Judge Gloria Shotz is the lady on the bench. I've been before this judge, Mr. Morebug. For our purposes next Monday, you're lucky to have drawn her. She runs her courtroom like a drill sergeant at boot camp. Postponements, even for legitimate reasons, rub her the wrong way. Since we'll be ready, I'd lay odds that any request coming from the prosecution will fall on irritated ears."

Morebug didn't look convinced. "But the trial date is just a week away. How can you be ready by then?"

"To realize our advantage, I must be. Don't worry. I'm familiar with the main thrust of the prosecution's case already, and I've got a week to get up to speed on the rest.

Now I must leave you. There are some interesting aspects of this case that I think could use additional investigation.''

"Additional investigation?" Morebug echoed. "I paid a fortune for the private investigator Sanders hired. Are you telling me the guy missed something?"

Graham rose. "Let's just say that I have access to a very special investigator that Sanders didn't. And she's the best."

Morebug had risen with Graham and now followed him to the front door. He shrugged his bony shoulders. "I'm always willing to pay for the best. What do you want me to do?"

Graham looked down at his new client, a man who barely came up to his shoulder, and knew Morebug's shortness would also carry a stigma with the jury.

"I'll stop by this weekend and we'll go over everything you remember about the day and night Warren Beaver died. Since your wife was out of town that week, I realize she can't be a witness on your behalf. Still, it will be helpful if she could be in court each day, beginning with the jury selection. And your son, too. Juries like to see family support."

Morebug nodded. "My wife will be there. But my son may be away on business."

Graham extended his hand. "Do what you can to get him to the trial."

Morebug's returning grip was intense. He struck Graham as a man who compensated for his small stature by being very good at something. As Graham left his client's expensive home, he decided that something must be making money. There was no law against that. What was important was that Morebug was innocent.

As soon as Graham had driven his old silver Mercedes out of Morebug's long driveway and gone through the electronic security gates, he picked up the car phone and placed his call to his great-aunt. As he punched in her number, he wondered what Morebug would have said if he had told him that his great-aunt was going to be his special investigator on the case.

Fran Tulip answered on the first ring, her sweet, elderly voice bringing a smile to Graham's face.

"I've got a case that is just made for your particular brand of social sleuthing, Fran."

Fran's voice tinkled in his ear. "Gray, how delightful! I was just saying to Violet and Mabel the other day how it had been much too long since we had a juicy case from you. This is juicy, isn't it?"

Graham smiled as he turned the nose of his Mercedes up Hunt's Point Road. "The juiciest. I'm defending Milton Morebug."

Graham wasn't surprised when the sharp mind on the other end of the line didn't even pause. "The county assessor accused of killing that so-and-so commissioner of public lands? Well, well. So you believe he didn't do it?"

"That's the reason I've taken the case. What I want you and the ladies to do is to dig up everything you can about Warren Beaver."

"Hmm. You know, Mabel and Violet and I suspected him of doing a lot of shady deals during his term in office."

"That's why I've come to you, Fran. As I recall, just before Beaver died, you had started to dig into those deals for the Environmental League by getting some of his friends to talk. I want you to resume the sleuthing."

"Shouldn't be a problem. As you know, the ladies and I keep up with the social functions that Beaver's family and friends attend. When do you want us to get started?"

"This is the part that gets sticky, Fran. I've gotten the case late. Trial begins Monday at nine-thirty."

There was a slight hesitation on the other end. "You mean a week from *today?*"

Graham could almost see Fran's minty blue eyes widen in surprise. He proceeded quickly before too much doubt could begin to diminish her enthusiasm. "My predecessor sent the prosecution the standard defense letter demanding a list of all the evidence the defense is entitled to see. I have that list, a bill of particulars about the crime and the transcripts from the preliminary hearing. I can be at your place in under thirty minutes, and we can go over the areas that look promising.''

''But it's already seven-thirty at night!''

Graham smiled at Fran's gentle reprimand. ''Yes, isn't it great that you've got all the rest of this week and the weekend?''

Fran gave a little laugh. ''Such an optimist! I'm gratified at your confidence, Gray, but discovering what you'll need to know by Monday morning—''

''I don't need everything by Monday morning, Fran. Just by the end of next week. As a matter of fact, I'm already feeling so ready for Monday that I'm beginning to feel sorry for the deputy prosecutor who's going to have to go up against me.''

DEPUTY PROSECUTOR Rosalind Hart sprinted toward the closing elevator on the fifth floor of the King County Courthouse, juggling a thick folder of documents in one hand and a packed briefcase in the other. She knew the doors were going to close and at the last minute, she gave it her best dash as four people already standing inside the elevator did mannequin imitations. As she nearly bumped into the closing doors, she swore there should be a law against elevator passengers who stood by refusing to push the Open Door button to assist a fellow traveler.

A quick glance at her watch and she decided she didn't have time to wait for the arrival of another one of the notoriously slow elevator cars. With a firm grip on her burdens, she shouldered her way into the stairwell and began to climb the two flights of stairs separating her from her goal, gathering emotional as well as physical steam with each step.

It was bad enough that her scheduled week of vacation had been canceled, but to get an involved murder case dumped on her at the last minute was unforgivable.

Still, it didn't surprise her. The county prosecutor was a workaholic and thought everybody else should be. As long as he ignored weekends, sick leave and vacations, he expected his staff to do likewise. It was no wonder her colleague, Judson Fry, had just suffered a heart attack at the tender age of forty-one. If she didn't watch out, it could be happening to her in another ten years.

Another ten years. Dear God, she was thirty-one. Every time she thought about it, she was amazed. Where had the time gone? She had promised herself no more than three years in bondage to the county prosecutor. Now six had passed.

Rosalind pushed the unbidden thought aside. She didn't need more distractions this morning. She had to concentrate on getting her postponement and then getting to her interview at Lloyd and Nash. It was the chance she'd been waiting for. If she was accepted as a junior partner in that prestigious law firm, this would be the last case ever dumped on her again. She could forget all about the county prosecutor's office with its overworked and underappreciated staff.

By the time Rosalind reached the seventh floor, she was out of breath and patience. She shoved her briefcase underneath her arm and pushed on the door lever to exit the stairwell, glancing down at her watch. It was 9:28. She had two minutes.

Rosalind barreled into the hallway and immediately felt a shoulder blow, which knocked her off balance and caused her to lose her precarious hold on the folder in the crook of her arm. It fell with a resounding splat as papers shot out of loosened spines, fanning out in several directions across the floor.

Rosalind sighed heavily as she dropped to a squat and grabbed for her trial notes. "Great. Just what I needed."

The suited, muscular, dark-haired man who had just bumped into her stooped to help. "You, okay, Roz? You shot in front of me so fast, I didn't even see you coming."

Rosalind gave the man a turbid look. "I'm fine, Max. Sorry to be cranky. It's just that now I'm going to be late for Judge Shotz's court, and frankly I'd rather have a root canal."

Detective Max Hill grabbed the remaining papers and jumped to his feet. "Know what you mean. Let's make a dash for it."

Rosalind looked at Detective Hill in surprise. "This is one of your cases?"

Max smiled as he dumped the retrieved trial notes into Rosalind's outstretched hand. "Ever since the Mercer Island PD realized they had a well-known victim and decided to let the sheriff's department take the heat. Let's make tracks."

Max took hold of Rosalind's arm and literally pulled her down the hall to W760—the courtroom of Judge Gloria Shotz.

Rosalind made no protest until they were just outside the door. There she extricated Max's hand from her arm and handed him her briefcase and folders while she smoothed back a few recalcitrant strands of long red hair into her circumspect braid at the back of her head. Then she reclaimed her things and straightened her shoulders.

"Well, here goes nothing."

Rosalind pushed opened the wooden door to the courtroom of Seattle Superior Court Judge Gloria Shotz. The first thing she noticed as she stepped inside was that Roger Horn, Shotz's tall, thin court bailiff with an unruly mop of yellow hair, was just coming through the door from the judge's chambers, a move that signaled the imminent emergence of her honor. Without hesitation, Rosalind set off at a run for the table on the right of the courtroom reserved for the prosecution.

Roger Horn's squeaky voice cracked in her ears like static. "All rise and come to order. Superior Court is now in session, the Honorable Judge Gloria Shotz presiding."

Rosalind was out of breath but standing in position when Gloria Shotz flew out of her chambers, proud and erect. She swooped into the judge's chair, black robes billowing like trailing wings. Rosalind never ceased to wonder at the commanding presence of the munchkinlike woman, considering she was barely five-two and needed to sit on four pillows to bring her head and shoulders above the bench. Still, despite her small stature, Judge Gloria Shotz possessed the voice of Orson Welles and the black piercing eyes of Poe's raven. And as any attorney who had come up against her could testify, she was a force to be reckoned with.

"Be seated," boomed Judge Shotz. "In the case of the State versus Milton Morebug, I understand we have a few pretrial changes in personnel."

Judge Shotz turned to Rosalind. "Who represents the state?"

Rosalind rose to her feet. "Deputy Prosecutor Rosalind Hart, Your Honor."

Judge Shotz nodded, made a note and then swung her dark head in the direction of the defense table. "Who represents Milton Morebug?"

"Graham Knight, Your Honor."

Rosalind's head jerked to the defense table, her eyes wide in disbelief and denial. It couldn't be *him!*

He rose behind the defense table, his lean, tall body moving with a sinuous ease. Rosalind had always loved the way he moved—smoothly and yet so full of barely leashed energy. Not a strand of his thick, dark blond hair dared to fall out of place onto the forehead of that classically chiseled face, handsome beyond all mortal fairness. She stared, her brain and body stunned.

For the briefest of moments their eyes met and Rosalind held her breath. A gleaming gray look swept over her, like the warm sun on the pewter waters of Puget Sound. She could clearly hear the drumbeat of her heart pounding in her ears.

But there was no flicker of recognition from Graham Knight, and for that Rosalind was inordinately grateful.

Judge Shotz was saying something. Rosalind wasn't hearing it. Her mind was a mass of confusion as forgotten memories and surfacing emotions bombarded her thoughts in an unrelenting barrage.

"Ms. Hart!"

Rosalind snapped to attention at the vehemence in the judge's voice, pulling herself together with an effort. "I'm sorry, Your Honor. Would you please repeat what you said?"

Judge Shotz's voice bellowed in Rosalind's ears. "Ms. Hart, I do not like having to repeat myself! You will pay attention to these proceedings. Do I make myself clear?"

Rosalind swallowed uncomfortably. "Yes, Your Honor. Please accept my apologies. It won't happen again."

"See that it doesn't. Now for the third time, are the People ready to proceed?"

Rosalind shifted her weight from one high-heeled shoe to the other. "Your Honor, the People request a continuance."

The already dark countenance of Judge Shotz darkened even more. She growled her question. "On what grounds?"

"On the grounds that the previous prosecutor of record, Judson Fry, suffered a heart attack and that I haven't had adequate time to acquaint myself with the particulars of the case. I am therefore unprepared to represent the People properly at this time."

Judge Shotz's dark eyes bored holes into Rosalind's face. "When did Mr. Fry suffer this heart attack?"

Rosalind stood straight. "Ten days ago, Your Honor."

"And you haven't been able to acquaint yourself with the facts of this case in that time?"

"I wasn't given the case until five o'clock last Friday, Your Honor. However, I understand that defense has also changed attorneys last week, so I believe my request for a continuance will satisfy the defense's need for more time as well as my own."

Judge Shotz turned to the defendant's table. "Does a continuance express your wishes, Mr. Knight?"

Graham was still standing, a small smile circling his lips. "The prosecution is mistaken, Your Honor. Defense is ready to proceed and urges that the deputy prosecutor's request for a continuance be denied on the grounds that it conflicts with Mr. Morebug's constitutional right to a speedy trial."

Rosalind stared at Graham with her mouth open. She couldn't have heard him right. He couldn't be prepared to go ahead with his defense with only a few days' preparation!

"Good point, Mr. Knight," Judge Shotz boomed. "Request for continuance denied."

Rosalind's eyes flew to the bench. "But, Your Honor—"

"Ms. Hart," Judge Shotz bellowed, "Defense is quite right. Milton Morebug is entitled to a speedy trial. Just because the prosecutor's office hasn't efficient backup systems in cases of illness, that is no reason to penalize this man. Mr. Morebug has a heavy accusation hanging over his head. He is due his day in court, and this is it. Now if you are truly unprepared to proceed, I am prepared to dismiss all charges against Mr. Morebug."

Dismiss all charges? Let a murderer walk? After nearly a year of hard work that might have even contributed to Judson Fry's heart attack? Rosalind took a deep breath and straightened to her full and considerable height. "No, Your Honor. That isn't necessary. The People will proceed now in the case against Milton Morebug."

Judge Shotz turned toward her bailiff. "Mr. Horn, has a panel of prospective jurors been called?"

"Yes, Your Honor," Roger Horn said in his high-little voice. "They are waiting in the jury assembly room."

"Then bring them in, Mr. Horn, and let's get this show on the road. Court will take a five-minute recess while the prospective jurors are given their entrance cue."

Judge Shotz rapped her gavel and descended from her pillows to flap toward the judge's chambers. Rosalind turned quickly to Detective Max Hill, desperately pushing down a swell of emotion that threatened to engulf her.

"I've got to make a call."

He wore a startled look. "Now? The jurors will be here in a minute."

Rosalind didn't answer. She was already halfway toward the door at the back of the courtroom.

"MR. RICE, THANK YOU for taking my call right away," Rosalind said as she leaned into the public telephone booth down the hall from the courtroom. "I'm afraid I'm not going to be able to make my interview at ten-thirty as scheduled."

Steve Rice's previously chipper voice developed a somber tone. "What's the problem, Ms. Hart?"

Rosalind took a breath. "I've been unable to secure a continuance on a case that came to trial this morning. I'll be in court at the time of our scheduled meeting."

Rosalind held her breath as the silence on the other end of the line stretched through several seconds. "That is most unfortunate, Ms. Hart. You realize I'll only be in Seattle this morning. I'm flying to Chicago this afternoon to interview another candidate, and then on to Atlanta Wednesday."

Rosalind licked dry lips. "I apologize for this short notice, Mr. Rice. I specifically asked for and was originally granted today as vacation so I could be sure nothing would interfere with our appointment, but the prosecutor revoked his approval last Friday when he dumped this case on me. Believe me, the situation is out of my hands."

"Hmm. I do sympathize, Ms. Hart, but as you know, the interviews for this opening were set up weeks ago. I've got to keep to the schedule in order to ensure that all candidates have been seen and evaluated in the time allotted for selection."

Rosalind shifted uncomfortably in front of the telephone as she watched the second hand on her watch count down the five-minute recess and listened to her future fading away. Her voice ascended in dismay. "Mr. Rice, are you saying that if I miss today's interview, I won't be considered for the job *at all?*"

Rice's tone turned tight. "Your trial experience is impressive, Ms. Hart, but an interview is essential to determine if you possess that compatible mixture of personality and presence that will complement our firm. My recommendation must be before the senior partners by the end of this week. I'm sure you understand the difficulty of my position.''

Rosalind understood all right. She wasn't getting the job. She gave Rice a hollow thank-you for his time and hung up. Her spirit felt leaden as she trudged back down the long hallway to the courtroom of Judge Gloria Shotz. There, waited a man she had hoped to never see again and a case for which she was totally unprepared. The last thing she wanted to do was go inside.

LEROY PONCE SAT in the back of Judge Gloria Shotz's courtroom and fingered the cool steel of the gun hidden in the pocket of his gray jacket. It was a relaxing way to pass the time, and it was important for him to relax. Relaxed people went unnoticed.

That was his gift—to be unnoticed until it was time to strike. Of course, he might not be required to kill. His client had been very insistent about that. "Just watch and wait," was his last written instruction.

So Ponce watched. Waited. And found an unexpected bonus to his assignment when Rosalind Hart appeared as the prosecutor on the case. A lucky turn of fate. When his assignment was over, he would settle an old score. And in the meantime, there was no reason why he couldn't have some fun. Ponce fidgeted in expectation and then caught himself. Mustn't get restless.

The false hairpiece and beard he wore itched, but he made no move to scratch. He looked down quickly and stayed perfectly still as the bailiff's eyes drifted in his direction. Those were the key ingredients—never make eye contact and don't move. People who didn't see your eyes rarely remembered your face, and calm people didn't attract attention.

Ponce didn't relish being in the courtroom every day. People who established patterns in his business got spotted. But he followed instructions, and orders were that he be here.

He was lucky that this trial was attracting media attention and there were other spectators. Still, it was a damn nuisance. But he had to play along until he got his money.

His money. Ponce's gray face sprouted a small frown despite his diligence to keep his countenance bland. It bothered him that he had to wait until the entire job was completed to get the bulk of his payment. It also annoyed him that he still didn't know who either his client, or his target was. There was a time when he wouldn't have agreed to take on an assignment under such circumstances.

But times had changed. He was older. And thanks to Rosalind Hart, he had a conviction. The offers for his services had dried up with that record. If he was going to spring his old man out of that state nuthouse, he had to have the money to grease the right hand.

The bailiff led in a jury panel and the judge read the indictment. A perceptible murmur rose at the mention of Morebug's name. For the next few hours, Ponce watched prospective jurors fill out questionnaires while a few were excused from serving by the judge because of personal hardship or preconceived ideas about the case from media coverage.

Not knowing who his quarry was, Ponce paid attention to everyone, particularly Rosalind Hart. Fate had thrown them back together, and he was determined to take advantage of his opportunity. He would think up something good for her while he waited for word from his employer. His fingers were beginning to perspire as they stroked the gun. He wanted the word to come soon. He wanted it to be to *kill*.

Chapter Two

Graham Knight watched Deputy Prosecutor Rosalind Hart with interest that expanded beyond his desire to assess her expertise at interviewing prospective jurors. The tall, gorgeous redhead was a knockout and a very unexpected added attraction.

She certainly wasn't the first female prosecutor he had faced, but she was far and above the most stunning. Contrasting with the fire in her hair was skin as smooth and white as milk. Her voice was a full contralto, deep and delicious as she addressed the first twelve people whose names had been drawn to sit in the jury box.

"Ladies and gentlemen, I'm Deputy Prosecutor Rosalind Hart. I will be representing the state in the matter of the People versus Milton Morebug. As the judge read to you earlier, Mr. Morebug, the county assessor, is accused of killing Warren Beaver, the state's commissioner of public lands. You have all sworn that you know neither of these men. When the judge read to you the list of the prosecution's possible witnesses, each of you indicated that no one on the list sounded familiar."

Graham watched the undisguised interest in the eyes of the prospective male jurors as Rosalind addressed them. Some looked as though they were already on her side, and that didn't bode well for his client. His initial anticipation of watching her in court for the next few weeks was replaced with concern.

Rosalind continued. "All of these precautions are made to find an unbiased jury, ladies and gentlemen. In legal terms, this process—questioning prospective jurors like yourselves—is called a voir dire and considered to be one of the most important features of our trial-by-jury system. That's because it's absolutely essential that Milton Morebug is judged by men and women who are impartial. Now to be absolutely sure of your impartiality, I'll be asking some additional questions. Please don't be offended if some of my questions seem personal. I'll just be trying to get to know you."

Graham could see Rosalind had the prospective jurors' attention. Her confident, erect posture projected a natural honesty and ease that were unmistakable.

Rosalind began by addressing each prospective juror by name without having to refer to the questionnaires they had prepared. She started off asking general questions about their lives. She listened attentively, more like an interested friend than a prosecutor. Graham watched the stiff apprehension in their hands and faces melt under her deft handling. She had softened them considerably.

"Ladies and gentlemen, I wish this crime had been witnessed. I wish I could tell you somebody would be taking the stand in this court and saying, 'I saw Milton Morebug shoot Warren Beaver.' That would make my job and yours much easier."

Rosalind paused and began to pace down the jury box. "But, that is not the case. You see, most murders are not witnessed by other people simply because most murderers take great pains to commit the act in private. They don't want to be caught. Warren Beaver's murderer was no exception."

Rosalind had walked the length of the jury box. She was now in front of seat number one. As before, she addressed the prospective juror by name. "Mr. Brown, do you think you could convict a person of murder even though no one actually saw that person commit the crime?"

Graham looked down at his copy of the juror's questionnaire. Brown was sixty, a retired military man who under earlier questioning had admitted to Rosalind he liked collecting stamps and constructing model ships. Graham's eyes raised to the contemplative look on the prospective juror's face as Brown answered Rosalind's question. "If the evidence of his guilt was compelling enough, yes, I could find him guilty."

Rosalind turned to juror number two. "And you, Ms. Tyrell. Could you find a man guilty of murder in the first degree even though no eyewitness came forward?"

Ms. Tyrell took a little longer in her answer. Graham identified her as a twenty-four-year-old cosmetics clerk for a downtown department store. Her heavily made-up face still looked uncertain when she finally answered. "I suppose so."

"You're not sure, Ms. Tyrell?"

"What evidence will be presented against him?"

Rosalind's tone was definite. "According to the law, the prosecution must prove means and opportunity. I will also present the motive to Mr. Morebug's crime against Warren Beaver. So you will have all three, Ms. Tyrell. Motive, means and opportunity. Can you convict based on them?"

The juror straightened her shoulders as though challenged. "Yes, if everything pointed to him."

One by one Rosalind went through the rest of the prospective jurors in the box. Each in turn gave some type of affirmative answer that they thought they could convict someone without eyewitness testimony to the crime if the other evidence was convincing.

Graham could see what Rosalind was doing. She was getting the prospective jurors to go on record that an eyewitness wasn't necessary.

Graham listened intently as Rosalind continued her mental maneuvering of the jury panel. He found himself admiring the way she gave her attention to each and let them feel the strength of her focus with the forward tilt to her head and immediate acknowledgment of their answers.

Without a doubt, this deputy prosecutor knew what she was doing.

He felt a small twinge. Under other circumstances, he would have enjoyed becoming more intimately acquainted with this lively lady who moved with such poise and professionalism.

But he was going to win this trial. For the sake of his innocent client, he must. He would be pulling out all the stops in an aggressive defense and throwing this deputy prosecutor off balance, hard and often. That didn't exactly make for an atmosphere conducive to the fostering of warm feelings.

He watched Rosalind give each of the prospective jurors a thoughtful look just prior to asking her final question. "Would you put aside all possible prejudices and agree to make a decision about the guilt or innocence of Milton Morebug based solely on the evidence presented in this trial?"

One by one they told her yes as she rewarded them with a brilliant smile. He knew she had them in the palm of her hand.

Judge Shotz turned toward Graham as Rosalind took her seat at the prosecutor's table.

"Mr. Knight?"

It was his turn to begin questioning the prospective jurors. He rose casually and carefully walked to within five feet of the jury box and smiled. "Good afternoon, ladies and gentlemen. My name is Graham Knight. I'm defending Milton Morebug."

Rosalind watched Graham move closer to the jury box, like an ardent lover sure of his welcome. Over the past couple of hours, she'd worked hard to win over those people. Now a knot of anxiety began to tie itself in her stomach as Graham's voice rode in on confident waves.

"As each of you responded to the prosecution just now, I couldn't help but admire how carefully you considered your answers. She asked some hard questions, didn't she?"

Graham nodded his head, and several heads of the prospective jurors joined him. "And from your carefully considered answers, I think you're all beginning to realize that the job of a juror is not an easy one."

Heads continued to nod as Graham paced sideways. "Yes, it's a difficult job, maybe the hardest citizens in a democratic society can perform. You see, you'll be carrying the life of another human being in your hands. And as thoughtful individuals, there are times when you'll be buffeted by swells of doubt. For the sake of Milton Morebug, I must know if you are strong enough for these dark and difficult waters."

Graham stopped to make steady eye contact with each of the prospective jurors. Rosalind saw the brightness of his smile flash like a lighthouse beacon to twelve lost ships on those "dark and difficult waters" he had described.

"What I will do now is test how strong you will be if given the precious burden of life to carry through to a just verdict. I'm going to ask you some questions. They are tough ones. Sometimes the answers will be even tougher. Share your honesty with me as you have with Ms. Hart. That's all I ask."

Rosalind watched Graham pivot and face Mr. Brown. The original knot in her stomach got another twist.

Brown's hands clasped together and folded over his ample tummy in a defensive position. During Rosalind's interview of Brown, Graham had noticed the man's hands had remained open on the arms of his chair.

Graham paced forward and watched Brown's knuckles turning white. The man's clasp had tightened. "You mentioned to Ms. Hart that you live in Bellevue off Highway 405. Do you own a home there?"

"Yes," Brown said.

Graham took a few paces away from Brown. As he paced forward again, he could see the tension once again gathering in the man's curling fingers. He tried a smile. "That's a lovely area."

"My wife and I think so."

Graham paced away again and Brown visibly relaxed.

Everything about Brown told Graham his comfort zone was a thin one where Graham was concerned. That was not the right way for a juror to feel about the defense attorney.

"You mentioned your wife is a real-estate agent?"

"Yes," Brown replied.

Graham stayed back, knowing Brown's tension would be less. "She must have seen a tremendous increase in the cost of homes over the last few years."

Brown's lips twisted. "It's ridiculous."

Graham cocked an eyebrow. "Ridiculous?"

Brown crossed his right calf over his left knee. "Hell, yes. We bought our current home ten years ago. In that time it's nearly doubled in value. Were we to buy that exact same house today, we couldn't afford it."

Graham nodded. "And with the increased selling prices of the homes around you, I presume property taxes are skyrocketing?"

Brown made a grunting noise. "Into outer space. My taxes went up fifteen percent in just this last year alone. Greed's running rampant."

Graham wore a mildly confused look. "Greed? Whose greed, Mr. Brown?"

"Why, the guys who keep jacking up the price of everybody's assessed valuation until pretty soon we'll be paying more money in taxes than we did to buy the blasted houses!"

Graham turned to Judge Shotz with a carefully regretful look on his face. "In view of this prospective juror's prejudicial statements regarding tax assessments, defense requests that the court dismiss Mr. Brown on cause, Your Honor."

Rosalind was on her feet. "Your Honor, may we approach the bench?"

Judge Shotz nodded and both Graham and Rosalind walked up. Rosalind's pulse beat faster as Graham stepped beside her, the arm of his suit coat lightly brushing hers. The scent of his familiar cologne filled her senses with all the tender memories of youthful expectation—and all the subsequent cruel disillusionment of dashed hopes.

Judge Shotz laid her hand over her microphone and tilted her head of short, dark straight hair.

Rosalind launched her protest with a forceful whisper.

"Your Honor, Defense is deliberating trying to make displeasure with property taxes an issue in this case. Mr. Morebug isn't being tried for improper tax assessments. He's being tried for first-degree murder. If Mr. Knight is allowed to dismiss everyone who doesn't want to pay property taxes from this jury, he'll be eliminating every home owner in King County!"

Graham shook his head. "Your Honor, Ms. Hart is missing a very important point. I'm defending the county assessor. An individual with a prejudice against the man who holds the county assessor's office clearly cannot be considered a fair and impartial juror in determining Mr. Morebug's guilt or innocence on any charge."

Rosalind turned toward Graham. "Mr. Brown never referred to the defendant even once while voicing his displeasure with his property taxes!"

Graham's face broke into a wry smile. "And just because he didn't refer to him by name you think he's forgotten Morebug is the county assessor?"

"That's enough!" Judge Shotz commanded.

Rosalind turned to face the judge's bright black eyes, feeling like a scolded child. "I've heard your arguments for and against," Judge Shotz said. "Now we will return to open court and I will rule on Mr. Knight's challenge for cause."

Graham and Rosalind returned to their respective tables. Judge Shotz gave them a moment then addressed the prospective jurors, removing her hand from her mouthpiece. "The court upholds Mr. Knight's challenge of Mr. Brown for cause. Mr. Brown, thank you for coming. You are excused."

As Brown left the jury box, Rosalind gulped down her disappointment. She had worked hard to cultivate Brown during the questioning and he had responded well. As a retired military officer, she felt confident that his sympathies would have been with the upholding of law and order and consequently favorable to the prosecution's case. He would have been a tough, solid ally on the jury, and Graham had gotten him excused without even using one of his peremptory challenges. This was not a good beginning.

Graham next turned to prospective juror number seven, Ms. Quiller, a forty-year-old supervisor at the telephone company. Rosalind liked the way Ms. Quiller had answered her questions with a quick confidence. She was intelligent and attentive. Rosalind wanted her on the jury.

As Graham began his questioning of Ms. Quiller, Rosalind watched the woman's interested face as she answered easily and pleasantly. She showed neither bias for or against the defense attorney. Finally Graham reached that point in his questioning that Rosalind dreaded. "Ms. Quiller, do you own a home?"

Rosalind held her breath. "No," Ms. Quiller replied.

Rosalind exhaled her breath thankfully.

"Have you always rented?" Graham asked.

"I've lived in the same apartment for nearly fifteen years."

"You must have a good relationship with your landlord," Graham said. "Ever talk about property taxes with him?"

"No," Ms. Quiller replied. "We don't discuss such mundane stuff. He's a retired police officer and has a lot of great stories to share."

"A retired police officer?" Graham echoed. "Ms. Quiller, tell me. Do you think police officers are less likely to lie than other people?"

Ms. Quiller shrugged. "I think they're more honest than the average person. That's why they become officers. They're concerned about protecting society against lawlessness."

Anticipation tied new knots in Rosalind's stomach. She knew where Graham was going.

"Ms. Quiller," Graham continued. "If a police officer took the stand and swore to tell the truth in this court, do you think he or she would ever lie?"

Ms. Quiller didn't hesitate. "Of course not."

Graham smiled and turned to Judge Shotz. "Defense moves to excuse Ms. Quiller for cause, Your Honor."

"Your Honor—" Rosalind began.

Judge Shotz raised her hand to stop Rosalind's protest. "I know what you're going to say, Ms. Hart. Before I rule on this, Mr. Knight, I'll ask my own questions to clarify."

Shotz turned her attention to Ms. Quiller in the jury box. "Are you saying, Ms. Quiller, that knowing nothing else about an individual other than he was a police officer, you would take his word over someone else's who took the stand in this courtroom and swore to tell the truth?"

"You mean if they didn't agree?" Ms. Quiller asked.

"That's right, Ms. Quiller. If the testimony of two witnesses—one a police officer and one not—conflicted, would you automatically assume the police officer was telling the truth?"

"Wouldn't you?" Ms. Quiller replied.

Judge Shotz screwed up her lips. "I'd say that's a whopping affirmative. Court upholds Mr. Knight's motion to excuse Ms. Quiller on cause. You may return to the jury assembly room, Ms. Quiller."

Rosalind sat on the edge of her chair, wondering who was next to get the ax, as Graham turned back toward the jury. It was a major surprise when Graham approached Ms. Tyrell, prospective juror number two. The young woman's face stretched into a smile that was blinding. Graham asked her some gentle, innocuous questions. Ms. Tyrell bubbled like warmed soda. Rosalind sighed. Well, those things had to be expected. Human nature being what it was, good-looking men just automatically had an edge with impressionable young women.

How well she knew. The years faded away and Rosalind saw herself as twenty-two again, the shy, gangly first-year law student in awe of Graham Knight, the suave, sophisticated third-year law student and editor of the *Washington University Law Review.*

Then with a start she suddenly realized that Graham had asked Ms. Tyrell a question she was having trouble answering. Cursing herself for her momentary lack of attention, Rosalind strained with every fiber of her being to try to understand what was causing the woman's pause.

Ms. Tyrell bit her bright coral lips. "Let me get this straight. You want to know what I would do if I was the only one on the jury who thought the defendant was innocent?"

"Yes, Ms. Tyrell."

Long coral nails scraped Ms. Tyrell's thin wrist. "Well, I'd try to convince the others I guess."

Graham's voice was low and gentle. "And if after all your effort they were still unconvinced?"

Her eyes stared up at him. "Then we wouldn't be able to come to an agreement, would we?"

Graham watched her adoring face for a moment before he spoke. "Ms. Tyrell, even if every one else voted guilty, could you still vote innocent if your conscience told you that Milton Morebug did not commit this murder?"

"Of course."

"Even if the other members of the jury got angry at you? Accused you of being wrong or obstinate? Maybe even yelled at you?"

Ms. Tyrell's straight little teeth clenched. "Yelling at me would do them no good. I never change my mind once it's made up."

Graham flashed her an award-winning smile and thanked her for her strength of character. Rosalind was sure after that deft maneuvering Ms. Tyrell had already made up her mind that the defendant was innocent and she would stick to it. She wrote "PC" next to her name for a later peremptory challenge. Graham had stepped toward prospective juror number four, Mr. Clam.

Another knot found its way into Rosalind's stomach. Clam was an accountant and Rosalind liked to have accountants on juries. They knew how to pay attention to details and add up the evidence presented. She kept her fingers crossed that Graham was just going to ask him the same type of "conditioning" questions as he had Ms. Tyrell.

"Mr. Clam, do you think Milton Morebug is guilty or innocent?"

Rosalind groaned inwardly. There was no way she could warn the prospective juror of the trap that had just been set for him. Clam shrugged. "I have no idea. There's been no evidence presented to convince me one way or the other."

Graham's smooth forehead sprouted an instant frown. "Mr. Clam, I'm sorry but our judicial system doesn't work that way. Each of us is presumed innocent under the law. No one has to present evidence to you that Milton Morebug is innocent. On the contrary, you *must* presume he is innocent. The burden of proving Mr. Morebug guilty rests with the prosecution."

Graham's voice rose, carrying throughout the courtroom. "And ladies and gentlemen, I want you all to understand why that concept of innocence is so important, why it must be fully and completely accepted in your minds before you proceed to judge the evidence presented in this trial."

Graham deliberately made eye contact with each of the remaining jurors before resuming what was turning into a statement rather than a questioning session of Mr. Clam.

"Each and every one of you should be convinced that Milton Morebug sits before you an innocent man."

Graham paused for effect before continuing. "And in order for any of you to change your mind, the prosecuting attorney must present compelling evidence that Milton Morebug killed Warren Beaver. And that evidence must be so compelling that you hold not even a shred of reasonable doubt that Milton Morebug is guilty."

Graham's arm slowly raised and extended, his open hand reaching toward the defendant. "And if the prosecuting attorney fails to present such compelling evidence, ladies and gentlemen, your job, no, *your sworn duty,* is to let this innocent man, Milton Morebug, go free."

He kept eye contact with the jury for a few moments more before dropping his arm and turning to the judge. "Your Honor, the defense regretfully excuses Mr. Clam for cause."

Rosalind slumped back in her chair. No doubt about it, Graham Knight knew exactly what he was doing. No prospective juror in that courtroom was thinking anything but that Milton Morebug was innocent at that moment.

She sighed. This was going to be a long jury-selection process. Still, King County's decent, hardworking citizens were depending on her to do her best to put lawbreakers behind bars, despite how good-looking or smooth talking their lawyers were. She was just going to have to be better and smarter than Graham Knight.

The brave pep talk brought confidence and a smile to her lips. It would feel good to beat Graham. He was so imbued with his own importance—so contemptuous of others' feelings. Well, there were other people in the world and it was about time Graham Knight found that out.

Rosalind rose to her feet. Let the jury-selection process take all week. After all, the more days it took to select this jury, the more nights she would have to get up to speed with this case. Fortified with this added logic, Rosalind stepped forward with renewed energy to begin the examination of the fresh batch of prospective jurors who had been called to replace the ones Graham had gotten excused.

GRAHAM FELT TIRED AFTER a long ferry ride and battling the heavy downpour and bumper-to-bumper traffic to get to his home on Bainbridge Island. The storm that had begun that morning showed no signs of abating. Being a native of Washington, he had long ago accepted the dark winter days and heavy precipitation, but that didn't mean he liked them.

He was glad to finally get out of the rain as he closed the door to his secluded wood-and-glass A-frame house tucked away on the southeast corner of the island.

Carefully he removed his soaked raincoat and hung it on the clothes tree by the door. Then he bent down to turn on the small lamp in the entry, dropping the Seattle newspapers that carried accounts of the opening day of the trial. Later he would read them. Now he headed toward the large built-in, brick-faced wood stove in the redwood-beamed living room and lit the wood and paper already stacked in its hearth. In a moment it was blazing warmly. He put his hands out, reaching for the licks of heat in the otherwise cold house.

He liked fires. They could bring warmth or scorch you if you got too close. They kept you on your toes. He bent down and threw another log onto the licking flames.

Now, as he stared into the white-hot glow encased in the blazing red flames, he began to receive an unbidden image of Rosalind Hart's flaming hair and white skin.

Graham decided she fit there—amid a conflagration. Every time he'd won a point that day, she'd sparked back hot and sizzling. He didn't know many attorneys who handled defeat so well. Her strength made defending his client more difficult, but he couldn't help but admire her for it.

Still, getting Milton Morebug acquitted was what he'd set out to do and it was what he would do. The jury-selection process was coming along well. If it continued to progress as it had today, it might take all week before the right twelve men and women and four alternates were chosen. Which meant the prosecution would begin its case on the following Monday.

It was a mixed blessing. On the one hand, a long jury selection gave him more time to prepare. On the other hand, from the way Rosalind Hart had memorized the first twelve prospective jurors' names and faces literally within minutes, he knew she was a quick study. No doubt she was reviewing the trial notes and investigative reports right now. It wouldn't be long before she was up to speed and any advantage he'd gotten from pushing her into trial early would be lost.

He'd best check with Fran to see what progress her special detective team had made. But as he reached for the phone, he could see the red light from the answering machine blinking impatiently away. He pressed the message button.

His ex-wife's voice pierced the air in a familiar whine. "Oh, Graham, the car got dented in the parking lot at the shopping mall! No one left a note. What am I going to do? It was so embarrassing to drive it home. Everyone was looking. The paint is all scraped and—"

Graham punched the message button to cut off a lament that he knew by heart. He sank into the couch and put his head in his hands. What a blind fool he'd been to marry Tami those three years before.

She was beautiful and she seemed to love him. At least it felt that way when she kept asking him what she should wear and what she should do about things. He thought she valued his opinion. But within a month after marrying her, he finally realized Tami sought his advice because she wanted him to make the decisions for her. And when he couldn't or didn't, chaos followed.

Overdrawn bank accounts. Overdosed pills. She hadn't even been able to keep the same psychiatrist for more than one session. Before the first year was up, Graham admitted defeat and filed for divorce.

Now when he looked back, he could see all the signs had been there, if only he had looked. At twenty-eight, she was still living with her parents. After seven years of flitting in and out of college, she still had no major, much less a degree. She had married him so he could assume the role her parents were performing—her keeper. And even now after he'd legally snipped the knot, she still hung on, trying to involve him with her personal problems.

When he didn't call her back, he knew she'd contact her parents and they would continue to give her the support that kept her a dependent child.

And one day maybe she'd stop calling and reminding him how foolish he had been to fall in love and get married. He hoped that would be soon. Graham Knight did not like to be reminded he'd been a fool.

ROSALIND SQUINTED AT Max Hill's investigative reports as she leaned over the kitchen counter of her apartment above Pike Place Market overlooking Puget Sound.

It was a tiny place with outlandishly painted walls, a different color for each room. When she had moved in six years before, she had told herself it was only until she could pay back her student loans. But the loans were paid and still she stayed. It was comfortable. It was home.

The market had closed hours before and quiet reigned beneath her floorboards. Her contact lenses were soaking in solution, and she had donned her backup glasses as the hour got late and her eyes burned from the strain of so many hours of reading. Her back ached from her bent-over position. She ignored the physical discomforts as she continued to flip the pages, huddled over the counter in her mustard-colored kitchen. There was still a lot of material to review.

Dinner had been a crisp Golden Delicious apple and a bowl of hot chicken noodle soup. Her stomach was reminding her that that had been many hours before. She hugged her bathrobe to her chilled frame, tucked her stocking feet beneath its flannel hem and blocked out everything but the task before her.

She could tell she'd inherited a strong case. Still, she knew she couldn't take conviction for granted—not as long as Graham Knight was Milton Morebug's attorney.

She tried to focus her attention back to the case notes, but it was no use. As soon as she'd thought of Graham again, his image clouded her thoughts like the thick smoke surrounding a freshly extinguished candle.

Giving up even trying to put him out of her mind, she scooted off the barstool and padded into the tiny, bright blue living room and headed directly for the bookshelves. It had been years since she saw the picture, but her hand fluttered to it like a homing pigeon, pecking it out of an old law book dictionary. She had filed him under *tort*—an injury committed to the person or property of another.

His thick blond hair crowned his head without an errant strand. His classic features showed to perfection in an easy polished smile that exposed perfectly straight teeth. He looked almost as good as he had looked in court today. Beneath this picture she had cut out of the university's yearbook were the notations of numerous awards received during his editorship of the *Law Review*.

There was another picture in the law dictionary. Its corner was sticking out of the page that defined corpus delicti, loosely translated—the victim's body. Rosalind slipped the picture out and she found herself staring at the unsmiling girl with the short red hair, thick-framed glasses and sturdy orange zits. The girl seemed a stranger to her, and yet behind those closed lips she knew hid a broken front tooth that the girl's parents had not had the money to fix.

It was fixed now. She, unlike Graham, had changed a lot in the past nine years. She caught a look at herself in the study mirror. Even wrapped in the old bathrobe and with the glasses back on her nose, very little remained of that terribly plain girl in the picture. No wonder Graham hadn't recognized her today. She barely recognized herself.

She looked back at the pictures and the years faded before her eyes, and once again she was that gangly first-year law student, hugging a chair in the back of the lecture hall and hanging on every word as third-year law student Graham Knight addressed her class. She had noticed him earlier walking around in his cashmere sweater, and she had drooled with the rest of the adoring one-L women. As he encouraged them to find time in their busy first year to help with research for articles on the *Law Review,* she saw a way to win his attention and approval.

She'd been first in line to volunteer and offered to research a criminal law case, having learned criminal law was his preference. It took her a month of grueling writes and rewrites, but finally she'd honed her analysis to perfection. Holding her masterpiece in shaking hands, she approached Graham with exultation in her heart. He would read her research and smile and tell her how good it was and all those memories of missed meals and sleep would fade in this, her shining hour.

But nothing had shone in that hour for Rosalind. Graham had snatched the pages from her extended fingers, given the first paragraph a glance and then dumped her work into his wastebasket. "Lousy case selection. There's nothing there that I find even remotely appealing."

Rosalind's thoughts returned to the present, feeling the pain shoot through her just as though it was yesterday. She looked away from the pictures in her hands and the one that burned in her mind's eye. The wind of the Sound pounded against her living-room windows as the early December torrent oozed across the panes in slimy little streaks. It had been raining on that night he broke her heart, too—small, hard pellet-size drops that had beaten her down in that long lonely walk back to the dorm.

Her eyes narrowed on the battering rain as a new determination rose in her like an angry wind. *Excuse every damn property owner and supporter of law enforcement in the county. It won't do you any good, Graham Knight. I'm no longer that adoring little law student you once so easily crushed with just a few words. I'm the prosecutor who's going to find twelve honest citizens who will convict your client!*

MILTON MOREBUG RETURNED to his Hunt's Point home very late Monday night after stopping for a dinner of prime rib with an old friend at Barnaby's, one of his favorite restaurants. He was feeling tired, but otherwise in good spirits. The first thing he did was flip on a light and dump his dripping raincoat on the hallway's tile floor. He headed for the Scotch decanter sitting on a table just inside the sitting room.

He didn't waste time turning on the sitting-room light. He grabbed the decanter and poured out three fingers full, then raised the glass to his lips. It went down smoothly until just before it cleared his throat. Then the bite came. He sighed in pleasure and then plopped into a chair, content to look out over Fairweather Bay to the drenched lights of Seattle's skyline.

Graham Knight had shown him a lot of savvy and solid legal maneuvering in court today. Morebug understood getting the right jury was ninety percent of the battle. After watching Knight's performance, Morebug was convinced that no matter how long it took, Knight would get the right jury to acquit him of murder.

Murder. The word soaked his mind like a smelly wet sponge. He took another swig of brandy in a determined, rinsing gulp.

"They say men who drink alone are alcoholics."

The unexpected voice in the dark, quiet room had Morebug jumping to his feet in startled reflex. In an instant, however, the familiar tone and dark silhouette against the windows returned Morebug's heartbeat to normal.

"Danny. You startled me, boy."

Morebug crossed the room to clap his son on the shoulder in welcome. Danny leaned away from his father's touch and switched on a lamp, illuminating the nineteenth-century furnishings.

Morebug dropped his hand as a look of concern descended into his eyes. "It's good to see you, Danny."

Danny's tone turned gritty. "Is it?"

Morebug frowned as he laid his hand on his son's arm. "Your mother is probably asleep upstairs. We'll have to be quiet so as not to disturb her."

Danny tore his arm away from his father's grasp. "A bit late to start worrying about her feelings, isn't it, old man?"

Morebug watched his powerfully built son saunter over to the fireplace. At twenty-four, his son had it all—health, looks, women, money. Why wasn't it enough?

Morebug suddenly felt very tired. He sank into the nearest chair. "Why are you here, Danny?"

Danny's olive green eyes flicked over to his father's face in scorn. "I need money, of course."

"Of course," Morebug repeated sadly. "I gave you thirty thousand no more than six months ago."

Danny shrugged. "So I spent it. Six months is a long time."

Morebug studied his son. Other than the eyes, he couldn't see anything of himself in the boy. But he saw a lot of his wife in Danny's curly dark hair and demanding ways. He'd been wrong to let her have so much say in the boy's upbringing. Hell, he'd been wrong to have a child by her in the first place. But when one was young and a woman beautiful—

"I need at least another thirty thousand," Danny said as he circled the room, touching its furnishings as though he was appraising their pawnshop value. "I've got some bills."

Morebug frowned as he watched Danny. "You mean you're gambling again, don't you?"

Danny threw his father a rancorous glare. "It's my life."

Morebug exhaled a tired breath. "I'm not trying to run your life, son. But I'm not a money tree, either. I have expenses of my own. I can't afford to—"

"Don't give me that crap. This is Danny, remember? A chip off the old block. I don't get the money, I might just start getting talkative."

Milton Morebug's eyes narrowed. He watched his son's face silently for several minutes before finally getting up and moving over to the wall safe. He deliberately kept his back to Danny when he entered the combination.

"I've changed my mind. I need fifty thousand," Danny called from behind him. "Yeah. Fifty thousand."

"You know I don't keep that kind of money on hand."

"So give me what you got."

Morebug shook his head sadly. "My attorney has suggested your presence could be of importance at my trial. Your mother is coming each day. Can I count on you, son?"

"As long as you get the rest of the money to me by Friday."

Milton Morebug looked back at the satisfied smirk on Danny's face. His hand brushed past the forty-five just inside the safe on the way to the cash. For a moment his hand hesitated near the gun. Sometimes he thought if it hadn't been for that green in Danny's eyes . . .

Chapter Three

On his way up to the seventh-floor courtroom Tuesday morning, Graham was delighted when the elevator stopped on the fifth floor and Rosalind Hart stepped in. With his most winning smile he wished her a good morning.

She returned a curt, cold nod and immediately faced in the direction of the closing doors.

Graham felt a twist of amusement. "Get up on the wrong side of the bed this morning, Ms. Hart?"

Rosalind turned a frosty face in his direction. "I don't see what small talk between us will prove, Counselor."

"That we possess good manners perhaps?" Graham offered.

The slight flash of chagrin in her eyes was all the encouragement Graham needed to press his point as the elevator doors opened on the seventh floor and they stepped out. "I called around to ask about you yesterday afternoon after court. Defense attorneys say you're fair, but none are eager to go up against you."

Graham noticed a slight thawing in the depths of her warm, brown eyes. He'd always found an honest compliment was the best way to approach a woman.

"You don't practice in King County often, do you?" she asked, and then looked like she was annoyed with herself for having descended into the depths of civility with him.

"As a matter of fact, I don't," Graham admitted, smiling at her discomfort. "I live on the other side of Puget

Sound, Bainbridge Island to be exact, and most of my practice is confined to Kitsap and Mason counties. I've probably only had half a dozen cases in King County since going into practice eight years ago.''

Rosalind felt annoyed that he'd been able to start a private practice right out of law school while she had to endure the long hours and low pay of the county prosecutor's office. She decided he was probably the spoiled child of wealthy parents.

She turned deprecating eyes in his direction. ''No doubt the substantial rate of billable hours you sock Milton Morebug with includes the time spent on the daily ferry rides.''

Graham picked up on the edge in Rosalind's words and was a little surprised at them. She really wasn't trying to be civil and that didn't fit with either her courtroom demeanor or her reputation. He also couldn't remember the last time he'd had such trouble charming a woman. He felt a racing in his blood, a surge normally only present in the challenge of courtroom battle.

''Actually I throw in the ferry-ride time for free, Ms. Hart,'' he returned with a wry smile. ''I'm always generous when I know I'm going to win a case.''

She stopped in front of the courtroom door and glared at him with fire in her eyes. ''You're not winning this one.''And suddenly, very clearly, he sensed that Rosalind had declared a much more personal war between them. A sharp thrill of anticipation zipped up his spine.

Smiling graciously, he made a great sweep of a bow as he opened the courtroom door and stepped aside to let her enter.

MAX HILL TOOK ONE LOOK AT Rosalind's expression as she approached the prosecution's table and gave out a subdued whistle. ''You look ready to draw blood. What's wrong?''

Rosalind exhaled heavily as she sank into her chair and dropped her briefcase onto the table. ''Knight was trying to be nice to me.''

Max looked perplexed. "And this is an occasion for anger?"

Rosalind realized she had spoken without thinking. The last thing she wanted to do was to explain her past dealings with the dashing defense attorney. She reached into her briefcase and pulled out the large stack of prospective jurors' questionnaires, letting the activity allow her to look away from the too-close scrutiny of Max Hill's eyes.

"I don't trust defense attorneys who try to butter up the prosecution. Now let's get on to the important stuff before court convenes. What do you think of the jury so far?"

Max looked at the diagram of the jury box Rosalind placed on the table before him and studied the names she'd penciled in the previous day. "Get rid of Tyrell as soon as you can. As a matter of fact, prospective jurors seven, eight and ten are the only ones I'd keep from this group."

Rosalind leaned closer toward the diagram and Max. "I agree about Tyrell, of course. And seven, eight and ten. But I would have thought that three was also a good bet, being a civil engineer."

Max shook his head. "Civil engineer or not, the woman's only twenty-six. I've heard a lot of prosecutors say they'd never put anybody on a murder trial jury under thirty. Young people are generally on the side of the defendant."

"If the defendant were in his twenties, too, I agree that a young juror generally shows such empathy. But we're dealing with a middle-aged defendant. I think the civil engineer possesses the type of demeanor that makes an attentive juror—someone who would listen to the evidence and feel its weight."

Max shrugged and sat back, locking his fingers behind his neck as his elbows winged next to his ears. "I still think you're making a mistake, Roz. Even if the other things are in her favor, women jurors in general are too easy on murder defendants."

Rosalind sat up straighter as she watched the attractive detective. "Max Hill, I can't believe it. In the six years I've worked with you, I never realized you were a chauvinist!"

Max's dark eyes flicked over Rosalind's face as he smiled. One of his arms draped casually across the back of her chair.

"Of course, I'm a chauvinist. But my particular brand heartily approves of female deputy prosecutors. Maybe you should have accepted one of my many invitations to dinner over the last six years and gotten to know me better. There's still time, you know. My calendar is clear tonight."

Max had leaned close and spoken his invitation softly in her ear. Rosalind remembered the occasions when he'd driven up in his racy 928 GT Porsche after court and confidently issued the offers. She knew her refusals had surprised him. "Max, I value our professional relationship too much to risk it."

The smile dimmed in Max's eyes. "That easy for you, huh? You're making a mistake, Roz. Rumor is I'm considered the best catch in the detective unit."

Rosalind laid a hand on Max's arm. "There's another rumor that says you're the best investigator in the joint, too. That's far more valuable to me than becoming another line in what is also rumored to be your very thick black book."

Max exposed an upper shelf of gleaming white teeth. "Even if I devoted an entire page to you?"

Rosalind laughed. "Even if it were filled in front and back."

Before Max could respond, Bailiff Roger Horn came charging through from the judge's chambers, his yellow mop bouncing as he called out the impending arrival of Judge Gloria Shotz. Rosalind dropped her hand from Max's arm and he dropped his arm from the back of her chair as they both rose.

Graham rose, too, but he was wearing a frown. Watching the prosecutor's table for the past few minutes, he was slightly irritated at the obvious physical familiarity between the deputy prosecutor and the investigative officer. His contacts in King County had told him Rosalind Hart wasn't involved romantically, but the image of Max Hill whispering in her ear as Rosalind's hand rested on his arm left Graham with an uneasy feeling.

He tried to shift his thoughts toward the important jury selection that could very well make the difference between his client's conviction or acquittal. But he found himself fighting down an unaccustomed annoyance.

LEROY PONCE SMILED as he watched Rosalind Hart strutting her stuff so confidently in court. This was the way he remembered her, so sure, so arrogant. Only the last time he'd had to watch her from the defendant's table, and he'd been locked up every night so he couldn't get at her. And when the trial had ended, she had succeeded in locking him away for eighteen fear-filled months when he was at the mercy of other inmates. Memories of those awful days fueled the fires of his revenge.

Throughout the week he'd followed her. He knew her car, her address, her unlisted telephone number and a thousand other little details about her life. It was the kind of thorough surveillance he normally did before a hit. But this was going to be different. He wasn't interested in killing her...yet. He wanted to see her live with fear, as she'd made him do. He wanted her to feel it, smell it, taste it. He wanted to see how confident she'd remain after he got finished with her.

ROSALIND WAS GLAD to come home to her little apartment above Pike Place Market Friday night. It had been a long day and an equally long week. Rain had pounded her every step of the way, and she felt wet and chilled as she closed her umbrella in the hall and hung her raincoat on the clothes tree. The next thing she did was step out of her high-heel shoes and ease her feet into fluffy, soft slippers from the hall closet. With a sigh of relief, she switched on the dull light of the long hallway and headed for the kitchen.

She didn't make it. There was no warning, no time for uneasiness to turn into fear. Just one incredibly unbelievable instant when her footing gave way and the world spun around with almost no sensation or judgment attached. The shock was too great for feeling because feelings were dependent on comprehension and Rosalind understood nothing.

Then she landed. In that split second, she became aware she'd fallen and was lying on her back, looking at the bright purple of the hallway ceiling. She felt pain and a lot of surprise. How could she have fallen?

Carefully, she moved her arms and legs and decided nothing was broken. She put her hand out to steady herself as she rose to a sitting position, but her hand slipped and she fell to the floor again. It felt silly to be so clumsy, and she chuckled.

She put out her hand more carefully this time.

It slipped again.

The chuckle died in her throat.

This wasn't clumsiness. A lick of fear shot up her spine. Something was wrong. Very wrong. She ran an exploratory finger across the hallway floor. It was as slippery as ice. But how? She hadn't waxed her floor.

She reached out to the wall, but her hand slid off it.

A wave of unreality washed over her as she continued to try to get some kind of a grip to help herself up, but her hands kept slipping away. When she tried to sit up without using her hands, her bottom literally slipped out from under her and she found herself on her back once more.

She fought down unreasoning panic. What kind of nightmare was this?

She must think. There had to be a way to get off this floor. Slowly she turned her head. No use trying to make for the kitchen. Although it was closest, its floor was of the same material. No way to tell if it was as slick as the surface she was on. Her eyes followed the dim hall light to where it just reached the bright blue carpet of the living room.

The carpet. Wherever this madness came from, the carpet's surface couldn't be slick like the floor's. She'd make for the carpet. Her destination decided, now all she had to do was figure out how to get there.

She looked around for some type of tool, but nothing was within reach. All she had were the clothes on her back.

Wait a minute. Her clothes. She could lay her clothes across the slippery floor and roll over on them to reach the carpet! The thought had no sooner entered her mind then she began to carefully maneuver out of her suit coat. It wasn't easy. With every move she slid. Whatever this stuff was, it was worse than the surface of an ice-skating rink.

Disciplining herself to slow her movements, it seemed to take forever for her to get out of her suit coat. When she had finally succeeded, she lay perspiring on top of it. Next came her blouse. Fortunately it was cotton, not a slippery silk or satin. Slowly, carefully she arched it onto the floor in the space between her and the living-room carpet. Despite her care, it slid close to the carpet, still leaving a considerable gap. There was no way around it. She'd have to remove her skirt and add it to her clothes bridge. Carefully, she wiggled out of it, slithering around the floor with each movement. The perspiration on her skin was clammy and cold when she finally held her prize in shaking hands, ready for its launch onto the floor.

She closed her eyes and took several deep breaths to steady her aim. Then she opened them again and gently launched the skirt. It landed right in the space between the end of her suit coat and her blouse.

Next she took off her slippers and added them to her clothes bridge. Well, it was now or never. She took a deep breath, tucked herself into a ball and with all her concentration rolled toward the carpet.

Buttons and zippers poked into her arms and back, bringing with them hard little knobs of pain. But when she opened her eyes after she came to a stop, the carpet was at the edge of her arms. She reached out for it, clinging to its comforting steadiness, weeping in relief as she dragged herself to it.

DETECTIVE MAX HILL shook his head as he tested the un-sanded part of Rosalind's linoleum floor with his finger. "Damn, that stuff *is* slick. It's a good thing I knew who to call to get a floor-sanding machine at this time of night. No way anybody could've walked on this surface."

Rosalind gave a heavy sigh as she looked at the difference between the sanded and unsanded sections of her hall-way. She'd called the sheriff's department instead of the Seattle police because she knew Max was the best. "What is it?"

Max shrugged as he got to his feet. "My guess is the floor and walls are saturated with one of those new silicon-based lubricants that harden slick when dry. Damn crazy thing to pour on a floor. You realize the even coating spread across the floor and walls means it's got to have been done delib-erately?"

Rosalind nodded as she took a gulp of coffee.

Max's voice became more gentle. "I've had my people check everything else, Roz. It looks like the floor and walls in here were the only things doctored. This MO isn't famil-iar. You're sure there's no one who's threatened you?"

Rosalind got off the barstool in the kitchen, feeling too jumpy to remain seated. "I've gotten the usual odd threats in my time, Max, but nothing in the last year or so. Frankly, this has me puzzled. Did you figure out how someone got in?"

"There are scratches on the lock where someone picked it. Wouldn't have taken much effort. Roz, this place is just begging for a break-in. Even if you got the best lock to se-cure your door, those back windows over there are easily accessible from the alley. You've got to move."

Rosalind frowned. "Move?"

Max shook his head. "Come on, Roz. This place isn't safe and it isn't much. You should have moved long ago, even without the impetus of this episode. Whoever slicked your floor this way is sadistic enough to try something even cuter next time. And you do realize that if you stay here, the odds are overwhelming that there *is* going to be a next time?"

Rosalind felt a small chill up her spine. She hugged her arms to her chest.

Max took a step closer. "Move, Roz. I'm leaving you my home number. Call if I can help."

Rosalind took Max's offered card. "Did you find any prints?"

"Just yours. Which means he probably wore gloves. He's not dumb. All the more reason why you should get out. Tomorrow."

Max gave her a pat on the arm and then left. He had a new police lock on the front door and had arranged for a Seattle PD patrol car to watch the place during the night. Rosalind looked at her apartment a little sadly. No, it wasn't much, but she'd been proud of it—after all, it had been the first place she had called her own.

And someone was forcing her out of it.

She shivered. It was late and she was tired. She secured the police lock and headed for bed. But in the early-morning hours, she was still awake, speculating on the kind of mind that thought up things like slicking someone's floors.

GRAHAM KNIGHT WORKED through his weekend just as he had for years. He poured over the evidence against Milton Morebug, planning methods of attack, trying out the effectiveness of each one.

He didn't bother working on an opening statement. He'd wait until he heard what Rosalind Hart had to say.

He was so engrossed that the telephone rang six times before the sound penetrated his mind. He scrambled for the receiver and said hello.

"It's Fran. Just wanted to give you an update."

Graham sat forward. "What have you learned?"

"Well, Beaver's family is one of the long-established wealthy residents of Mercer Island, so they're pretty close-mouthed. His father bought land on the island when the only way to get to it from Seattle was by ferry. Those old families are the real power behind the island's government."

Graham frowned. "Are you saying you can't do it, Fran?"

"Gray, I'm surprised you don't know me better than that. Mabel, Violet and I will do it, all right. It's just I'm not sure how long it will take. Things are opening up. Next Monday I have a luncheon scheduled with the widow, and next Monday night Mabel and Violet are attending a dinner with several of Mercer Island's elite."

Graham took a breath. "Opening arguments are scheduled for Monday morning."

"I know, Gray. But this hasn't been an easy task you've assigned your great-aunt. Which reminds me. Mabel and Violet have even given up their Monday night at the theater to attend the dinner, which leaves me with two extra tickets. I hate to go alone. Will you come?"

Graham leaned back and smiled. "I'd be delighted. I can't remember the last time I went to a play. Who are you going to give the third ticket to?"

"Come to dinner tonight and I'll give you both of the extra tickets. Then you can bring a friend."

"Maybe. Fran, are you sure there's nothing you've learned yet about Warren Beaver that might be of some help to me?"

Fran's tone was hesitant. "Well, when we opposed him on all those antilogging issues, you know we always suspected there were some under-the-table deals he might have going?"

Graham's tone was eager. "Yes?"

"I've hesitated to tell you because it's all hearsay with no specifics at the moment, but word is that those deals existed, all right. And he even cheated the people who were in on those deals with him. Is that helpful?"

Graham smiled. "Forget about preparing dinner tonight. You just earned a night out at your favorite restaurant."

ROSALIND APPROACHED the newly sworn-in jury Monday morning to present her opening statement. She had used her peremptory challenges to get rid of Ms. Tyrell and several other prospective jurors who seemed to show bias in the defense's favor. Naturally, Graham had done the same with jurors he envisioned as biased in the prosecution's favor.

Now, sitting before her were twelve men and women and four alternates who, although she couldn't call them her first choice for a jury, were at least outwardly unbiased.

She took a deep breath, preparing herself to draw a picture for them, using her words, her voice and every mannerism and nuance in her repertoire to get them to feel like eyewitnesses.

"Ladies and gentlemen of the jury, I'm going to take you back to January eighth of this year, eleven months ago. The weekend before, a storm had blown through Seattle, leaving a white carpet of snow on the streets. Like a clean kitchen floor trampled on by a mother's returning brood, the snow had soon become streaked with commuters' black tire tracks. The vehicles slipped on the ice as temperatures dipped into the single digits.

"But it was warm and inviting at Milton Morebug's place, a French Provincial mansion on exclusive Hunt's Point, across from the brilliance of Seattle's night sky. The maid had turned on many of the room lights and adjusted the heat to a comfortable setting. She'd even lit the fire in the card room. And as instructed by her employer, she had prepared the card table there and left sandwiches and beverages for those soon expected to take part in a weekly card game. Then no longer needed, she left. Milton Morebug awaited his guests alone.

"Three visitors arrived shortly after seven that night. The first was Warren Beaver, the state's commissioner of public lands. Morebug and Beaver had known each other for several years. But Warren Beaver was not a normal attendee at Milton Morebug's weekly card game. In fact, this was his first invitation."

Rosalind paused and looked questioningly at the jury. "You may wonder why this was so. We did, too. It seems that Milton Morebug told his friends he didn't trust Warren Beaver and that's why he hadn't included Beaver in his weekly card games before.

"Why did he do so on this night? Well it seems one of Morebug's normal cardplayers and his former attorney, Harold Sanders, had become ill with a sore throat and couldn't make it. So Beaver, we find out, was a last-minute replacement.

"Soon after Milton Morebug had welcomed Warren Beaver to his home on that fateful January evening, Morebug's two regular cardplayers arrived. Raymond Hogg, the owner of a logging mill, was the first. He was soon followed by Brian Wreckter, a local land developer and longtime friend of Morebug.

"All four men help themselves to a drink, sit down around the card table, lean back and look forward to a long evening of entertainment. They laugh and joke, their chatter jumping from football to food to the fall of the next card. Joyce Beaver, the victim's wife, calls to the house around ten to ask her husband to buy her favorite chocolate ice cream on the way home.

"Over the first few hours, the winnings are distributed fairly evenly. But then the wheel of fortune makes a decided turn toward Warren Beaver. He wins twelve games in a row."

Rosalind's voice slowed and deepened. "Tension is now heavy in contrast to the previous atmosphere of light camaraderie. The players hunch over their cards. Their hands perspire. The pot is the largest of the evening. The game is five-card stud."

As Rosalind paused, she sensed the courtroom was quiet enough for her to hear a pin drop. Her voice deepened even more.

"The betting increases as the cards are dealt. 'It's too rich for my blood,' Raymond Hogg finally says as he drops out of the game. Next Brian Wreckter folds.

"Two players are left—Warren Beaver and Milton Morebug. Beaver has three jacks showing. Morebug has three aces. The stakes are raised again. And again. Neither will back down.

"Finally Morebug calls Beaver to show his hole card. Beaver turns over the fourth jack and, smiling in triumph, circles his arms around the money in the pot.

"But Morebug's hand shoots out to halt Beaver's progress. He hasn't shown his hole card yet. Can it be the fourth ace? Now he turns it over and audible gasps and cursing can be heard around the room. No, it's not a fourth ace. It's a jack!

"But how can it be a jack? Beaver's hand shows four jacks already. There aren't five jacks in a deck of playing cards!

"Suspicion balloons into the hot air. Suddenly Warren Beaver's recent winning streak is seen by Milton Morebug in a new light. He jumps to his feet and swings at Warren Beaver across the card table, screaming 'cheat' at the top of his voice. A blow connects and Warren Beaver is knocked to the floor. Hogg and Wreckter hold Morebug back as he lunges toward the fallen Beaver. Beaver scrambles to his feet and rushes for the door.

"Hogg and Wreckter have a quick drink with Morebug. Then they leave for their respective homes as Warren Beaver has done.

"However, Warren Beaver never gets home. On a lonely stretch of road only blocks away from his home on Mercer Island, Warren Beaver's car is run off the road and he is shot three times in the chest. As he lays dying beneath the clear, cold sky, he tries to leave a message. With blood-stained fingers, he desperately digs the letter M in the cold carpet of snow. Then his strength fails him and he dies."

Rosalind stopped as her own index finger drew a big letter M in the air before the jury.

"Warren Beaver's body is found shortly after. When the police hear about the argument at Milton Morebug's home the night before, they get a warrant to search Morebug's premises. They find a recently cleaned .38 in Morebug's possession. It's registered in his name. Ballistics prove it to be the murder weapon. There is only one fingerprint found on the weapon. That fingerprint belongs to Milton Morebug.''

Rosalind once again paused in her narrative and began to pace in front of the jury box. ''Ladies and gentlemen, in the next week, one by one, the prosecution's witnesses will come forward and you will hear the evidence of the events I have just described. One by one, these pieces of evidence will add up to one thing and one thing only.''

Rosalind extended an accusatory finger at the defendant.

''And that one thing is that this man, Milton Morebug, enraged over Warren Beaver's card cheating, got his gun, loaded it, shoved it into his pocket and took off after Warren Beaver. He knew Warren Beaver would be delayed as he picked up the ice cream for his wife. He was determined to catch him. And when Milton Morebug caught up with Warren Beaver, he forced Beaver's car off the road and shot Warren Beaver three times, until he collapsed into the snow, his life's blood draining away.''

Rosalind was quiet for a moment as she stood in front of the jury, her arm still raised, her finger pointing in accusation, her words seeming to echo in the still courtroom. Then slowly, her arm descended.

Rosalind's head went up, high and proud. ''Ladies and gentlemen, I have a job to bring the guilty to justice. I'm going to show you the evidence that will convince you beyond a reasonable doubt that Milton Morebug killed Warren Beaver.''

Rosalind stood very still. In that moment she reminded Graham of one of those beautiful, carved wooden ladies that adorned ship's bows, chin up to the wind.

''And as jurors you, too, have a job,'' she continued. ''It's to evaluate the evidence that will be presented in this court according to the law as the judge explains it to you. And when you do your job to the best of your abilities, I know you will find Milton Morebug guilty as charged.''

As Rosalind glided back to the prosecution table, Graham watched the faces of the jury and swallowed hard. Were they to take a vote now, he had no doubt it would be for conviction, despite the fact that no evidence had been presented.

"Mr. Knight?" Judge Shotz prodded.

Graham got up slowly and moved until he was several feet in front of the jury. He took a deep breath. "Ladies and gentlemen, Ms. Hart is a fine speaker. I don't know about you, but she paints a picture with her words that still lingers before my eyes."

Graham looked up in the air as though he was trying to remember something. "What was the phrase she used? Ah, yes." Graham extended his right hand and moved it horizontally through the air. "'Like a clean kitchen floor trampled on by a mother's returning brood, the snow had soon become streaked with commuters' black tire tracks.' Very picturesque."

Graham lowered his arm and paced down the length of the jury box, his eyes alighting on each juror in turn. "The rest of her story was equally well drawn. You could almost hear the men's chatter becoming somber as Warren Beaver won game after game. The tension of betting in that final hand. The turn of Warren Beaver's hole card. The sinister implications of Milton Morebug's turning over a fifth jack."

Graham nodded. "Without a doubt, very well drawn."

He suddenly stopped his pacing and looked up as though just caught by a thought. "But did you notice that her account of Warren Beaver's murder was not nearly as clear?"

Graham stood silently, looking at the jury while he let his question sink in.

"There's a reason for that, ladies and gentlemen. The prosecution can present direct evidence about the weather on the night of January eighth, the road conditions and the happenings at the card game at Milton Morebug's home."

Graham shrugged. "But quite frankly those events have nothing to do with the murder of Warren Beaver. They may be interesting and, thanks to Ms. Hart's gift for words, very picturesque, but those events are not evidence of murder."

Graham drew a mental line in front of the jury box and walked it, never losing eye contact with the jury.

"So where is the evidence of this murder? It certainly can't be found in the fact that Milton Morebug became angry over being cheated. Do you know of anyone who wouldn't be angry if someone cheated him or her at cards?"

Graham paused, watching the jurors' faces, seeing the ones he had reached already and zeroing in on those still undecided.

"Of course, you'd be angry. So would I. We're human beings just like Milton Morebug. But just because we get angry at someone doesn't mean we're going to murder them. If that were true, I'd estimate there wouldn't be a person in this courtroom who wouldn't be either dead or behind bars!"

Graham paused as the murmur of polite chuckles echoed throughout the courtroom. His tone turned into a scold. "No, ladies and gentlemen, the prosecutor is sucking an empty straw by trying to insist the motive for Beaver's murder was because the man was caught cheating at cards. And making such a preposterous statement doesn't get us closer to the truth because it isn't even evidence—it's only conjecture."

Graham began to pace along the jury box again.

"As a matter of fact, the only real evidence relating to the murder of Warren Beaver that will be presented in this courtroom will show that he was shot to death nearly fifteen miles *away* from Milton Morebug's home, at least an hour *after* the card game broke up, and for what reason and under what circumstances no one will be able to say, and by a gun that many people had access to on the night of the murder. That will be the evidence.

"Now it's also true that you'll hear about some scratching in the snow near the body. But no one is going to be able to say they know for sure who made the scratching, what it meant or if, indeed, it meant anything at all."

Graham paused in his pacing and wiggled his index finger. "Oh, yes. I almost forgot. The evidence will show one other thing, ladies and gentlemen—one very important fact, because it gets us closer to the truth. It will show you that Warren Beaver was not a well-liked or ethical man. And because he wasn't honest in his dealings, he made enemies. Lots of them. And more than likely it was one of those enemies who lay in wait for Warren Beaver on that lonely stretch of road on the night of January eighth and took his life."

Graham scratched his head in a precise air of confusion. "Unfortunately, I doubt we're going to find which one of his enemies took Warren Beaver's life. The fact is, the police have been barking up the wrong tree for so long, the real fox has had plenty of time to cover his tracks."

Graham's hand fell to his side, confident, assured. "No, we can't find Beaver's killer. But we can put a muzzle on those—" his arm quickly shot out to point a finger at the prosecution's table "—who have lost the guilty scent and are baring their teeth in desperation at this innocent man."

Graham's hand dropped to the jury rail as he leaned forward in fervent supplication. "Don't be pulled along on Ms. Hart's leash, tugging and yapping for Milton Morebug's blood, ladies and gentlemen. Hold your conclusions until all the evidence has been presented. I'm sure once you hear it, you will be convinced none of it ties Milton Morebug to the murder of Warren Beaver. Because the truth is, Milton Morebug is innocent."

As Graham took his seat, Rosalind almost expected a loud burst of applause after that spectacular performance. It was hard not to admire his style.

Of course, she did take exception to his characterization of her as a yapping hound. And he had the gall to call her words picturesque! More and more she realized she was going to need every ounce of her training and experience to overcome the doubt he'd placed in the minds of the jurors.

But overcome it she would. She'd hammer every shred of evidence home. She had to. Milton Morebug was a murderer, and as she had promised the jury, her job was to get him convicted. And as she had promised herself, Graham Knight was due for a beating.

Chapter Four

Graham entered the County Terrace coffee shop on the second floor of the King County Administration Building, and immediately spied Rosalind sitting alone, head down, pouring over papers and her lunch at a window table. He stepped into the line and filled a plate with prime rib, green beans and red potatoes, a combination advertised as the Holiday Dinner Special, a label that might refer to the just-passed Thanksgiving or the upcoming Christmas season.

He didn't hurry to the cashier, but deliberately waited until the room filled up to the point where no vacant tables remained. Then he paid for his meal and walked over to where Rosalind sat.

"Mind if I join you, Ms. Hart?"

For one unguarded moment, her startled eyes gazed up into his. They were a deep, lush brown. As he saw the question in them get answered, a dark curtain closed over their warmth and her full lips narrowed. "I'm trying to work, Mr. Knight."

Graham sat down. "Then I'll just sit here and eat quietly as there are no other free tables in the room."

Rosalind turned her head to check the other tables, obviously unwilling to take his word. A small frown wrinkled the whiteness of her brow as she lowered her head again to the pages in front of her without comment.

Graham ate his lunch and watched her read. His eyes traveled from her high forehead to her determined chin, but they lingered on her full lips, and for the briefest of moments he thought he saw something familiar there. Then the fleeting image was gone and he found himself wondering what her red hair would look like full and free from the tight braid that fell to the middle of her back.

When her eyes stayed on the same page for five minutes, he smiled to himself. Despite her bold front, he knew he had interfered with her concentration. He was sure from her earlier strong reactions to him that she couldn't ignore him. Whatever was boiling beneath her surface, it certainly wasn't indifference.

He drank the last of his coffee and leaned forward. "I have an extra ticket for a preview showing of a new play at the Bagley Wright Theatre tonight. It's a production of the Seattle Repertory Theatre Company, part of their Stage II season. I have no idea what the story line is, but it might be entertaining."

Her head came up, surprise in her eyes. "Excuse me? You're offering this extra ticket to me?"

Graham smiled. "I can't think of any other reason why I would have brought it up."

He reached into his wallet, but Rosalind put her hand in a halt position. "No, no. Absolutely not."

She rose to her feet, gathered up her papers, stuffed them into her briefcase and grabbed her luncheon tray. Before she could leave, however, Graham rose and placed a restraining hand on her arm. "No strings attached, Ms. Hart. It really is an extra ticket."

Rosalind yanked her arm away. "I'm not interested in anything extra *you* have to offer, Mr. Knight."

As Rosalind strode away, Graham wondered what it was about him that turned the fiery prosecutor off so dramatically? And what was it about her that made him so attracted to her? Whatever the reasons, the lady was definitely a challenge, and he'd never shied away from challenges. He whistled as he picked up his tray and started for the door.

"I THOUGHT YOU TOLD ME you were ready to proceed on this case, Ms. Hart," Judge Shotz said in an irritated voice after court was reconvened following the lunch recess.

Rosalind shifted on her feet. "We are, Your Honor. It's just that in order to present a continuity of events to the jury, Ms. Stephanie Pond should be the prosecution's first witness, and she isn't available to testify this afternoon. So if Your Honor will grant me a continuance until tomorrow—"

"Why isn't this witness available?"

Rosalind swallowed. "She's maid of honor at a wedding."

Judge Shotz leaned forward in her chair as her voice pounded into Rosalind's ears. "And you thought that sufficient reason not to serve your subpoena?"

Rosalind steeled herself for another tongue-lashing by Judge Shotz, feeling particularly uncomfortable because it was about to happen in front of the jury. She was flabbergasted when it was Graham who spoke.

"Your Honor, defense is not adverse to a continuance until tomorrow morning. In fact, it would be of assistance to us, as I need to speak with a colleague this afternoon to confer on the case."

Judge Shotz's black-raven eyes flew to Graham, then back to Rosalind. Her suspicious look accentuated her sharp and uncompromising tone. "Approach."

As commanded, Graham and Rosalind walked up to the judge's bench. Shotz put her hand over her microphone. Her whisper was like a hiss. "Be warned, both of you. I will not tolerate collusion between prosecuting and defense attorneys to delay this trial. Now step back."

As Rosalind regained her position behind the prosecution's table, Shotz's voice boomed out irritably. "Court will reconvene tomorrow at nine-thirty."

The judge rapped her gavel, rose from her chair and flew toward her chambers.

Rosalind fell back into her chair in relief.

"That was an odd thing for Knight to have done," Max Hill whispered beside her as the jury filed out. "He could have gotten you tongue-lashed and his continuance without opening his mouth. Why did he?"

Rosalind shook her head. Max had just voiced her own thoughts quite clearly. "I've no idea. Certainly didn't make any sense, but I'm not complaining. Have you got the on-scene officers lined up for tomorrow morning?"

Max nodded. "They'll be waiting outside to go on the stand right after your bridesmaid. By the way, why didn't you force her in today?"

. Rosalind frowned at the detective. "Find your heart, Max. She's a bridesmaid at an old friend's wedding that's been planned for months. Yanking her out of it at the last minute so she can testify she did the right thing when she found a body nearly a year ago isn't what I call justice."

"You're getting soft, Roz. Or have you always been?"

Rosalind got to her feet, shoving papers into her briefcase and an edge into her voice. "Why don't you reread my conviction rate, and then you tell me."

Max's hands came up in surrender as he rose beside her. "Okay, okay. No need to bring out the heavy artillery. Hear you found a new apartment Saturday. What's it like?"

Rosalind sighed. Her nerves were more on edge than she had thought. "It's in a modern building with state-of-the-art security. I should be satisfied."

"But you're not?" Max asked.

"Let's just say I haven't had much time to notice. I'm still trying to grasp all the details on this case."

Max nodded. "I get the picture. You stay home reading the case rather than unpacking?"

Rosalind shrugged. "Something like that."

Max eased the stiff cuff of his white dress shirt over the Rolex watch on his wrist. "Remember the All Work And No Play adage. By the way, I'm meeting with the chief tomorrow morning, so I won't be in court. You want me here for the rest of the trial?"

Rosalind's voice softened. "If your schedule permits. I have no idea what Knight might have up his sleeve. I'd be thankful for a clear head beside me."

Max's smile was rueful. "That's me—the clear head. Pity you can't find uses for the rest of this body."

Rosalind gave Max's arm a good-natured consoling pat as she turned to leave. From the corner of her eye she could see Graham talking with his client and the client's family, and her earlier question returned. What was going on? Why had Graham so openly supported her request for a continuance until the next morning?

She was still mulling the mystery over in her mind as she made her way back to her office on the fifth floor of the courthouse. She stopped by the front desk and retrieved her messages from the receptionist. Among the yellow telephone slips was a white envelope with her name scrawled across it.

She dropped her briefcase onto her desk as she walked into her small rectangular office, crowded floor to ceiling with files. It took just a moment to slit the envelope with a letter opener. Graham's business card and a ticket for the play fell onto her desk. Rosalind picked up his card and turned it over. The message on the back read, "In case you change your mind."

GRAHAM HEADED TOWARD the public phones after court recessed for the day. Although he had deliberately spoken up in court to save Rosalind from Shotz's anger, he hadn't lied to the judge. He was eager to confer with Fran to see how the ladies were coming along. Graham snatched up the phone and placed his call.

Fran answered on the first ring, advising him she had just returned home. "As I expected, luncheon with Joyce Beaver went well, Gray. Of course, she wasn't openly forthcoming about her late husband, but I didn't expect her to be. We'll have much better luck with one of the other women in the circle."

"How's progress in that direction?" Graham asked.

"The ladies are getting themselves close to the best sources," Fran assured. "My maid is in contact with the Beaver family's domestic staff. Violet and Mabel are attending a Mercer Island political dinner tonight, and at lunch today, I got myself invited to a charity fund-raiser with the Beavers' friends and neighbors on Wednesday."

"Have you learned anything new?" Graham asked.

"The ladies and I have heard bits and pieces of gossip from various sources that Beaver had an unusual quirk that didn't ingratiate him with hosts. Seems after he visited some people's homes, they'd notice something small and valuable missing."

"You mean Beaver was a kleptomaniac?"

"No one could prove anything, but many suspected."

Graham drummed his fingers on the side of the pay phone. "Seems Beaver had some eccentric wrinkles even we didn't suspect. I'm more concerned about the shady deals, however."

"I understand. It's just a matter of time before I learn who was involved and the other particulars."

"Time is tight, Fran."

"I understand, Gray dear. But as you know, our type of investigation is delicate. We're after information these people would never tell the police. We have to have some patience."

"I'm an impatient man."

"Hmm. One of your less endearing qualities as I always told your uncle Jack. We're still going to the play tonight?"

Graham smiled. "Never dream of standing up my favorite lady. I'll be at your place at six-fifteen. By the way, a woman may be joining us at the theater. You don't mind, do you?"

Fran's pause was a startled one. "Of course, I don't mind! Gray, I had no idea there was someone special. It's about time you settled down to just one again."

"Who says I have?"

Fran's excited voice dropped. "Oh. Well I just thought since you were letting me meet her—"

Graham frowned. "No future great-nieces on the horizon, Fran. Besides, a man's on trial for his life. Nothing must distract me from giving him the best defense possible."

Fran was clearly disappointed. "You are very single-minded, Gray. I realize that is probably one of the reasons you're so successful, but I wonder if you're ever going to stop and smell the roses."

Graham's frown went deeper. "I did that once, Fran. Remember? What I found was that roses are beautiful to look at, but it's when you lean down to smell them that you discover their thorns draw blood. I've got to go now. I'll see you tonight."

ROSALIND CAME OUT of the shower of her new apartment Monday night with no intention of going to the Bagley Wright Theatre. No intention at all.

She had a lot more important things to occupy her mind than a frivolous play. Besides, she was still surrounded by packed boxes. And if she couldn't convince herself to unpack them, then there were always trial documents she could review. And even if she didn't want to do either of those things, she certainly didn't want to spend her evening with Graham Knight.

She spied the ticket sitting on her nightstand and picked it up, turning it over and over in her hand. Despite the fact he'd risked the judge's ire to save her that afternoon, Rosalind reminded herself she didn't owe Graham anything.

Nothing good, anyway, considering their past history. Still, his behavior with the judge and this ticket perplexed her. It didn't seem to fit the callous, self-serving attitude she had previously attributed to him. And if there was one thing that bugged her, it was inconsistency.

Unless he'd pulled that stunt in court just to pressure her into going out with him? Was he really that conniving and manipulative? Only one way to find out. And only one way to answer such arrogance. She headed for the closet and snatched one of her nicer outfits off the hanger.

WHEN GRAHAM SAW ROSALIND walk into the theater lobby that night, he did a double take. He was prepared for her to show up, but he wasn't prepared for how she would look. Her dress was clinging golds and greens, and her hair was loose and framed her face like dancing fire. When she strode up to him, her eyes held a distinct dare. She was beautiful and she was ready for battle.

He found it an irresistible combination. Her challenge tingled his blood as he stepped toward her. As the lushness of her perfume invaded his senses, his physical desire for her lurched ahead, unheeded by his mental restraint.

With an effort Graham collected himself, carefully schooling his voice into nonchalance. "Ms. Hart, nice to see you could make it after all. I'd like you to meet my great-aunt, Ms. Tulip. She is the benefactor of our tickets this evening."

Fran sent Graham a puzzled look. "Ms. Hart? Ms. Tulip? Gray, whatever has gotten into you to be so formal?" She stepped forward and offered her hand. "Please call me Fran. What's your first name, dear?"

"R-Rosalind."

Graham was pleased to see Rosalind completely taken off guard by his great-aunt's presence. All her fiery defiance seemed to go up in smoke as Fran clasped her hand.

As always Fran immediately took over the social duties, as she deemed it was her right, and hogged the conversation. Graham didn't mind. He was content to watch and listen as his great-aunt's steady stream of observations from the continuing rainy weather to the marvels at the aquarium overwhelmed Rosalind.

He had judged right. The fiery prosecutor was not a woman easily approached. Yet Rosalind's suspicions of his motives were obviously fleeing in the face of Fran's lightning-quick subject changes. He was pleased that Rosalind's ticket was for the seat on the other side of Fran.

At least part of him was. That part that hoped to conquer her defiance by keeping her constantly guessing. But there was another part that craved her beside him, defiant or not. That part he determinedly kept in check. He had no intention of showing his hand so soon with this lady.

Fran was still directing the conversation. "Normally Mabel and Violet, a couple of my friends, join me for these plays, Rosalind. But since they're busy, I'm so glad it's you and Gray who'll keep me company. It's always so much more pleasant to share things with someone, don't you think?"

Rosalind couldn't help but feel comfortable with Fran's irresistible charm and innocence once she got over the initial surprise of finding her there. "Yes, I do, Fran," she replied as she smiled at the little, white-haired, doll-shaped woman who was eighty-five if she was a day.

"Do you have any family living nearby?" Fran asked.

"My parents live over in Seabeck, on the Hood Canal. I'm a second-generation Washington native."

"How terrific! Any brothers, sisters?"

"No. I was a late-in-life baby for my parents. A total surprise. My mother was forty when she had me."

Rosalind soon found herself telling Fran all about her retired fisherman father and homemaker mother and their modest home at the base of the Olympic Mountains. There was something about Fran Tulip that made her very easy to talk to. Maybe it was the abject interest that shone in her minty blue eyes. Or the encouraging tilt to her head of snow white curls.

Fran's eyes sought hers. "Are you much of a playgoer?"

Rosalind began to realize she'd given Fran a lot of personal information over the last few minutes. It began to make her feel uneasy as she remembered Graham was standing right beside them. She fiddled with the clasp of her evening clutch. "No, I'm afraid I'm generally too busy."

"Really? What do you do?"

"I'm a deputy prosecutor for King County."

Fran's eyebrows raised. "A deputy prosecutor? How wonderful! Such extraordinary things young women do today. Don't you think so, Gray?"

Graham saw the matchmaker light gleaming in Fran's eyes and knew he should have expected it. "Yes," he agreed amicably.

Fran beamed back at Rosalind. "Of course, many women of my vintage did work outside the home. But most of us were content to raise families and volunteer for community service. Did you and Gray meet on a case?"

Graham watched new embarrassment erode over Rosalind's face. "I...we're..." Her voice broke off awkwardly.

Graham kept the smile off his face and out of his voice as he came to the rescue. "Rosalind is the prosecutor in the Milton Morebug trial, Fran."

Fran's eyes blinked rapidly. "Milton Morebug?" She shot her great-nephew a look. "Gray?"

Graham patted her arm. "They're flashing the lights. I think we'd best hurry to make it to our seats."

ROSALIND COULDN'T GET her thoughts or feelings straight. She'd been sure Graham had offered her the ticket to the play as a ploy to make a move on her. She'd been prepared to reject his slightest overture publicly and loudly, savoring her revenge while looking her best, of course. But after being introduced to the sweet Fran Tulip, Rosalind didn't know what to think.

Except that she'd been invited to a very good play—a real old-fashioned romantic comedy. From the opening dialogue to the last line, she smiled and laughed and even, once or twice, felt a tear in her eye. And throughout it all she was conscious of Fran's faint, rhythmic tinkles beside her and Graham's deep rumbles two seats away.

She was in such a good mood that when they walked out into the cool, rainy night air and Graham suggested they go down the street for a light after-theater supper, Rosalind agreed without a thought.

After a bowl of clam chowder and several slices of hot cheese bread, they all sat back in the snug booth of the small restaurant in comfortable silence.

Graham was the first to break it. "It's hard to find a good play these days—one that isn't filled with gloom and doom that the cynical critics rave over. Thanks for sharing this one with me, Fran."

Graham had voiced her thoughts so accurately, Rosalind looked over at him as though he'd read her mind. She was very surprised at his favorable reactions to the warm and funny play.

Fran patted Graham's arm with her wrinkled white hand. "You've always enjoyed a romantic ending, Gray. I remember when Jack and I took you to the movies when you were just a youngster and—"

Graham's hand folded over Fran's and gave it a restraining tug. When his eyes flicked over to Rosalind, Fran got the message and eased back in her chair. "You were always appreciative," Fran concluded.

Rosalind was sure those words were not what Fran had been about to say, but had been substituted so as not to embarrass Graham. The idea that Graham could be embarrassed came as an unexpected revelation.

Rosalind watched Graham's comforting hand on his sweet great-aunt's arm. Fran Tulip related to him with sensitivity and tenderness, and he returned the behavior in kind.

An uneasiness grew in Rosalind born of inconsistency. This isn't the real man, she told herself. She had met the real Graham Knight nine years before. He was an insensitive lout who had treated her like dirt and thrown her work into the trash. Memories of that insult flashed once again in her mind and propelled her to her feet.

"Thank you very much, Fran. I enjoyed the play. But it's getting late and I must be going now. It's been a pleasure meeting you."

Rosalind reached into her purse to extract the money for her meal. She placed it on the table.

Fran's surprised eyes blinked up into hers. "You're leaving so soon, Rosalind? But I thought you and Gray—"

Graham's hand once again tightened on his great-aunt's arm and she broke off whatever it was she had been about to say. He rose slowly to face Rosalind and stretched out his hand formally.

"Thank you for joining us, Ms. Hart."

Rosalind took his hand because she knew it would be rude not to. But she was unprepared for the feel of his warm flesh wrapping around hers, shooting arrows of excitement through her body.

A mindless heat coursed through her veins. She wanted to pull her hand away, but somehow she couldn't. Her eyes rose to his and she read the open invitation there, and something deep inside her yearned to answer.

"Shouldn't you walk Rosalind to her car?" Fran asked.

Fran's voice acted like a hook yanking sense back into Rosalind's head. She tore her hand away from Graham's touch. Turning toward Fran, she tried not to let her emotions show through. "That's not necessary."

"Of course, I'll walk Ms. Hart to her car," Graham said. "My manners reflect your training, Fran. I won't disgrace you."

Rosalind knew she couldn't refuse Graham's offer, not without appearing totally rude in front of Fran. To buy herself some time wherein she could regain her composure, she excused herself to visit the ladies' room.

As soon as Rosalind was out of sight, Fran turned to her great-nephew. "Gray, why does Rosalind act as though she's angry with you?"

Graham retrieved the money Rosalind had left on the table and sat down next to his great-aunt. He gave himself a moment. Physical contact with Rosalind Hart and the look in her eyes had proved to be more exciting than even he had anticipated. "Good question, Fran. I'd sure like to find the answer to that one myself. So far, I've been a perfect gentleman."

Fran's eyebrows arched. "So far? Graham you've become a scoundrel. As you should have discovered by now, many women have an antenna for men who target them. My guess is the lady is picking up your intentions and responding accordingly. You should be ashamed of yourself!"

Graham felt amused at Fran's reprimand. There were times when she still treated him as though he was twelve. "Think so?"

Fran ignored the twinkle in his eye. "And why in heaven's name you've got designs on the deputy prosecutor on the case you're trying is beyond my comprehension."

Graham stirred some cream into his after-dinner coffee. He'd wondered about that one himself. "She's a beautiful woman, Fran. Surely I don't have to point that out to you?"

Fran leaned toward him. "She's also a dangerous one to get involved with, considering you're on the opposite ends of a court battle."

"Who said I intended to get *involved* with her?"

Fran shook her white curls. "Gray, dear, another notch on your belt isn't the way to happiness. Not for a man like you. You're still a romantic in your soul, no matter what your experiences have been. You see, I know you, dear. You can't fool me."

Graham saw the moisture gathering in Fran's eyes, and he felt a sad little tug at his heart. His disillusionment with love and marriage seemed to have hit her harder than it had even hit him. He wrapped his large hands around her small ones and smiled. "It was a good play tonight, wasn't it?"

GRAHAM ROSE WHEN Rosalind approached the table again, and told Fran he'd return to her shortly. He said nothing as he escorted Rosalind out of the restaurant. As they stood under the awning at the entrance, Graham helped Rosalind get into her raincoat, inhaling her sweet scent and lightly brushing her arm twice to be sure she didn't forget he was there. When he was finished, he was certain the light flush to her cheeks wasn't caused by the chilliness of the rain-swept breeze.

He opened her umbrella. "Where are you parked?"

He watched her catch her breath before answering and smiled. "Down at the end of the street in the public parking lot."

Graham turned in that direction and gently wrapped his arm around her shoulder. She withdrew from it as he had anticipated, but she had to stay close beside him so as not to get wet as he held the umbrella over her fiery hair. He had anticipated that, too. He walked slowly.

"I'm glad you decided to come tonight, Ms. Hart. As my great-aunt said, a play is always better when you can enjoy it with someone. And Fran and I both enjoyed your company."

He watched Rosalind open her mouth as though to protest something he had said, then close her mouth as she realized he'd said nothing she could protest. It was obvious to him that she was a battle just pining to be fought and it was frustrating the hell out of her that he was giving her no opportunity to cross swords.

"You seem close," she said carefully.

"We are. Fran raised me ever since I was twelve. She was the one who encouraged me to go to law school. Now that my great-uncle Jack has passed on, Fran's the only family I've got."

Graham could feel Rosalind's eyes reaching up to search his profile. "Your parents are dead?"

Graham felt a bit annoyed with himself. He wasn't sure why he had even spoke of his past. Since he had, her question was a natural one. In an effort to avoid an answer, he pointed toward the cars in the lot they had just approached.

"Shall I guess which one is yours?"

He could still feel her eyes as she hesitated briefly. "All right, if you think you can."

The lot was full. Graham really had no idea what kind of car she would drive. He had just used the question as a diversionary tactic. But even if he had known what car she drove, he sensed that it would be more helpful to their future relationship if he should guess wrong and give her a feeling she was still in control.

His eyes scanned the lot for the least likely vehicle, determined it would be his choice. But his search was distracted when he spied the well-kept, older Chrysler LeBaron, about twenty feet away. He walked up to the white car, trying to get a better look through the rain, wondering why it was nearly a half foot lower than the cars on either side of it.

It took but a moment to see that the car sat so much lower than the others because all of the tires were slashed and it was supported by its wheel rims. There was a savageness to the strewed steel-belted rubber that left Graham with a very uneasy feeling. He heard Rosalind's small sound beside him.

"Looks like some kind of vandalism," he said. "Maybe one gang harassing another."

Rosalind's voice was deep and emotionless beside him, belying her earlier exclamation. "It's not."

Graham was surprised at the unequivocalness of her statement. "How do you know?"

When she didn't immediately answer, Graham turned to her. It was only then he saw how deathly pale her face was and realized something was terribly wrong. "Rosalind?"

"I know because this is my car," she said.

Chapter Five

Graham admired Rosalind's calm as they walked back to the restaurant and she called the police. He wondered at how she could remain so resolutely in control until he saw how badly her hands shook as she held on to the telephone receiver. Feeling a need to help, he went back to the table to explain things to Fran, then ordered Rosalind a brandy. He was back at the telephone booth holding it out to her when she got off the phone.

She shook her head. "I don't need a drink."

He wrapped his warm steady hand around her cold, shaky one as he placed the drink in it. "Consider it medicine."

Under the open caring of his look, Rosalind felt her resolve slipping. She took a gulp of the brandy. The warming vapor exploded inside her throat and traveled like a hot poker into her chilled chest. She gasped.

"A little more slowly," Graham directed.

Rosalind shook her head and shoved the drink toward him. "That was sufficient, thank you. I'm not interested in dulling my senses when I have work to do."

"Work?" Graham was sure she was too emotionally distressed to be serious. "You're not thinking of involving yourself personally in the investigation of who slashed your tires?"

Rosalind didn't appear to be listening. She spoke aloud, but Graham was convinced she was talking to herself, not him. "More than likely it's one of the people I helped to put away or some angry family member out for revenge."

Despite the boldness of her words, Graham didn't like watching the way Rosalind clutched her hands about her. He tried for a soothing tone. "Maybe this had nothing to do with a personal attack on you. Maybe it's just some teenage vandalism done on a dare."

Rosalind looked up at Graham. "Slashing just *my* tires in a parking lot full of cars? Not likely. Much more likely this is another incident in a pattern of incidents."

Graham's hands went out to circle her arms without conscious thought. He looked deep into her eyes and saw the flicker of fear. It sent a momentary chill up his spine. "*Pattern* of incidents? Your tires have been slashed before?"

Rosalind's head shook. "No. Someone broke into my apartment last Friday and slicked my floor."

Graham swallowed uncomfortably at her words. "What?"

Her rueful smile was a painful affair. "Crazy, huh? It seems I'm being sent a message."

ROSALIND TOOK the courthouse stairs Tuesday morning, preferring to walk the two flights rather than risk another chance encounter with Graham Knight in the elevator.

She was tired and edgy. She'd hardly slept after finishing with the police following the tire slashing the night before. They had told her what she already knew—that chances of catching the person responsible were slim—at least not without some fingerprints or hair samples or something concrete to give to the lab. They said they could only hope they'd get lucky and find something the next time.

The next time. Thinking about the next time was why Rosalind hadn't slept. "We'll get him," Max Hill had promised when he appeared at the scene to take over the investigation before Rosalind could flag a taxi home. But she kept wondering when and where and how "the next time" would emerge.

Get your mind on something else, an inner voice cautioned. Rosalind took a deep breath and forcibly switched her thoughts to the Morebug trial.

As she reached the courtroom of Judge Gloria Shotz, she saw a young woman she guessed to be her first witness of the day, Stephanie Pond, pacing in front of the courtroom doors, twisting the strap of her purse in some anxiety. Rosalind walked up to her and held out her hand.

"Ms. Pond? I'm Rosalind Hart."

Stephanie Pond turned to Rosalind and took her hand. It felt clammy in Rosalind's grasp.

"Are you nervous, Stephanie?"

Stephanie's long dishwater hair swished from side to side. She was barely twenty-one, with facial hair so light, her eyelashes and eyebrows looked nonexistent. When she saw the doubt in Rosalind's eye, she smiled. "I guess. A little."

Rosalind guessed a lot. She gave Stephanie a reassuring pat on the arm. "Don't worry about today. It's like I told you on the phone last week. I'll ask you the same questions Judson Fry originally did in the preliminary hearing. Why don't you have a seat on this bench here, and when it's time for your testimony, the bailiff will come to the door and motion you inside."

Stephanie's pale blue eyes filled with surprise as she sat. "Why can't I sit in the courtroom?"

Rosalind sat beside Stephanie. "I realize that television's 'Perry Mason' always has the people involved in a case sitting in a courtroom when the real killer is revealed, but in real life, witnesses are excluded from the trial except during their testimony."

Stephanie looked confused. "Why is that?"

"Well, if a witness like yourself were to hear the testimony of other witnesses, it might sway your judgment and change your testimony. So, as a safeguard, you are kept separate from others who will testify. That's also why I've cautioned you not to discuss your testimony with anyone else. I want you to get up on that stand this morning and answer all questions as clearly and concisely as you can to the best of your recollection, not someone else's. Does that make sense?''

Stephanie nodded. Rosalind gave her a reassuring smile.

When Rosalind rose, she caught sight of the two Mercer Island police officers who were also scheduled to testify that morning. She went over to them and renewed their brief acquaintance of a week before. Assured her witnesses were ready, she checked her watch and headed for the door.

When she walked into the courtroom, she purposely didn't look at the defense table as she made a beeline for the prosecution's table.

Max Hill wasn't there. She remembered he'd mentioned he would be out of court this morning. But as Rosalind approached the prosecution's table, she saw the single long-stemmed red rose lying across it.

There was a small, white envelope pinned to the cellophane wrapping. She put down her briefcase and opened the envelope, a puzzled frown on her face at the money she found inside. Then she found the note folded in half and opened it. "Supper was my treat. You have a friend should you decide you need one. G.''

Rosalind's fingers closed over the note in her hand as she felt the blood rushing into her neck. Graham Knight had been very gentle with her after the tire-slashing incident. Very nice and considerate. And that was precisely why she was trying to avoid him.

Nine years ago she had learned of his cold indifference. She knew how to respond to both it and his arrogance. But she didn't know how to respond to his tenderness. Of its own accord, her head turned toward the defense table. Graham looked at her and smiled.

Rosalind looked away, fighting against the sudden pounding of her heart. What was Graham Knight's game? And what treachery was this that her own body was turning against her?

"All rise and come to order. Superior Court is now in session, the Honorable Judge Gloria Shotz presiding."

Rosalind crushed the paper in her hand, digging her nails into the soft flesh of her palm. She didn't need this confusion. Not on top of everything else. With every shred of her control, she refocused her attention. As soon as Judge Shotz gave her the go-ahead, Rosalind called her first witness.

Stephanie Pond took the stand and told the court about how she had been driving home on the night of January eighth on West Mercer Way on Mercer Island, east of Seattle, when she spied what looked like two sets of skid marks in the snow at the side of the road.

"Two sets?" Rosalind asked.

"Yes. One set of tracks had gone over the bank. The other had curved and swerved back onto the road like one car had run the other car off the road."

"Objection," Graham said. "Speculation."

"Sustained," Judge Shotz ruled.

Rosalind had expected the objection, but she knew Stephanie's words had been heard by the jury and that the image would be hard for them to erase despite the judge's ruling.

"What did you do, Ms. Pond?"

"Well, I pulled my car into a shallow turnout just ahead of the skid marks and stopped. You see, it's kind of dark and steep on that stretch of the road. After looking at those skid marks going over the side, I thought somebody might need help."

"What did you do after you stopped your car?" Rosalind asked.

"I got a flashlight out of my glove compartment and I got out of the car to take a look. I followed the skid marks."

"What did you see?"

Stephanie's young voice suddenly sounded older. "There was a car there all right. It had gone over the embankment. Looked like it had hit a tree on the sloping ground down there."

"Did you see anything else?"

Stephanie nodded. "The driver's door was open and there was a man lying in the snow beside the open door."

Rosalind's voice turned gentle. "What did you do then?"

"I slid down the embankment, knelt next to the man and I put my fingers on his neck to see if he was alive." Stephanie demonstrated by placing her finger against the pulse in her neck. Then her hand dropped.

"The man wasn't alive?"

Stephanie shrugged. "I'm not trained in first aid or anything but I didn't find a pulse."

"All right. You felt for a pulse in the man's neck. What did you do next?"

Stephanie's hands twisted in her lap. "Well, I knew I couldn't do anything for him. I went back to my car and I drove home. I was only three blocks away. I called 911."

"And then?"

"Then I drove back to where I'd found the man and waited for the police. They arrived a few minutes later and after them a paramedics unit came. The paramedics said the man was dead."

"Thank you, Ms. Pond. That's all the questions I have."

As Rosalind returned to the prosecution's table, Graham rose and buttoned the front of his deep gray suit coat. As she passed, he gave her a small smile. It caused her heart to skip a beat and she was immediately annoyed at him and herself.

Graham watched the confused flash in Rosalind's eyes and chalked up another point for his side. But the light-heartedness he normally felt while in pursuit of a beautiful woman was overshadowed by the events of the previous evening. Rosalind Hart was obviously the target for some lunatic and no matter how hard he tried, he couldn't wipe away the savage image of her slashed tires.

Particularly since she had refused his every offer of help. She'd been so frustratingly self-reliant that it irritated him. Curious. Tami's inability to cope had been intolerable. And now he was finding this woman's ability to cope equally intolerable. What was wrong with him?

Graham forcibly brought his mind back to the trial as he stopped approximately ten feet away from the witness stand

and watched Stephanie quietly for a moment without speaking. He knew something was wrong with her testimony, but at this point he couldn't put his finger on it. All he was sure of was the young woman's inability to keep her hands still.

"So, Ms. Pond, you stopped your car while driving along West Mercer Way on Mercer Island because you thought an accident might have occurred?"

"Yes."

"You said the marks looked like skid marks. How did they differ from regular tire tracks?"

Stephanie's hands shifted in the air. "Well the snow was sort of pushed aside."

"Like it might be if someone drove over it?"

"Well, I guess."

"Isn't it true, Ms. Pond, that it's very difficult to distinguish skid marks from regular tire tracks in snow?"

Her hands twisted in her lap again. "I guess so."

"Then why did you say these were skid marks?"

"Well, that's a dangerous turnout. The bank slopes down quite steeply. Seeing the two sets of tracks that looked like one had forced the other—"

"So you inferred the marks were skid marks?"

"I guess."

"Just like you inferred the other tracks in the snow, the ones that had turned back into the road, had occurred at the same time?"

"I guess."

Graham stared at her. "Yes, it sounds like you do a lot of guessing. Isn't it true that those tracks could have been made at any time after the snowfall of the previous weekend?"

"I g—" Stephanie caught herself. "Yes."

"Did you see any footsteps in the snow leading from those tracks to the bank?"

"I really didn't look."

"So you got out of your car and walked over to the man lying in the snow beside the open door of his car."

Stephanie's hands twisted. "Yes."

Graham looked away as he paced sideways. "There was a lot of snow along the side of the road. How did you walk in it?"

"I was wearing boots."

"How far did you have to go before you saw him?"

"I followed the tracks over the bank. About twenty-five feet from the road. Then it dips down about ten feet." Stephanie's hands curved and dipped to demonstrate. "The car was at the bottom, its nose up against a tree."

"You saw that from the top of the bank?"

"No. The flashlight beam didn't reach that far. I followed the tire tracks down to the bottom of the ravine. That's when I saw the car and the man."

"Was the engine still running on the man's car?"

"No. The lights were off, too."

"How long did it take for you to reach the man?"

Stephanie Pond's hands were still nervously shoving back her cuticles. "I'm not sure. A few minutes maybe."

"Then what?"

"I leaned down and tried to feel for the pulse in his neck."

"And when you didn't find it?"

Stephanie's cuticles got a vicious jab. "Like I told Ms. Hart. I drove home to call the police."

Stephanie's hands told Graham she wasn't telling all. What could this young woman be hiding? He pressed. "Ms. Pond, refresh my memory. What time was it again that you stopped for this presumed accident victim?"

"About two-thirty in the morning."

Graham shook his head. "You're quite a daring young woman, Ms. Pond. Alone, you get out of your car at two-thirty in the morning and track through the darkness and snow over a treacherous bank because you *think maybe* an accident might have occurred. Wouldn't it have made more sense to have simply reported the tracks to the police when you reached home?"

Stephanie bit at the end of her fingernail. "I thought if it was an accident I might be able to help."

Graham looked deliberately confused. "But I thought you testified you aren't trained in first aid? Are you?"

Stephanie brought another fingernail into her mouth. "No."

"Then how could you have helped?"

"I . . . might have been able to do something."

Graham paced closer to the jury so that Stephanie would have to look in their direction to answer his next set of questions.

"Ms. Pond, you testified you were on your way home that night?"

"Yes."

"What time did you arrive at the turnout?"

"Around 2:25."

"And what time did you drive home to notify the paramedics?"

"Right after."

"Say around two-thirty?"

"Yes."

"You live with your parents?"

"Yes."

"Where had you been?"

"At UW. I had been helping to put the paper to bed."

Graham's interest immediately rose. "The paper to bed? By that I take it you're a journalism major at the University of Washington and you work on the school paper?"

"Yes."

"What position do you hold?"

"I'm the news editor this term."

"And what position did you hold last January eighth, the night of Warren Beaver's death?"

Stephanie's hands curled around the arms of the witness chair. "I was chief photographer."

Chief photographer? A glimmer of an idea began to grow in Graham's thoughts. He gave the witness a long, hard stare. "Ms. Pond, have you told this court everything you did when you found the dead man on the night of January eighth?"

Stephanie's fingers gripped the chair arms. "I don't know what you mean."

It was the reaction Graham had been hoping for. It told him he was on the right track. "Don't you? Ms. Pond, were you carrying a camera in your car on the night of January eighth?"

Stephanie's fingernails dug into the fabric on the chair arms as Rosalind rose to her feet. "Objection. Question has no relevance."

Graham turned toward Judge Shotz. "I'm about to establish the relevance, Your Honor, if the court will grant me some latitude."

Gloria Shotz nodded. "I'll allow the question."

Graham turned back to Stephanie Pond. "I repeat, Ms. Pond, did you have a camera in your car?"

Stephanie's voice dropped to barely a whisper. "Yes."

"Please speak up so that the court can hear you, Ms. Pond."

Stephanie's chest heaved as though she was making an effort to suck in more air. "Yes!"

Graham circled about eight feet in front of the witness careful not to get too close since close proximity to a witness would be considered threatening. "So a newspaper's chief photographer happens on what she thinks to be the scene of an accident. And she has a camera in her car—"

Stephanie had begun to shake her head. "I didn't—"

"Perjury is a very serious crime, Ms. Pond," Graham interrupted. "You can be imprisoned for it. Now answer yes or no. Did you go back to your car and get your camera when you found the dead body of the man in the snow?"

Stephanie choked out her reply. "No!"

Graham's eyebrow raised. "No? A news photographer didn't even think of taking pictures of a dead body?"

"I—"

"Yes, Ms. Pond?"

Stephanie exhaled in defeat. "I already had the camera with me."

Graham leaned forward eagerly. "So you *did* take pictures?"

Stephanie's hands wrapped around her body and hugged it. Her face crinkled in misery. "All right! I took pictures!"

There was a murmur through the courtroom as Judge Shotz rapped her gavel for order. Rosalind shook her head over the unexpected and unwelcome turn of events.

Graham waited until the murmur had died down before he pursued his questioning. "Why did you take pictures?"

Stephanie's head drooped. "I thought I might be able to interest the newspaper in a story about the accident."

"The university's newspaper?"

"No. The *Seattle Times*. The university won't run anything that isn't related to the school. But I thought the *Times* might, considering who the dead man was."

Graham's eyes narrowed and his pulse raced as the implications of the witness's words sunk in. He circled to get as close to the witness as he dared. "Considering who the man was? Ms. Pond are you saying that you *knew* the victim?"

Rosalind's spirits continued to sink at the unexpected revelations of her first witness. The woman's testimony should have been just a brief recital of her having found the body. She had no idea how Graham had figured out Stephanie Pond had been withholding information, but somehow he had and was capitalizing on it for all it was worth. And now it looked like Stephanie Pond had known the dead man!

Stephanie's nails ripped at the fabric on the arms of the witness chair as Judge Shotz rapped for quiet in the courtroom. When order was once again attained, Graham repeated his question. "Ms. Pond, did you know the victim?"

Stephanie's light eyes had begun to water. "I wasn't exactly sure at the time. It was so dark and the flashlight beam was dull and I never really talked to the guy when he was alive."

"But?" Graham prodded.

"But it looked like him," Stephanie admitted. "Warren Beaver had played golf with my dad at the country club."

Graham emphasized his words. "Your father knew Warren Beaver, the state's commissioner of public lands?"

Stephanie nodded. "He only lived a couple of miles down the road from us. A lot of Mercer Island's families know one another. It's because of who he was that I took the pictures. I didn't mean any harm. I mean he was already dead, and I didn't know he'd been shot."

"You didn't see the blood on his chest?"

Stephanie's nails were back to ripping at the fabric on the chair's arms. "I saw the blood, sure. But I thought it was as a result of the car accident. I swear it!"

"You needed some time to take these pictures. When did you really arrive at the scene of Beaver's death?"

Stephanie hung her head. "Maybe two-fifteen."

"And you left to phone the paramedics when?"

"Two-thirty. Like I said before."

"Was your father home when you arrived to call the police?"

"No. He and my mother were in San Diego on vacation."

"Did your father and Warren Beaver get along?"

Rosalind was on her feet. "Objection. Irrelevant."

"Sustained, " Judge Shotz pronounced.

Graham had expected the objection. He went on undaunted.

"How about you, Ms. Pond. Did you like Warren Beaver?"

"I told you I didn't even know him!"

"But surely your father must have talked about his dishonesty. How he was always cheating people?"

Rosalind flew to her feet this time. "Objection!"

"Sustained. Mr. Knight, you know better. No more evidentiary remarks concerning the character of the deceased."

Graham turned toward the judge. "Sorry, Your Honor."

Rosalind shook her head. He looked anything but sorry.

Graham faced Stephanie again. "How many pictures did you take, Ms. Pond?"

"A dozen or so."

"You had a flash attachment?"

"Yes."

"Still, you'd have to get pretty close in order for a flash attachment to be effective at night, wouldn't you?"

"Yes."

"So how close did you get, Ms. Pond?"

"Five feet maybe."

"And you walked all around the body in order to photograph it at different angles?"

"Yes."

"Obliterating any other footprints?"

"Objection!" Rosalind said. "Leading and calls for a conclusion."

The implications of Graham's statement had sunk in and Stephanie Pond immediately went on the defensive as Graham had expected she would. She leaned forward in the witness chair.

"I wasn't the only one. The two cops who came didn't care where they were stepping. And the paramedics even dragged that cart—"

Rosalind interrupted. "Objection, Your Honor. Please instruct the witness to wait until a ruling is made."

Judge Shotz glared at Rosalind. "I know my job, Ms. Hart." She turned toward the witness stand. "Ms. Pond, please do not answer a question from either counsel when an objection has been made until I rule on it. Do you understand?"

"Yes, Your Honor."

"Good. Ms. Hart's objection is sustained."

Graham didn't care the ruling went against him. Stephanie had already told the jury what he wanted them to hear. "Ms. Pond, did you watch the scene of the crime get trampled on by the police and paramedics crew?"

Rosalind was up again. "Objection! 'Trampled on' is suggestive and leading. And any questions regarding the physical scene of the crime calls for an expert conclusion and the witness is hardly an expert nor are any of her conclusions admissible."

Graham turned toward the judge. "Your Honor, the witness was there. She can testify to what she saw."

Judge Shotz shook her head. "Rephrase your question, Mr. Knight. Let the witness use her own words."

Graham turned back to Stephanie. "Ms. Pond, what did the area around the body of Warren Beaver look like after the police and paramedics were finished? In your own words."

"There were a lot of footprints. The snow was smashed down pretty good."

Graham smiled. "Smashed down" was as good as "trampled on" any day. "What happened to the pictures you took?"

Her fingernails were back to ripping at the chair's fabric. "They didn't come out too well."

Graham wasn't sure whether she was holding something back or was just embarrassed. "You didn't submit them to the *Times?*"

Stephanie fidgeted in her chair. "It wasn't any use. I'd written the story as an accident report and before I could even submit it, the radio report came on saying it was murder."

Her hands rested on the chair flat and defeated. Graham decided she was telling the truth. "What did you do with your story?"

"I threw it away."

"And the pictures?"

"I threw them away, too. They really weren't too clear."

"And the negatives?"

Stephanie nodded. Graham shook his head as he slowly walked back to the defense table. Gloria Shotz's booming voice followed him. "Mr. Knight, are you finished with this witness?"

"Yes, Your Honor."

"Any redirect, Ms. Hart?"

Rosalind would rather have throttled Stephanie Pond at this point than question her, but she held her temper as she rose behind the prosecution's table. "Yes, Your Honor."

She took her time circling the desk so that there was a clear field between herself and Stephanie. She wanted the young woman to see the anger in her eyes. "Ms. Pond, are you aware that you've altered a crime scene, and withheld information and evidence pertaining to a crime and that the penalties for these actions can be very severe?"

Stephanie's eyes got big. "I didn't mean to! I swear I didn't think about it as being evidence. It was just a story."

"Are you serious about pursuing a career in journalism?"

"Yes."

"Are you aware that what you did was unlawful and unethical and if you had been a professional journalist you could have been fired from your job?"

Stephanie Pond hung her head. "I can see that now."

"But you didn't see that then, did you?"

"No. I wasn't thinking straight."

"Is that why you didn't tell the investigating officer about all of your activities on that night?"

Stephanie's head came up and her hands flew through the air. "Look, I'm sorry. Really. I just figured my taking a few pictures had nothing to do with Mr. Beaver's death."

"You're sure that was your only motivation?"

"Yes! I swear it! I was just trying for a scoop. I didn't even know Warren Beaver. And I wasn't the one who ran him off the road and shot him. Everyone knows that was Milton Morebug."

Graham was on his feet. "Objection, Your Honor."

"Sustained. The jury will disregard that last comment."

Stephanie had made the point Rosalind was hoping for—that her behavior on the night of Beaver's death, however reprehensible, had nothing to do with the crime of murder. She smiled internally as she sat down. "I have no more questions of this witness, Your Honor."

Judge Shotz turned to the witness box. "Ms. Pond, you may step down. I shall leave it to the prosecutor's office to take whatever steps deemed necessary to address your very questionable behavior in this matter."

Stephanie Pond slunk out of the witness chair and exited the courtroom like a whipped puppy.

Rosalind's next two witnesses were the Mercer Island police officers who responded to Stephanie Pond's call to 911. They both testified the call had come in at 2:35. They described arriving at the scene and finding the dead body. Rosalind considered their testimony perfunctory in most respects, presented only to give the jury a feeling for the sequence of events. But in each case, Graham got the officers to admit to having left quite a few footsteps in the snow around the scene of the murder.

When the paramedics next took the stand, he got them also to state that they walked all over the scene.

Rosalind didn't think it would help him much. The prosecution wasn't presenting evidence of Milton Morebug's footprints from the crime scene. She realized Graham's thrust had to be to throw as much doubt on every one of the prosecution's witnesses as possible, even if it had nothing to do with evidence of the crime. She made a note to be sure to point out that fact in her closing remarks to the jury.

For now she had to concentrate on meeting each one of his points with a counterpoint. She couldn't let up a second.

By the time Graham had finished cross-examining the second paramedic, it was lunchtime and Judge Shotz adjourned court. It had been a busy morning and Rosalind felt famished. With little enthusiasm, she visualized going back to her office and dropping her freeze-dried envelope of soup into some hot water. What she needed was a real lunch in a real restaurant.

Graham's voice spoke up beside her. "I'd like to talk to you about the case, Ms. Hart. If you have no plans for lunch, perhaps you wouldn't mind combining the two?"

Rosalind looked up into his gray eyes, wondering at this uncanny skill he seemed to have to read her mind.

"I don't think—"

He put a hand up to stop what she was about to say. "Look, I'm hungry. Aren't you?"

For a moment she battled with conflicting emotions—irritation, hunger, wariness and curiosity. The hunger and curiosity won out.

"All right. Let me just check my office first for messages."

Fifteen minutes later they were at the Metropolitan Grill on Second Avenue, a place Rosalind chose because of her greater familiarity with the area. It was a nicely appointed lunch establishment with quick service for the business crowd. After they had given their order to the waiter, Graham leaned forward in the booth, his eyes studying her face.

"Did the police find anything last night?"

Rosalind avoided his eyes as she picked up her dinner napkin. "Nothing helpful."

"I wish you had let me drive you home. From those circles under your eyes, I can see you didn't get much sleep."

Rosalind glanced up frowning. "Always full of compliments I see. Are they part of your routine?"

A small smile circled Graham's lips. "Why is it that every time you look at me, Ms. Hart, I feel I'm about to get my face slapped?"

"Maybe, Mr. Knight, because you deserve to." Rosalind's gaze dropped to her napkin. She studiously avoided looking at the handsome face so close to hers, to the eyes filled with humor. "Look, I'm here because you said you wanted to talk about the case. So talk about it."

Graham couldn't miss the brusque irritation in her voice, but her hands told him a different story. The napkin she held was twisted tight. Very tight. He speculated on what emotions would unravel should she let them. His gut tightened as he anticipated the exciting possibilities.

He leaned back in the booth. "All right. Let's talk about the case. I'm going for a motion after lunch to bar the crime-scene photographs from evidence. Rather than make it a fight before the judge, I suggest you pull them voluntarily."

Rosalind's eyes raised to Graham's face. "Voluntarily pull the crime-scene photos? Are you mad?"

Watching her shocked expression, he couldn't help but grin. "Not yet certifiably. Look, you and I both know the death scene was substantially altered by Stephanie's impromptu photo session and the Mercer Island PD and the paramedics. There's no way any pictures taken after that much traffic went through can be seriously considered as evidence. The judge is going to have to throw them out."

Rosalind shook her head vehemently as she leaned forward, her voice full of fight. "On the contrary. You know perfectly well that those shots clearly show the position of the body in relation to the vehicle and also reveal the bloody letter M that Beaver scratched in the snow. Those photographs are germane to my case and I will fight to the death to keep them in."

Graham smiled at her terminology. "To the death, Ms. Hart?"

Rosalind shrugged away her dramatic words. "Take your best shot, Knight. It will do you no good. I'm putting those photographs into evidence. This afternoon."

Graham studied the flushed determination in her face. That familiar tingling began to pulse in his veins. He leaned forward. "We're adversaries, Rosalind, not enemies. Call me Graham."

The warmth in his eyes seemed to draw out the moisture in her throat. Rosalind reached for her glass of ice water and took a gulp. It didn't help.

"I don't see—" she began.

His hand covered hers as it lay on the table. "No, I guess you don't. When we're in that courtroom, I expect you to use all your legal skills to oppose me. As a matter of fact, I'd be disappointed if you didn't. But outside of the courtroom, Rosalind, outside—"

Fortunately for Rosalind's dissolving demeanor, the waiter arrived with their food and Graham removed his hand.

Rosalind deliberately didn't look at her luncheon companion again. She concentrated on her food. Yet despite her hunger, she ate her poached salmon in dill sauce without really tasting it, because with each bite she could feel Graham's watching eyes.

"CONTINUING WITH THE People versus Milton Morebug, I understand you have a motion to suppress certain exhibits, is that correct, Mr. Knight?" Judge Shotz asked in a booming voice prior to the jury being brought in at the beginning of the afternoon session.

"Yes, I do, Your Honor," Graham said as he rose from behind the defense's table. "In light of the testimony of the prosecution witnesses, I move that all subsequent photos taken of the turnout off West Mercer Way in the early morning hours of January ninth be stricken from admissible evidence. As the court clearly heard, the contamination of that crime scene was so pervasive as to render such pictures worthless."

Judge Shotz pursed her lips. "Ms. Hart?"

Rosalind rose. "Your Honor, it's true that foot traffic in the area might have destroyed imprints in the snow made by the murderer, but none of the footprints destroyed the position of the victim's car and body nor did they obscure the scratched letter M in the snow beside the victim's hand. These visual facts are evidence and should be admitted as such."

Graham didn't let a pause intrude. "Your Honor, since the crime scene was disturbed, we can't be sure the body of Warren Beaver wasn't moved or that the paramedics didn't inadvertently cause the scratching in the snow that the deputy prosecutor insists on interpreting as a letter M. Therefore, no pictures can be presented as accurately depicting the crime scene."

Judge Shotz turned to Rosalind. "Well, Ms. Hart? The counsel for defense makes a persuasive point."

"Your Honor, if each photograph of a crime scene had to be an accurate depiction of the crime immediately following its commission, I'd venture to say we wouldn't have any photo exhibits in any court. After all, who's to say that the murderer after killing his victim doesn't himself attempt to alter the scene so as to confuse and delude the police? All we can do is to take the pictures as promptly as possible and in the most professional way available to us and then use experts to help us interpret the evidence that might be there."

Rosalind stopped a moment and turned toward Graham. "If defense is concerned about the scene having been tampered with, then he has the right to cross-examine those experts in that regard and let the jury consider both his challenges and their answers. After all, it is the jury who is ultimately responsible to determine the truth in this matter, not the defense attorney."

Judge Shotz nodded. "Well argued, Ms. Hart. Motion denied, Mr. Knight."

Graham sat down as the jury was led in. He wasn't surprised his motion was denied. He knew he'd had a slim chance of getting it through with Rosalind as an opponent. Despite the circles beneath her eyes, she'd just proved she was up to the fight. He recognized that in some unfathomable way, that made him glad.

"Prosecution calls Susan Mast to the stand," Rosalind announced after the jury had been installed back in their box.

Susan Mast, a tiny blonde with short, curly hair, strode confidently up to the witness chair. The bailiff swore her in and Rosalind established her credentials before the court as a professional crime-scene investigator.

Using two-foot by three-foot blowups of the crime-scene photos taken by the Mercer Island PD, Rosalind began.

"Based upon your ten years as a crime-scene investigator, and your status as an expert witness in this court, Ms.

Mast, can you tell us if the victim was shot in his car or out of it?''

"He was out of it."

"And you know this because?" Rosalind prompted.

"There was no blood found in the car or in the snow around the car. If the victim had been shot there, logically blood would have been found there."

"So Warren Beaver was standing away from the driver's door of his car when he was shot?"

"Yes. Approximately five feet. That's where he fell."

"And, again, the reason for this conclusion?"

"Bloodstains around the body were localized to that area."

Rosalind circled to the easel exhibit. "Ms. Mast, I now direct your attention to the blowup of the area identified as People's exhibit number three. Would you say that was a letter M the victim had scratched in the snow just below his hand?"

"Objection," Graham protested. "Leading and calls for a conclusion."

Rosalind turned to the bench. "Your Honor, the court has ruled that Ms. Mast is an expert witness. Based on that classification, she should be allowed to give her opinion."

Judge Shotz shook her head. "Then ask for it properly, Ms. Hart. Objection sustained."

Undaunted, Rosalind turned back to her witness. "Ms. Mast, did you have occasion to examine the area below the victim's fingers as pictured in this photograph?"

"Yes."

"And what if anything did you find?"

"I found what appeared to be the victim's attempt to scratch something in the snow before he died."

"Objection," Graham said.

"I'll allow it," the judge ruled.

"Why do you think it was the victim who made these markings?" Rosalind asked.

"There was dried blood embedded in the indentations. When we tested it, we found it was the victim's blood. His fingers were also caked in dried blood."

Rosalind stepped in front of the jury, looking at them now.

"That's why you concluded the victim had scratched this letter M in the snow?"

"Objection! Assuming information not in evidence. Nothing has been introduced to determine what the scratching represents."

Rosalind pointed at exhibit three with incredulity in her voice. "Anyone who has eyes can see it's a letter M."

"Objection, Your Honor."

"Sustained. Ms. Hart, you are not here to give evidence. You are here to present it."

"I'm sorry, Your Honor. I have no further questions."

Graham waited almost a full minute before he began his cross-examination. Rosalind had managed to make the crime-scene investigator's testimony far more damaging than it should have been. She was clever. But he was no slouch. He rose carefully and approached the witness as close as he dared.

"Did you find the victim's blood in places other than the scratch marks?"

"Yes."

"Where, Ms. Mast?"

"Underneath the body. His clothing was soaked with it and it had seeped into the snow."

"So the victim bled a lot?"

"I'm not sure what you mean by a lot, Counselor."

Graham's eyebrows went up in incredulity. "You said his clothing was soaked in blood and it had seeped into the snow. I assume that's more than a little?"

Susan Mast shifted in her seat, uncomfortably. "More than a little," she agreed.

"And this blood had all collected beneath his body?"

"Except what was in the scratches next to his right hand."

Graham paced. "Oh, yes. And the blood on his hand. How did he get blood on his hand?"

"Objection," Rosalind protested as she got to her feet. "Calls for a conclusion."

"Your Honor," Graham said, "Ms. Mast is the prosecution's witness and has been granted expert status by this court. Surely after ten years of viewing crime scenes it isn't too farfetched to be asking her how a victim got blood on his hands?"

Gloria Shotz nodded. "I'll allow it."

Graham turned back to the witness. "Ms. Mast?"

"Since the victim received no hand wound, he may have gotten blood on his hand by clutching at his chest, perhaps in pain or fright, right after being shot. That's not an uncommon gesture."

Graham nodded. "Not uncommon at all. If a person was falling, what would that person commonly do just out of reflex?"

"Objection," Rosalind called. "Irrelevant."

Judge Shotz's eyes narrowed at Graham. "Mr. Knight, where are you going with this?"

"Your Honor, Ms. Mast has given us a reasonable explanation for the victim having blood on his hand. I think with a little patience, she may also provide us with a reasonable explanation for the scratches in the snow."

"Overruled," Shotz said.

Rosalind didn't like the look in Graham's eye. She found herself on the edge of her seat, ready to object.

"Well, Ms. Mast," Graham said, "what would your reflexes dictate you do if you were falling?"

"I suppose I would try to put out a hand to stop myself."

"With fingers extended, Ms. Mast? So that when your hand impacted with the snow those fingers would dig in and leave three scratches like those shown in exhibit three?"

Rosalind flew to her feet. "Objection!"

"Overruled," Judge Shotz said. "You may answer the question, Ms. Mast."

Susan exhaled deeply. "That's possible."

"And if that's possible reflex behavior for you, Ms. Mast, might it also have been possible reflex behavior for the victim, Warren Beaver?"

"Anything's possible, Counselor."

Graham's eyes narrowed. "I'm not asking you about anything, Ms. Mast. I'm asking you about the night Warren Beaver was mortally wounded and falling to the snow. Might he have put out his hand to stop his fall and might his extended fingers have put those scratches in the snow?"

Susan's answer hissed through locked teeth. "Yes."

Graham was already on his way back to his seat. "Thank you, Ms. Mast. I have no more questions for this witness." He had the nerve to flip Rosalind a smile.

Rosalind rose in determination. "I have a few redirect. Ms. Mast, if you were falling, as defense counsel has described, would your reflexes have just one of your hands stretching out to block your fall?"

Susan shook her head. "No. I would judge that both hands would be placed in motion as a natural reflex."

"Both hands?"

"Yes."

"And from your examination of the death scene of Warren Beaver, was there any evidence he put his left hand out to block his fall?"

Susan gave her a grateful smile as she answered. "No. None at all."

Rosalind grinned deliberately over at Graham. "Thank you, Ms. Mast. I have no further questions."

LEROY PONCE GROUND his teeth in dissatisfaction. Rosalind Hart showed no signs of fear. He obviously hadn't reached her yet. That would be rectified.

She had to be taught to fear. And lesson number one, she'd learn that moving to a different apartment hadn't bought her security. He'd been at his profession a lot of years. He was a master at getting into electronically controlled buildings.

He had plenty of opportunity to work on his plan while he sat in court each day. By this time he knew the defendant's wife and son by sight and the name and face of every reporter and the one or two courtroom groupies who were always in attendance. Of course, they were used to seeing him now and that wasn't good.

Still, he was stuck until he got word. The post office box where he received his messages from his employer had been empty for nearly a week.

It was irritating. He wanted this business over with. He wanted his payoff. Particularly since the female head of security at the county nuthouse, who he was bribing to take care of his old man, had been bugging him for more money. "Getting tougher to switch shifts," she had complained. "I've got expenses. You better get me more money."

"Don't take no lip from no woman," his old man's voice echoed in his ears, just like he'd told him a million times before. Well, he certainly didn't intend to take any lip from that witch. But he had to placate her. At least for the time being.

And he had to think up a real treat for Rosalind Hart. He smiled. Something a bit more pointed.

Chapter Six

Rosalind's last witness Tuesday was David Inch, a tall, thin medical examiner with thick glasses and a nervous shoulder twitch. He was an old-timer in the medical examiner's office and had testified often. He knew his stuff, but his jerky movements on the witness stand always made Rosalind uneasy.

"Dr. Inch, you did the autopsy of Warren Beaver?"

"Yes."

"When was that?"

"Four-thirty on the morning of January ninth."

"What did you find as the cause of death?"

Inch's shoulder twitched. "Beaver died from injuries sustained as the result of three bullet wounds to the chest fired from approximately ten feet away."

Rosalind placed a blowup of the pre-autopsy photo of Warren Beaver's punctured bare chest on the easel for the jury to see. Inch pointed to it as he described the bullet entries and got specific as to which bullets had entered which organs and which one might have been the fatal bullet. He identified three expended slugs as those he removed from the murdered man.

"And based upon your medical experience, when did Warren Beaver die, Doctor?"

His shoulder twitched again. "Approximately two a.m."

"And you base this determination on?"

"The degree of rigor mortis and the amount of lividity from pooled stagnant blood."

"For the jury's benefit, Doctor, can you tell us what rigor mortis is?"

Inch adjusted his glasses farther back on his beak of a nose. His shoulder gave another twist. "Rigor mortis is the muscular stiffening that follows death."

"And lividity?"

"It's the discoloration of the skin that occurs when the body's blood pools in response to gravity after death. Since Warren Beaver died while lying on his back, his blood collected there."

"And based on these two items, you determined death occurred at approximately two a.m.?"

"Yes. Rigor mortis was nonexistent and lividity was only slight. Both of those findings point to a recent death."

Rosalind zeroed in on the critical area of the doctor's testimony. "Based upon your medical experience, Dr. Inch, would you say Warren Beaver died immediately after being shot?"

"Not necessarily. Conceivably he lasted several minutes."

"And during those several minutes, would Beaver have been conscious and able to move his hand?"

"Objection," Graham called. "Question is outside of this witness's expertise. Dr. Inch is an expert on human remains. Any comments he may make regarding living persons is outside his realm of expertise."

Rosalind shook her head. "Your Honor, Dr. Inch has been with the medical examiner's office twenty-five years. He's a licensed medical practitioner. He knows what the human body can and can't do."

"I'll allow the question," Judge Shotz ruled.

Rosalind turned back to her witness. "Doctor, I ask you again. During the several minutes that Warren Beaver may have survived his mortal injuries, could he have been conscious and could he have moved his hand?"

"Yes."

"Thank you, Dr. Inch. I have no further questions."

Graham approached the witness stand to his usual six feet. He stared at David Inch until the man's hands clasped the arms of the witness seat.

"Doctor, you said you based Warren Beaver's time of death on the lack of rigor mortis and small amount of lividity. Was it because of those factors that you said death occurred at two?"

"Yes."

"But doesn't rigor mortis and lividity only point to an approximate time of death?"

Inch's shoulder twitched. "His death was recent. Not more than two or three hours from the time I examined him."

Graham paced. "So what you're saying is that Warren Beaver could have died before two a.m.?"

Inch's shoulder twitched. "Not much before. The roads were icy. He had to have sufficient time to get from Mr. Morebug's home at Hunt's Point to that turnout on Mercer—"

"Later than two a.m., Doctor?" Graham interrupted.

"Well not much later since by the time the paramedics examined the body at 2:50—"

Graham interrupted again. "So what you're saying, Doctor, is that you really used information from the police and the paramedics to determine the time of death?"

"Well, I—"

"Isn't it true, Doctor, that based on minimal lividity and the lack of rigor mortis, Warren Beaver could have died at any time between one-thirty and four in the morning?"

"Well, when the other things are taken into consid—"

"Just answer yes or no, Doctor."

Inch scowled. "Yes."

"And isn't it true that you really determined the time of Warren Beaver's death based on the police reports?"

Graham had caught Dr. Inch, and the man showed his discomfort as he twisted in his seat. His shoulder twitch had developed into a jerk. "I used my observations on rigor mortis and lividity, and my judgment."

Graham's tone dripped in sarcasm. "And your judgment," he repeated with a crooked smile. "Which was formed by reading the police reports. Was it also after reading further on those same police reports and finding out about the snow scratches that your *judgment* decided Warren Beaver could have been conscious and could have used his hand?"

Rosalind flew to her feet. "Objection!"

"Sustained."

Graham was already walking back to the defendant'stable, a look of disgust on his face that clearly showed he didn't care what the court ruled. "I'm through with this witness."

Judge Shotz turned to Dr. Inch and excused him from the stand. His shoulder jerked all the way out of the courtroom as Rosalind tried to tell herself that Graham's cross-examination of the medical examiner hadn't been as bad as she was imagining.

Judge Shotz's voice boomed. "As it is approaching five o'clock, court will adjourn until nine-thirty tomorrow morning."

"It's a shame we couldn't have picked another medical examiner," Max Hill whispered beside her as they rose. "I was watching the jury. Inch didn't come across too creditably."

Rosalind groaned internally. Those were precisely the words she hadn't wanted to hear.

GRAHAM GAVE Fran's cheek a brief kiss before sitting down to dinner in her Capitol Hill home, the table laid with a snow-white cloth and sparkling as usual with the elegance of its bone china and crystal goblets.

Fran and his great-uncle Jack had had many prominent people to dinner in this fine old dining room of this old house. He knew she missed Jack and their very full social life.

That was the real reason he had begun to involve her in his cases five years back, after Jack's death. She had stopped going out and entertaining and it worried him. He had needed a confidential inquiry made into the background of a prominent Seattle politician and he thought by asking for her help, he might be able to coax her back into a social life. He didn't really think she'd be able to find out anything.

But with the help of two of her eighty-year-old "girl-friends," Mabel and Violet, she'd brought him facts about that Seattle politician that had been amazingly revealing and helped Graham to successfully press an age-discrimination case. And more importantly, she had positively glowed doing it. Just as she was glowing now.

Fran waited to share her news until the maid had put a bowl of soup in front of Graham and left the room.

Graham tried the soup. It was cream of asparagus and quite tasty. But he put the spoon down because he could tell Fran was eager to relate her findings.

"Violet and Mabel came by today to tell me what they learned at dinner last evening. They were able to confirm Warren Beaver wasn't trusted because he involved both his personal and business associates in different kinds of underhanded dealings."

"Did they get any specifics?" Graham asked.

"The group the ladies talked to were very closemouthed about the particulars. Mabel said they were left with the feeling that Beaver orchestrated these 'deals' ostensibly as favors to those around him and then later when they fell apart, Beaver acted surprised."

"But the people who were involved with him on the scams thought he did know what was coming?"

Fran beamed. "Exactly, Gray. But because the deals were shady, they had no recourse when they fell through."

Gray fingered his spoon. "Did Beaver need the money?"

"No. He was very well off. The feeling the ladies have gotten is he did it for the sport of the thing—just to see if he could pull it off—if you know what I mean."

Graham nodded. "It's a shame Mabel or Violet couldn't have gotten a specific incident we could look into. I'm particularly interested in anything involving Hogg, or Wreckter, the two other men at the card game."

"We're not giving up, Gray. There's still that charity affair I'm attending tomorrow with a very close friend of Joyce Beaver, the wealthy widow. Now that I have a little better idea of what to ask, my questions will be better focused."

Graham ate the rest of his soup without really tasting it as his mind wrestled with the possibilities. He looked up as Fran's next question changed the direction of his thoughts.

"How is Rosalind?"

"She seems to be holding up quite well, at least if her courtroom performance is any indicator. I shouldn't worry."

"But you are worrying, aren't you, dear?"

Graham looked up at his great-aunt. Sometimes it was damn uncomfortable being around someone who could read him so easily. Seeing the concern in her eyes, he exhaled, giving up any further attempt at pretense. "Yes, I'm worried. It sounds to me like Rosalind is being stalked. She doesn't know who it is, and she's stubbornly refused all of my offers to help."

Fran cocked her head as she studied her great-nephew. "Such spirit and strength. Quite different from Tami, isn't she?"

Graham looked at Fran suspiciously. "Which means?"

Fran concentrated on looking innocent as a small, knowing smile circled her lips. "Oh nothing, dear. Just an observation."

ROSALIND WAS getting ready for bed by nine o'clock Tuesday night. After eating her microwaved dinner of sole and rereading her notes for the next day in court, she just couldn't keep her eyes open another minute. Yawning with weariness, she climbed into bed, set her alarm and was asleep before her head hit the pillow.

The call came after midnight. Rosalind didn't at first realize what had awakened her. She squinted bleary-eyed at the illuminated time on her clock radio. The next ring sent her fingers groping on the nightstand. She found the receiver and brought it to her ear. She got a blast of dial tone.

She groaned as she dropped the receiver back on the base and turned over on her side. She was almost asleep a minute later when the phone rang again. She got to the receiver more quickly this time and said hello.

The voice was deep and breathy. "Rosalind Hart?"

She yawned. "Yes."

"I'm from the Twenty-Four-Hour Fix-it Service."

Rosalind's eyes again sought the illuminated digits of her nightstand clock, not believing a salesman would have the nerve to call this late. Her voice rose in indignation. "For God's sake, do you know what time it is?"

The deep breathy voice laughed. "I'm a professional. Time means nothing to me. Fix your floor. Fix your tires. I'm here to fix you, Rosalind."

She shot up in bed as his words thrust her awake. This was the man who had broken into her apartment and who slashed her tires outside the theater. Her heart began pounding in her ears. Her voice croaked. "Who are you?"

The breathy voice laughed unpleasantly. "You'll never know, Rosalind. You see, that's the fun of it. I'm going to kill you and you're never going to know who or why or how... or when."

The sudden loud dial tone shot like a cannon through her eardrum. The receiver slipped from her hand and dropped to the hardwood floor, clanging loudly as it dragged the base with it off her nightstand. Rosalind stared at them both, much as she would some hideous, poisonous snake.

Trickles of fear ran cold and clammy down her back as she hugged the covers around her. There was no question anymore of what her tormentor wanted. The man intended to take her life.

"ROSALIND?"

Graham watched her jump as she jerked around to face

him at the call of her name. The dark smudges beneath her eyes were even deeper today, despite the light makeup she had dabbed there to camouflage them. The flicker of fear in her eyes turned to a look of guarded relief as she recognized him. She didn't exactly relax, but there was a perceptible easing of the tightness across her shoulders. "Yes?"

Graham didn't wait for an invitation but pulled his chair next to Rosalind's at the prosecution's table. He was glad Detective Hill had not shown yet. After seeing her obvious distress, he wanted to talk with her alone.

"There's been another incident, hasn't there?"

A frown appeared on her brow. "How did you know?"

His voice was gentle. "I only had to look at you, Rosalind."

She let out a trapped breath.

"What happened?"

"Why do you want to know?"

"I want to understand. Please."

Rosalind studied him intently before answering. There was no gleam in his eyes, no challenge to his lips this morning, just a note of worry in his voice that Rosalind found amazingly soothing. Before she knew it she had told him about her call of the night before.

His mouth set grimly and his brow furrowed as he heard the news. Then he rested his hand on her arm. "Is your telephone listed?"

"No. That's why when I moved this last weekend, I had the same number reconnected in my new apartment. I didn't want to go through the long process of contacting all the people who had my old number."

Graham was watching her, a deep frown still on his forehead. "So he could have gotten your number when he was in your old apartment by looking at the telephone number strip?"

Rosalind nodded. She was beginning to realize that she hadn't followed some basic security precautions. She'd rectify that soon enough. "My number is being changed today."

Graham nodded his approval. "There's only one reason he would call you. Whoever is doing this wants you afraid, Rosalind. He needs your fear. Don't let him think he's succeeding. If he doesn't get satisfaction, maybe he'll quit. Or make a mistake."

"Who's going to make a mistake?"

Rosalind and Graham looked up to see Detective Max Hill had approached the prosecution's table just in time to overhear Graham's last comment. Rosalind rose and so did Graham, but he didn't remove his hand from where it circled her arm and he noted Hill's eyes flicked in that direction.

"Max Hill, I don't think you've formally met Graham Knight."

Graham released Rosalind's arm to extend his hand. Max took it with an easy smile, but the tightness of his grip transmitted a different message.

Max turned back to Rosalind. "The office just told me about the call you received last night. Why didn't you try to get me at home right away?"

Rosalind shrugged. "It was late, Max. I didn't see any reason to disturb you. I knew there wasn't anything you could do."

Before Max could respond, Court Bailiff Roger Horn's head emerged from the judge's chambers as he began to call court to order. Graham scooted his chair back to the defense table. He gave Milton Morebug and his wife and son a reassuring smile as he stood beside his client, but his mind was whirling with thoughts of Rosalind Hart and most of them had nothing at all to do with their adversarial role in the courtroom.

As he had feared, someone was after her. Someone who wanted her scared first. But who? And why? And what in the hell could Graham do about it? And why was he so determined he should be doing something?

"I THOUGHT YOU DIDN'T trust defense attorneys who tried to butter up the prosecution?" Max's slightly teasing tone said beside Rosalind.

"What makes you think I do?" she asked.

"You went to a play with him Monday night and today I find you sharing confidences. If that's how you act with someone you don't trust, what do you do when you trust them?"

Rosalind frowned at the mild accusation in Max's words. It annoyed her all the more because she could see the truth in what he said. Rosalind bit her lip and forcibly turned her attention back to the trial.

Detective Max Hill was Rosalind's first witness of the day. As he strode up to the witness box, Rosalind noticed the women on the jury were giving him a closer look now that they were seeing him out from behind the prosecution table. It was understandable. Max Hill was very attractive.

Rosalind took Hill through a cursory description of his observations at the crime scene. Some of the testimony covered the same ground as that of the two Mercer Island police and Crime Scene Investigator Susan Mast, but Rosalind considered that as a helpful aid in establishing continuity for the jury.

Once the preliminaries were over, Rosalind directed the testimony to the important areas. "Detective Hill, in the course of your investigation, what if anything did you learn about the victim's activities on the night of his death?"

"That he had played cards at the home of Milton Morebug."

"Did you find out who else was at that card game?"

"Yes. Milton Morebug, Raymond Hogg and Brian Wreckter."

"Did you have occasion to question the attendees at that card game about their evening's activities?"

"Yes."

"And how did they answer?"

"Mr. Hogg and Mr. Wreckter described a physical altercation between Milton Morebug and Warren Beaver."

"And after learning of this physical altercation, what if anything did you do with that information?"

"I obtained a subpoena and a search warrant and served them on the defendant at his Hunt's Point home."

"And what if anything did you find pursuant to that search?"

"I found a .38 special revolver in Morebug's study."

Rosalind went over to the exhibit table and picked up a gun. She turned toward Judge Shotz. "May I approach the witness?"

"Yes."

Rosalind walked up to Max Hill and handed him the gun. "Is this the weapon you found in Milton Morebug's home?"

Max took the gun. "Yes. It has my identification tag."

"Did you check who owns this weapon?"

"It's registered to the defendant, Milton Morebug."

He handed the gun back to Rosalind and she returned it to the exhibit table. "Your Honor, Prosecution moves to place this revolver into evidence as People's exhibit five."

Rosalind didn't have any more questions of Max Hill. As Graham rose from behind the defense table, he kept remembering Hill's tight squeeze as they shook hands. He watched those hands now. They were resting easily on the arms of his chair. The man's relaxed manner annoyed Graham almost as much as learning that Rosalind had Hill's home telephone number.

"Detective Hill, did you conduct a paraffin test on Milton Morebug's hands to see if he'd recently fired a weapon when you placed him under arrest on January ninth?"

"Yes."

"And what were your findings?"

"Negative."

"So Mr. Morebug hadn't fired a gun?"

"Not necessarily. He could have worn gloves or washed the evidence away."

"But your test was negative, isn't that right?"

"Yes."

Graham circled the witness box. "Detective Hill, when you searched the defendant's home, did you find exhibit five buried in some drawer under lock and key?"

Hill's fingers started to tap on the chair. "No."

"Where was it?"

"It was in a display case in the library."

"Sitting out for all to see?"

"Yes."

Graham went over to the evidence table to pick up the gun. "This isn't a normal .38 special, is it?"

Hill didn't play dumb. Graham judged he wouldn't with the shining evidence staring the jury in the face. "No. It's a 24-karat gold-plated World War II commemorative revolver."

"And it was displayed in plain sight?"

"Objection," Rosalind said. "Asked and answered."

"Sustained."

"Detective, is it your experience that a person who has used a weapon in the commission of a crime will later try to hide that weapon?"

"Objection. Hypothetical and calls for a conclusion."

Graham turned toward Judge Shotz. "The witness certainly has expert status in this field and considering the circumstances, the situation is hardly hypothetical."

Judge Shotz nodded. "I'm inclined to agree. You may answer the question, Detective Hill."

Max Hill sat back easily. "It depends on the personality of the perpetrator."

Graham frowned. "Could you explain that please?"

His fingers tapped some more. "If the perpetrator is worried about being caught, he might try to hide the weapon he used."

Graham's voice took on its incredulous tone. "He *might*, Detective Hill? I would think that it would be a foregone conclusion that he would hide it."

"Objection. Argumentative."

"Sustained."

Graham put the gun down. He knew he'd made his point. Morebug hadn't been trying to hide the murder weapon. He turned back to Hill. "In your investigation of this death, have you had occasion to delve into Mr. Beaver's business activities?"

Detective Hill repositioned himself in the witness chair. "I learned he was commissioner of public lands."

Graham watched the man's fingers as they increased their beat. "You learned nothing more?"

Hill smiled. "Perhaps you'd like to be more specific."

Graham smiled back. "All right. Did you learn that Warren Beaver had the reputation of a cheat and a liar and frequently ran scams against his business associates?"

"Objection," Rosalind said. "That question is leading and carries evidentiary value."

Judge Shotz shook her head. "It sounds to me like the witness opened himself up to be led, Ms. Hart. And as to the evidentiary value of Mr. Knight's question, I would say that depends on what Detective Hill's answer is. Overruled."

Graham looked expectantly at Detective Hill. Despite the detective's bland countenance, his fingers were tapping quite rapidly now. "Well, Detective?"

"I uncovered no evidence that Warren Beaver scammed anyone."

Graham looked purposely astounded. "None of Warren Beaver's associates said anything negative about him?"

"There were some complaints," Hill admitted.

"What were they, Detective?"

"A couple of people told me they had had business with Beaver and would not choose to do so again."

"Did they tell you why, Detective?"

Rosalind rose. "Your Honor, I object to this whole line of questioning. The victim is not on trial here."

"I'm going to allow it. You may answer, Detective Hill."

Hill's fingers were beginning to circle the chair's arms for support. Even his bland look seemed to be slipping a bit. "They said they didn't trust the man to keep his word."

"Detective Hill, did you thoroughly investigate these people who had bad business dealings with the deceased, the ones who didn't trust him to keep his word?"

Rosalind rose, anticipating Graham's direction and not liking it. "Objection. Irrelevant, Your Honor."

Judge Shotz looked undecided. "Mr. Knight, where are you going with this?"

"Your Honor, these questions are important in establishing the thoroughness of the police investigation. If Detective Hill took the easy way out by arresting the first person who appeared to have a motive—"

"Objection!" Rosalind shouted.

"Sustained. Strike Mr. Knight's last sentence and the jury will disregard. Let's have no more of that, Counselor. Defense may only proceed in this line of questioning if prudence is exercised."

Rosalind didn't think Graham's attempt to throw doubt on others had worked. Max Hill was no novice, either as an investigator or as a witness in a courtroom.

Hill went on to testify that he had thoroughly investigated anyone who had expressed displeasure with doing business with the deceased but that none of these leads had proven fruitful. All evidence had led to Milton Morebug.

By the time Max Hill left the stand, Rosalind felt he had come across very creditably. She just prayed her judgment wasn't getting clouded with her hopes.

Rosalind's next witness was the ballistics expert.

He took a long time explaining how distinctive markings were left on a bullet as they traveled through each individual gun barrel and how those markings could identify the weapon used. Then, with enlarged photo exhibits, he showed the markings on the bullets taken out of Warren Beaver's body and compared them to the markings on bullets he had subsequently fired from exhibit number five, the .38 special that belonged to the defendant. He pronounced them a match.

Graham waived his cross-examination. He knew trying to discredit a ballistics expert these days was a lost cause.

Television police and courtroom dramas had convinced the population of the infallibility of that science. Besides, the thrust of his defense in this area didn't require him disputing that Morebug's .38 special was the murder weapon.

Rosalind's next witness was Jane Day, a fingerprint expert. Rosalind carefully established the woman's credentials by listing her education and then experience in analyzing several hundred crime scenes. She received concurrence from the defense that Day would be accepted as an expert before the court.

"Ms. Day, I'm holding in my hand exhibit five, a gold-plated .38 special." She walked toward her witness and handed the weapon to her. "Do you recognize this gun?"

"Yes. It has my identifying tag. I dusted that weapon for prints."

"And what if any did you find?"

"I found a partial left index fingerprint on the smooth metal portion just in front of the trigger cavity."

Rosalind held the gun in a firing position with her right index finger on the trigger and her left index finger on the space just in front of the trigger cavity. It was a position suggesting that the fingerprint had been placed there when the gun was fired. "Here?" she asked the witness, tapping her left index finger.

"Yes."

Rosalind let Ms. Day take the floor then and carefully go over a set of pictures placed on the courtroom easel, comparing an enlarged print she had taken off the gun with another enlarged print labeled at the top to be Milton Morebug's left index finger. She marked each matching identification point on each whorl-shaped print for the jury.

When she was finished, Rosalind asked her final question. "As a result of your experience and expertise, have you formed an opinion as to whose fingerprint it was on exhibit five?"

"Yes. It belongs to Milton Morebug."

"Thank you, Ms. Day. I have no further questions."

Graham remained standing behind the defense table as he asked his questions of the fingerprint expert. "Ms. Day, did you consider it unusual to find Morebug's fingerprint on his gun?"

"On the contrary. I would say it would be quite natural to find the owner's fingerprints on his possession."

"So you would have been surprised if you hadn't found Milton Morebug's fingerprints on the weapon?"

"Objection, Your Honor. Asked and answered."

Judge Shotz turned to Graham. "Get on with it, Counselor."

"Yes, Your Honor. Ms. Day, did you find any other prints on exhibit five when you examined it?"

"No."

"Didn't you think that strange?"

"Objection. Calls for a conclusion."

Graham looked toward Judge Shotz. "Your Honor, Ms. Day is an expert. Her conclusions regarding the likelihood of fingerprints on an object are part of her expertise."

Judge Shotz nodded. "Objection overruled."

Graham looked back at the witness expectantly.

Ms. Day obliged. "I didn't think it was strange not to find other prints because the gun had recently been cleaned."

Graham paused, looking thoughtfully at the jury to gain their complete attention before asking his next question of Jane Day. "So after the gun had been used to murder Beaver, you're saying someone cleaned it, wiping off his prints, but leaving Milton Morebug's?"

Rosalind was on her feet. "Objection, Your Honor! Leading, evidentiary, calling for a conclusion, assuming facts not in evidence—"

Judge Shotz held up her hand. "I get your drift, Ms. Hart. Objection sustained."

Rosalind could see Graham looked amazingly satisfied with himself as he advised the court he had no further questions of the witness. He should be, she thought. He'd just managed to leave the impression someone was trying to frame his client.

Damn, he was good. Despite the unsavory memories of their past, she couldn't help but admire his courtroom technique.

Judge Shotz called the noon recess. Graham came over. "Let's have lunch. I've got a couple of ideas I'd like to share about this creep who's trying to terrorize you."

Before Rosalind had a chance to respond, Max Hill chimed in. "Roz is having lunch with me. I'm assigning a bodyguard to her."

Rosalind watched Graham's face darken. He didn't look pleased at Hill's dismissal of his offered help. His tone wasn't particularly social as he took a step forward and glared down at Max who was two inches shorter. "And is there going to be someone watching Rosalind's residence and car, too?"

Max's chin went up, as though to try to even the height between him and Graham. "If necessary."

Graham's voice rose. "Someone's broken into her home and slashed the tires of her car and you're questioning if it's *necessary* to post a guard?"

Rosalind didn't like the glare in Max's black eyes as his hands balled into fists and he took a step closer to Graham. "Just who do you think you are, Knight?"

She rose and stood between the two men, annoyed at the sudden animosity that had arisen between them. "Look, I don't have time for this, or either of you. All I want is a nice quiet lunch at my desk. And that's where I'm going right now. Excuse me."

Rosalind trudged off, uneasy at the exchange she had just witnessed and wanting very much to get into her small, crowded, safe office and close the door against the world and put her head down for an hour. The last couple of virtually sleepless nights were beginning to catch up with her. She desperately needed a respite before the afternoon court session.

She ignored her messages at the front desk and headed down the two corridors to the dark, rectangular hole she called hers. She walked in and closed the door behind her, not bothering to turn on the light. She headed directly for the chair in front of her small metal desk and slumped into it, dropping her briefcase on the floor and kicking off her shoes. She scissored her arms on the desk top and rested her head inside them, letting out a long sigh. She felt beyond weary.

She must have actually fallen asleep for a few minutes before something dragged her back to consciousness. When she opened her eyes, she felt groggy. At first all she was aware of was the dark stillness of her office. And then she felt an uncomfortable moistness on her lap. She scooted the chair away from the desk and felt the top of her suit skirt. It was wet and sticky. Damn it. Her lunch must be leaking.

Except the chicken sandwich that comprised her lunch was still in her briefcase. What was this stuff? She rose and padded in her stocking feet to the wall light switch. The fluorescents blinked on tentatively and then with more determination. She studied the navy blue fabric of her skirt and saw the dark wet stain there. She felt it with her fingers. It was sticky to the touch. Perplexed, she walked back to the desk and bent down.

There. She could see the steady stream. The center drawer was dripping. Dripping? From what? She slid it open.

Rosalind gasped, her own jagged breath choking her as she shrank back in terror at the obscene sight stabbing her eyes. Shoved into her desk drawer was some kind of raw bleeding animal heart with a knife stuck in it. The bloodied note impaled with it read: "One more Hart to die."

From some primitive part buried deep inside her, Rosalind screamed.

Chapter Seven

Graham was writing a quick note to Rosalind at the receptionist's desk when he heard the scream. It took him less than five seconds to drop the pen and navigate the one left and then two sharp right turns to reach her office. He didn't pause to knock on her closed door, but turned the knob and shot inside.

It was with immense relief that he saw her flattened against the wall across from her desk, apparently unharmed. But before he'd even caught his breath, his concern returned as he noticed the fixed stare of her eyes and followed their path to the opened desk drawer. He approached warily.

As soon as he saw what it was, he understood why Rosalind had screamed and why she still looked so pale and frightened. Without a thought, he gathered her in his arms. She felt cold and stiff, but she didn't resist.

"What's going on in here?"

It was the voice of the stout, fiftyish receptionist who had been behind the counter of the central lobby of room 554 when Graham was writing his note. She had followed him back into the interior offices.

Graham barked his order to her. "Call the police. Someone has broken into Ms. Hart's office."

The receptionist nodded wordlessly and turned to go.

Rosalind stirred in Graham's arms. "No, contact the sheriff's department on the first floor. It's Max Hill's case," she called to the retreating receptionist.

Graham could see Rosalind's cheeks were still pale, but the way she was issuing orders told him she was recuperating fast despite the nasty shock she just had. This was not a lady who would fall to pieces. Even now he could see the determined rise to her chin. It was while studying her face that the sweet scent of her skin and hair reached his awareness and of their own accord, his arms tightened around her.

She took a deep breath and drew away. "I'm all right now. It was just the shock of finding...it."

Graham dropped his arms reluctantly. "I understand. Who has access to these interior offices?"

"The county prosecutor's staff. Nearly everyone is at lunch now. It never occurred to me he could—"

Rosalind shivered and wrapped her arms around herself tightly. Graham could see that despite the brave talk, she was far from recovered.

He resisted a strong impulse to take her in his arms again and instead concentrated on the office complex layout. "It might not have been too difficult for someone to walk past the receptionist. If she was busy answering calls or talking to someone at the desk, she might not have noticed. Do you normally keep your office door locked?"

"Not during the day."

"Well it looks as though it wouldn't have been much of a trick to gain access. Let's wait in the hall for the police. We'll be less likely to disturb anything."

Rosalind felt calmed by Graham's composed and supportive demeanor. He scrounged around for a couple of chairs from the other offices and she gratefully accepted one as he rolled it toward her in the hallway. As she sat down next to him, his arm brushed up against hers, sending soothing warmth throughout her body. A feeling of unreality encased her, shuttering her mind into a comfortable blank.

Two sheriff's deputies arrived several minutes later and Graham gave them a brief statement and then excused himself. He headed for the chambers of Judge Gloria Shotz and was surprised but not disappointed to find her eating a hard boiled egg at her desk. When he explained the situation, the judge shook her head. "Why isn't the prosecutor's office conveying this information to me, Mr. Knight?"

"I'm sure they intend to, Your Honor. But at present Ms. Hart is giving her statement to the police. As an officer of the court, I felt it was my duty to inform you as soon as possible."

Judge Shotz scooped the firm yellow center out of her egg and popped it into her mouth whole. She chewed on it for a full minute before swallowing. "All right, I'll excuse the jury for the rest of the day and reconvene court in a few minutes to announce a continuance until tomorrow morning. But if the deputy prosecutor is being harassed to the point that she cannot perform her duty, then the prosecutor better replace Ms. Hart so we can get on with this trial."

ROSALIND WAS TRYING to be patient as the young, male crime-scene investigator carefully went over everything in her office. She was disappointed that Max Hill hadn't been available to respond to her call. Dealing with strangers was not very conducive to her current feeling of slipping security. Nor was the quickly passing time. The closer it got to one-thirty—the time Judge Shotz's court was scheduled to reconvene—the more agitated she became.

At one-twenty-five she decided she could wait no longer. She picked up her briefcase and shoulder bag and turned to the deputy who had been first on the scene. "I'm due in court. You'll have to do the rest of this without me."

Then she turned and headed down the hall, which was full of her curious fellow workers now returned from lunch. Promising to talk to them all later and explain what was going on, she navigated around them and out of the glass doors of the prosecutor's offices. She came to a surprised halt as Graham stepped in front of her and gently took her arm.

"We have a continuance until tomorrow morning. Come on. We'll have to move quickly to avoid the reporters."

He whisked her down the hall and into the elevator so fast that Rosalind barely had enough time to react. Just as the elevator doors were closing, Rosalind caught sight of the reporters barreling her way, microphones extended. Graham punched the Close Door button and it swished shut in front of them.

Rosalind turned surprised eyes to Graham. "They know about the attempts?"

Graham nodded. "Unfortunately the media were in the courtroom a few minutes ago when Judge Shotz read the explanation into the record of why court was being dismissed for the day and would reconvene tomorrow morning."

Rosalind shook her head. "But how did Judge Shotz know?"

"I told her, Rosalind. After what you've been through, I knew you weren't in any condition to continue the trial today."

Rosalind felt herself bristle at his words. "Now just wait a minute. *You* didn't think I was ready to argue my case in court? Am I supposed to believe that you arranged for a continuance so that *I* would be better prepared to prosecute *your* client tomorrow?"

Graham smiled internally at the fight in her tone and the steady gleam in her eyes. She was back to doing battle and that was enormously reassuring. He smiled. "I want you at your best in court so that when I beat you, you'll know it was fairly done."

Rosalind's fiery eyes burned into his as her chin shot toward the ceiling. "When you beat me? In your dreams, Knight."

Graham let his laughter out as he walked Rosalind to her car in the underground parking lot, but she didn't crack a smile. He easily recognized the white Chrysler LeBaron with the four new tires. She shoved her keys into it with a vehemence that underlay her state of mind. She yanked open the driver's door and then rested against it as she swung to look at Graham.

"You've got to be playing some angle, Knight. I don't see you riding to the rescue this way."

Graham felt himself drawn to her flushed face, turning its cream to pink. He stepped closer. "You don't, Rosalind? You mean to tell me I've donned all this shining armor for nothing?"

He was standing so close that Rosalind could smell his fine cologne mixing with the exciting heat of his body. As she looked up into his gray eyes she noted the laughter still dwelling there and something else so intense that it robbed her of breath. Her lips parted to speak, but nothing came out. Then slowly, very determinedly his mouth descended to hers until it was just a whisper away.

When her name became that whisper, it was Rosalind who closed the distance.

Her kiss was like a flash fire zipping through him, hot and sweet. He had meant to carefully control this seduction, let it build until he was ready to claim her, but suddenly it was he who was being seduced. He forgot all his subtle patient moves and crushed her to him with fierce abandon. Her body fitted into his tightly, perfectly, answering a need far deeper than the one he had thought existed.

Rosalind couldn't seem to get enough of the warm arduous lips that scorched hers or of the hard body that grasped her so closely. She wrapped her arms around him and held on tightly as the world spun. Tears sprung from her eyes as the feel of him freed something inside her almost painful in its yearning. She knew that on some level she had craved this moment with Graham Knight for a long time.

A long time. To that first day she saw him in class. When she was that plain, pitiful girl whose hopes and dreams he had so cavalierly smashed. The memory acted like a sudden bucket of ice water, drenching her physical desire. Rosalind found the emerging need for emotional survival even stronger than that which had driven her into Graham's arms. With a hardened resolve nurtured over the years, she pushed away.

She lashed out, a moment's inspiration borrowing his own hurtful words from the past. "There's nothing there that I find even remotely appealing, Knight."

Then without looking at him or waiting for a reply, she swung into the driver's seat and slammed the door shut. In an instant, she'd gunned the engine and driven away.

Graham stared after her feeling marvelously stirred and stunned. She had kissed him as no woman ever had, and he knew with every burning fiber of his being that she wanted him as strongly as he wanted her. But despite victory in that battle, a victory that seemed to belong to them both, she'd just confirmed that war still raged. And it was hotter than ever.

What a delicious, delightful challenge she was. He hurried to his car before she got out of sight. He was determined to see her safely home from a discreet following distance. He was not going to lose her now, although the complete ramifications of that thought were left unformulated in the back of his mind.

LEROY PONCE WATCHED Rosalind drive away and was just ready to follow when he spied the defense attorney taking off after her. Damn. He'd had another little surprise all planned to spring. Now he'd have to wait for another time.

At least his last surprise had gotten her attention.

Still, he couldn't let his revenge on Rosalind Hart screw up the deal he had going. More and more it was getting critical for him to get his payoff and spring his old man. He'd used up all the money he had left in bribing that damn greedy Mrs. Ryan at the hospital.

Leroy's hands balled into fists. He couldn't stand the idea of his old man in a loony bin. So what if he had beaten that woman attendant to death when he'd gotten in his rage at the rest home? Damn broad probably deserved what she got. If only he hadn't been in the joint when it happened, he could have figured a way to get his old man clean away right then. But he had been locked up, thanks to Rosalind Hart.

And they had dragged his old man into court and judged him legally insane and locked him up. He'd gone to see his old man to try to explain that he was going to get him out. He hadn't gotten through. His old man had looked at him like a zombie.

An acrid bile swam up to choke Leroy. Yes, she was going to pay. Rosalind Hart was really the cause of it all. Just as soon as he got his money he'd take care of her.

His money. Thinking about it made him decide to swing by the post office box early. It was only a couple of blocks away. He gunned his old, beat-up green Honda and squealed his tires on the next turn. Maybe there would be something there from his mysterious employer. Maybe he would have a chance to kill soon.

ROSALIND ARRIVED home to a ringing telephone. She replaced her lock securely and waited for the answering machine to pick up the call. A relieved breath she didn't even know she'd been holding escaped when she heard her boss's voice. She dropped her briefcase and shoulder bag on the table and leaned over to pick up the receiver.

"How did you get my new number so fast? I don't even know what it is yet."

"I'm the county prosecutor, remember? Now tell me, what's all this business about you being terrorized?"

Rosalind briefed him as succinctly as possible. After assuring him she was just fine and quite capable of proceeding with the prosecution of Milton Morebug, he hung up seemingly satisfied. She knew dealing with threats against his staff was routine for him.

But not for her. Her fright over being stalked and her inconsistent feelings for Graham both tormented her. A wise voice inside her asserted that all her emotions were probably being exacerbated because of lack of sleep. She had to get some rest. But her nerves were raw. If she went to bed now, she knew she'd just toss and turn. Rosalind stepped out of her heels and walked into the bathroom.

She bent over the open but still unpacked box that contained most of her bathroom items and looked for the sleeping pills. When she finally found the full bottle, the date on it was two years past its discard date.

She threw the pills into the trash. She went into the bedroom and stripped off her skirt and jacket and then her slip when she realized the bloodstain had seeped into it also. She shivered as she saw the faint red discoloration on her thighs. Gritting her teeth, she draped her discarded garments over a chair in the corner and sat on the bed, reaching for the phone.

Her mother's voice sounded very good to her tired ears. After warning both her and her dad of what they might be seeing or hearing about her on the six o'clock news, she sat back and listened to their warm and comforting concern.

But neither tried to talk her into coming home or giving up her work. It was one of the things she loved most about her parents. They had always encouraged her to face life and make her own decisions. And although they hadn't been able to help her financially in her pursuit of a law degree, they had contributed something far more valuable—their absolute belief in her ability to do it.

It was their belief that helped her keep up her grades in law school while working long shifts as a waitress to support herself. It was that same belief that came through to her now. It both soothed her raw nerves and made her feel strong. She hung up the phone, unplugged it, put her head down and slept.

GRAHAM HELD the telephone receiver tightly as Fran's voice related her findings from her political luncheon. Possibilities were literally popping through his brain.

"Gray, is that the information you wanted?"

Graham's eyes gleamed as he stared into the fire. "Yes, Fran. That is just the information I needed. You're a peach.

If you'd agree to accept a salary for your work, I'd write you a check for a million dollars.''

Fran laughed. ''And it would bounce.''

Graham smiled. ''One day it won't. One day I'll begin to pay you back for all the sweet—''

''No, Gray,'' Fran interrupted. ''What I do for you I do in love. There's no price on love, dear. Besides, you know this old lady thrives on being in the thick of things. Now I'm going to meet Mabel and Violet for dinner. Call me after court tomorrow and let me know how things went.''

Graham agreed and hung up the phone. But he sat for a long while studying the notes he had made based on Fran's findings, carefully planning the best ways to apply his new knowledge in court the next day.

He was looking forward to some interesting cross-examinations. But even his anticipation of those couldn't override the memory of Rosalind's kiss or his growing concern over her safety. That afternoon he'd assured himself of her apartment's security before leaving.

And tomorrow he'd be out in front of her place ready to follow her into court to be sure she got there safely. He knew that despite the fact that she'd probably be resisting his every effort, he'd be looking for ways to stay close from now on.

Maybe it was her persistence in not asking for his help that made him so determined to give it. Maybe it was the valiant way in which she stood alone against this terrorizing creep that drew him to her side. Maybe it was simply he would have found any excuse he could to pursue the woman whose lips he could still feel hours after her kiss.

ROSALIND WAS BOMBARDED by reporters Thursday morning when she got off the elevator on the seventh floor. Television lights blinded her as voices yelled from black silhouettes.

''Ms. Hart, is it true that Milton Morebug is behind these attempts on your life?''

"Ms. Hart, would you care to comment on the report that the prosecutor is going to be pulling you off the Morebug case because he no longer thinks you can cut it?"

"Ms. Hart, what about the reports that you've faked these incidents to incite the jury against the defendant?"

Rosalind couldn't believe the inflammatory questions reporters had the nerve to ask. She "no commented" all the way to the courtroom, pushing through the mass of bodies.

She felt better today. She'd had a good long rest, and a hearty breakfast. So even though the rain still poured in unrelenting sheets, she decided the world was definitely looking up. After verifying her first witness was present and ready outside, she stepped into the courtroom with a spring in her step.

Graham gave her a smile as she approached the front of the courtroom. She nodded curtly in return as an exciting warmth battled with her desire to be aloof. She headed for Max Hill who was already sitting at the prosecution table.

Max held the chair out for her. "Sorry I wasn't available yesterday for that business in the office. I called you at home in the afternoon, but I didn't get an answer."

Rosalind took her seat. "I unplugged the phones."

Max smiled as he sat down beside her. "Looks like it did you some good. I've checked the records of murderers you've gotten convicted and found five who could have been likely candidates for retribution. Problem is, all five are still doing time."

"Any vindictive relatives of those five in the vicinity?"

Max shook his head. "Now that is going to take a lot more time to check out. But I want you to know that I've already gotten a couple of the guys started on it."

Rosalind nodded in approval as Roger Horn emerged from the judge's chambers to call court to order. The normally crowded courtroom was now packed with journalists and the curious.

"Ms. Hart, are you prepared to call your first witness?"

"Yes, Your Honor. The prosecution calls Raymond Hogg."

Hogg rolled into the courtroom behind the leading bailiff like a short, burly, rough-hewn log. His nut-colored hair was plastered to his round head like moss and the ends of his thick mustache dug into his cheeks like woody twigs. As he raised his hand prior to ascending to the witness chair, a voice like a buzz saw promised to tell the truth.

As with most witnesses in her case, Rosalind had an opportunity to speak to Hogg only by telephone concerning his testimony. She kept her fingers crossed that he would present a creditable appearance to the jury. She circled from behind the prosecution table and faced him in the witness box.

"Mr. Hogg, what is your profession?"

"I own and run Hogg's Logging."

"And where is the location of your business?"

"Wherever there are logs to cut." A smile surfaced beneath the bushy mustache.

Great, she thought. *My own witness is sarcastic.* Aloud she tried again. "Do you have a physical office?"

"Yes. In Redmond."

"And you live?"

"At Hunt's Point. Quarter mile up from Morebug's place."

"And how long have you known Milton Morebug?"

"About ten years."

"Where were you on the night of January eighth?"

"I was at Morebug's house playing cards."

"When did you arrive?"

"Around 6:50. I was a little early because I wanted to give myself extra time in case the roads were icy."

"Who was there when you arrived?"

"Morebug and Warren Beaver."

"And who if anyone else arrived later?"

"Brian Wreckter arrived around 7:20."

"And can you describe to this court the events of that evening?"

"Well, sure. We were having a few drinks and a sandwich or two while we played poker."

"What was the general feeling among Mr. Morebug and his guests at the beginning of the evening?"

Hogg grinned. "Damn good. We talked sports. Drank beer. Played poker. It don't get no better than that."

"Were you playing for money, Mr. Hogg?"

"Is there any other way to play?"

"I assume you mean yes. Who won?"

"Well, at first, everybody seemed to be about even. Then Beaver started to win steadily. It began right after his wife called about the ice cream."

"What can you tell us about that telephone call?"

"Well, Morebug's answering machine picked up the incoming call and when Beaver heard it was his wife, he got up and talked to her on the phone."

"And is it your testimony that you heard her asking him to pick up some ice cream for her?"

"We all did. That was the message she was leaving on the answering machine. She wanted this special double-chocolate stuff that is sold only at this all-night grocer just outside of Bellevue. Said as long as the grocery was on his way home, she wanted Beaver to swing by and get her a gallon."

"And that's when he picked up the phone?"

"Yeah. He didn't want to detour for the ice cream so he picked up the receiver and suggested *she* go out the next day and get it if she wanted it so bad. They argued a bit about how the roads were getting worse and more snow was expected for the next day and then he finally agreed to get the ice cream on his way home and hung up the phone and came back to the table."

"How did he act then, Mr. Hogg?"

"Oh, he looked pretty ticked. Said something uncomplimentary about wives and we all laughed. Then the conversation shifted back to sports and then the game when he began to win steadily."

"When you say win steadily, how many games are you talking about?"

"Twelve."

"Is twelve an exact count?"

"Yeah, I think so. After Beaver won three in a row, we all remarked how it was the first time someone had done it that night. Then of course it was easy to count each additional win from there."

"Mr. Hogg, what was the atmosphere in the room after Warren Beaver started winning so steadily?"

"It got real quiet. We'd all had quite a few beers by then. I don't know about the others but I was trying to concentrate on the cards I was playing."

"Did anyone make any comments about Beaver's steady winning streak?"

"Not until after the thirteenth game Beaver won."

"Mr. Hogg, could you please tell us everything you remember about that thirteenth game?"

Raymond Hogg leaned forward, his buzz-saw voice cutting easily to every corner of the large courtroom. "It was five-card stud."

"And for the jury's benefit, could you briefly explain the game?"

"Well the dealer deals one card facedown to everybody and the next four cards are dealt faceup. Players can bet after each round of new cards."

"And who was the dealer?"

"Beaver. The deal always went to the winner of the previous hand, so Beaver had dealt the last twelve hands."

"What happened next?"

"It was the damnedest thing I ever saw. Morebug got dealt three aces and Beaver three jacks. Betting was pretty steep right from the first ace and jack. By the time the third ace appeared in front of Morebug, hell, I knew I didn't have a chance so I folded. Wreckter hung in there until the last card before he dropped out."

"So Milton Morebug and Warren Beaver were the only two left in the game?"

"Yeah. And they started going crazy, raising each other right and left. When the betting finally stopped, there must have been close to twenty thousand in the pot."

"Twenty-thousand dollars?"

"Yeah. I tell you they went crazy. We never had more than five hundred going in any one game before. Beaver had written a check to cover part of his bet and Morebug had gone to the safe to get more cash. There was more money in that one pot than there had been wagered all night."

"What happened then?"

"Well, Morebug finally called Beaver. That's when Beaver got this big grin on his face and turned over the fourth jack. He began to laugh as his arms surrounded the money."

"What did Milton Morebug do?"

"Well, he leaned across the table and grabbed Beaver's arm to stop him from taking the money in the pot. Beaver looked kind of surprised and sat real still. That's when Morebug let go of Beaver's arm, leaned back and turned over his hole card. Hell, my eyes nearly popped out."

"What was so surprising about Morebug's hole card that caused your reaction, Mr. Hogg?"

"Why, it was a damned jack, too!"

Judge Shotz rapped her gavel as a perceptible murmur swept throughout the courtroom. When order was restored, Rosalind continued with her examination. "What happened after the fifth jack was exposed on the card table, Mr. Hogg?"

"Well, Wreckter and I just stared at it kind of stunned like. But Morebug shot to his feet and grabbed Beaver by the shirt. Then he called him a dirty cheat and took a swing at him. Beaver raised his arm in defense and Morebug's fist ended up connecting with Beaver's forearm. Still, it was a powerful enough blow to knock Beaver to the floor."

"Then what happened?"

"Well, Wreckter and I came to our senses about then and we each grabbed one of Morebug's arms."

"And why did you think it necessary to do that, Mr. Hogg?"

"Well he was headed for Beaver where he lay on the floor and he had blood in his eye."

"Objection!" Graham called.

"Sustained. Strike 'blood in his eye' from the record. The jury will disregard."

Rosalind went on undaunted. "You said Mr. Morebug was headed for Beaver, isn't that right?"

"Yeah. So like I said, Wreckter and I held him back until Beaver got off the floor and left."

"So Warren Beaver left?"

"Yeah, real quick like."

"And what time was that?"

"Around one in the morning."

"And were there any further exchanges between Milton Morebug and Warren Beaver before Mr. Beaver left?"

"Oh yeah. Morebug yelled at him that he better get out or else."

"Or else what, Mr. Hogg? Did Milton Morebug say what he was going to do to Warren Beaver?"

Hogg's buzz-saw voice cut into the courtroom. "He said, 'Or else I'm going to kill you, you cheating bastard.'"

Chapter Eight

Rosalind paused for almost half a minute before asking her next question, partly to let the courtroom settle down and partly to leave Raymond Hogg's last words hanging in the jury's ears.

"And after Milton Morebug threatened Warren Beaver's life, what did Mr. Beaver do?"

"He left. Real quick like."

"And when Warren Beaver left the Morebug residence on the night of his death, did he take the winnings in the final game with him?"

"No. The money was left on the table."

"What happened to it?"

"Well, Morebug gave Wreckter and me about fifteen hundred apiece to compensate us for what we probably lost throughout the evening because of Beaver's cheating. Then he took the rest."

"What happened after Morebug gave you and Wreckter your money back?"

"Well, we all had a final drink and Wreckter and I left."

"And what was the reason for that final drink?"

"Just a friendly drink. To improve the atmosphere soured by Beaver's cheating."

"Nothing more?" Rosalind pressed.

"Well, I wanted to be sure Morebug had cooled down."

"When you say cooled down, what do you mean?"

"Well, Morebug was real angry at Beaver, knocking him down and all. I didn't want him going after the guy and killing him."

"So you thought he might?"

Graham was on his feet. "Objection, Your Honor!"

"Sustained."

Rosalind didn't think she could slip that question past Graham, but it had been worth the try. "Mr Hogg, how long would you say it took to divvy up the money and have that last drink?"

"Probably no more than ten minutes."

"And then you and Brian Wreckter left?"

"Yeah. I was home in five to ten minutes. Like I said before, I live at the northernmost end of Hunt's Point."

"Thank you, Mr. Hogg. That's all the questions I have."

GRAHAM BUTTONED his suit coat as he rose from the defense table. He knew he had a lot of damage to repair as a result of Raymond Hogg's testimony. But he also felt he possessed the right verbal hammer and nails for the fix-up. He took a moment before beginning his cross-examination to silently study the witness. Throughout his testimony, Hogg's hands had remained out of sight on his lap. To Graham that was a sure sign he was hiding something. Thanks to Fran, he was pretty sure he knew what.

"Mr. Hogg, you testified that you and Brian Wreckter had a final drink with the defendant after the poker game broke up to be sure Mr. Morebug had cooled down. Is that correct?"

"Yeah."

"And were you convinced Mr. Morebug had cooled down?"

"Yeah."

"What convinced you?"

"Well, he was calm. Even joking after a swig or two of Scotch. I didn't think he'd go after Beaver."

"And what about you?"

"Pardon?"

"I'm asking about you, Mr. Hogg. Had you had time to cool down?"

Hogg's hands remained hidden at his sides. "I wasn't the one who was angry."

"Really? You expect this court to believe that you had been cheated all night by Warren Beaver, and when you found out you weren't angry?"

Hogg shifted in his seat. "Well, I wasn't smiling."

"You weren't smiling," Graham repeated as he faced the jury. "Mr. Hogg, how long have you known Warren Beaver?"

"I guess since he got elected four years ago."

"Not before that?"

"Not to my recollection."

"Then it's also not to your recollection that you contributed a quarter of a million dollars to his campaign?"

Hogg swallowed hard.

Rosalind was on her feet. "Objection, Your Honor. I see no relevance to this line of questioning."

Judge Shotz turned to Graham. "Where are you going, Mr. Knight?"

"To this witness's motives for killing Warren Beaver."

"Your Honor, I object," Rosalind protested. "Raymond Hogg is not on trial here."

Graham chimed back quickly. "Maybe he should be."

"Your Honor—" Rosalind began.

Judge Shotz held up her hand. "Mr. Knight, you know better. No more innuendos about this witness. Ms. Hart, defense is within his rights to challenge the witness's motives and state of mind. I'm going to allow this line of questioning."

Graham turned back to the witness, encouraged by the judge's ruling. "Well, Mr. Hogg? Did you contribute a quarter of a million dollars to Warren Beaver's election campaign?"

Hogg's answer sounded like it was being dragged from his lips. "Yeah."

"So you did know Beaver before his election to office?"

"Yeah."

Graham smiled. "I'm glad your memory seems to be improving. Were you good friends?"

Hogg squirmed. "More like business acquaintances."

"Oh? And what business would that be?"

Hogg seemed to be having difficulty clearing his throat.

"Mr. Hogg?"

"He told me about upcoming state timber sales so I could submit a closed bid to get the logs processed through my mills. It was perfectly legal."

"Were these bids he personally received?"

"They were handled through the timber program of DNR."

"DNR?"

"The state's department of natural resources."

"But isn't the DNR part of the commissioner of public lands' responsibilities?"

Very reluctantly, he said, "Yes."

"And wasn't it Beaver who opened the sealed bids?"

Hogg had begun to rub his sweaty palms on his pants. "I have no idea."

"You have no idea, Mr. Hogg? Then why did you contribute a quarter of a million dollars to his election campaign? And why is it that your mills received three of the last four shipments of state timber?"

Rosalind was on her feet. "Your Honor, Defense is issuing compound questions and not giving the witness time to answer."

Before Judge Shotz could rule, Hogg buzzed his reply. "I was the highest bidder! That's how I got the contracts."

Shotz shrugged. "One question at a time, Mr. Knight."

"Yes, Your Honor." Graham bore down. "How much was your last bid?"

Hogg shook his head. "The bids remain confidential, even after the work is awarded."

Graham walked toward the jury. "How very convenient. The man you gave a quarter of a million dollars to was the sole judge of who submitted the highest bid and he never had to divulge the amounts of those bids. That's like a license to steal, isn't it?''

"Your Honor—" Rosalind began.

"Sustained," Judge Shotz interrupted.

Hogg wiped his mustache with a sweaty hand. "Look, I'm just a businessman. I operate a few sawmills. What with all those damn environmentalists clamoring about the spotted owl habitat and all the Asian buyers offering ridiculously high stumpage prices, I was going under. So four years ago Beaver approached me and told me he was in favor of protecting the state's logging industry by reserving state timber for domestic mills. I jumped at a chance to contribute to his campaign. Anyone in my position would have. That's no crime."

Graham's eyes narrowed. "But Beaver paying you back by deliberately circumventing the closed-bid process and selling you those crops of raw logs is a crime, isn't it?"

"No! That was done by closed bid. You've got nothing on me!"

Rosalind stood up. "I object to this whole line of questioning, Your Honor. Whatever the past dealings between the deceased and Mr. Hogg, they're not relevant to this case."

"Your Honor," Graham said quickly. "If you will just bear with me a moment more."

Judge Shotz looked far too interested in Hogg's testimony to let it end. "Objection overruled. Go ahead, Mr. Knight."

Graham circled as close to Hogg as he dared. "Beaver agreed to pay you back for your large campaign contribution by giving you the timber deals, isn't that right, Mr. Hogg?"

"No!"

"Come on. Do you expect this court to believe—"

Hogg sat forward as though something had just struck him. "If Beaver and I had such a deal going, then why didn't I get the contract for the last shipment that was four times as big as the three prior ones put together?"

Graham smiled. "Yes, that must have really irritated you, Mr. Hogg. He threw a few smaller jobs your way, but when it came down to the really big payoff, he sold out elsewhere didn't he?"

Hogg's face was rapidly turning red. His lips were clamped shut so tightly, his mustache had rolled into one long log.

"Yes, I can see that it did," Graham said. "On the night of Warren Beaver's death, did you enter the library of Milton Morebug's home?"

Hogg's tone turned surly. "So what if I did?"

"Just answer yes or no, Mr. Hogg. Did you enter Milton Morebug's library on that night?"

Hogg crossed his arms across his chest in a defensive gesture. "We all did. You had to walk through the library to get to the john."

"So you were in Mr. Morebug's library alone on several occasions during the evening, weren't you?"

"Yeah, I walked through it alone."

"And were you aware Mr. Morebug owned a commemorative World War II .38 special?"

"He had guns all over his library walls."

"Mr Hogg, I didn't ask you about other guns. I asked you about the commemorative World War II .38 special. Were you aware that Mr. Morebug owned that gun, yes or no?"

Irritated now. "Yeah, yeah."

"And when you arrived at Mr. Morebug's home that evening, what did you say to your host when you found out that Warren Beaver was going to be one of the players?"

Hogg's right hand shot up to rub his mustache quite violently. "I don't remember."

Graham smiled. "Well then let me refresh your memory. Could it have been, 'That double-crossing bastard. Who invited him?'"

"Your Honor—" Rosalind began.

"Save it, Ms. Hart," Judge Shotz interrupted. "I want to hear what the witness has to say."

"Well, Mr. Hogg?" Graham asked. "Is that what you said?"

Hogg looked down at his lap. "I might have."

"Speak up, Mr. Hogg, so the jury can hear you."

Hogg's head came up with a snap, anger in both his face and voice. "Yeah, I called him a double-crossing bastard! You gonna hang me for it?"

Graham paused and just looked at the witness for a minute. "That's not my job, Mr. Hogg. I leave the hanging of murderers to Ms. Hart."

"Your Honor," Rosalind began again.

"Mr. Knight—" Judge Shotz started.

"You're quite right, Your Honor," Graham interrupted. "I apologize to the court and withdraw my comment from the record. I have no further questions of this witness."

Rosalind watched him stride back to the defense's table and give her a wink. The damn man oozed charm. She was still on her feet from her last objection. "A few questions on redirect."

"Go ahead, Ms. Hart," Judge Shotz said.

"Mr. Hogg, earlier you testified that after you left Milton Morebug's house you drove straight home, is that right?"

"Yes."

"And what time did you arrive?"

"About one-fifteen. One-twenty at the latest. Like I said, I only live five minutes away, although that night it probably took me about ten minutes because of the slippery roads."

"And where were you at about two in the morning, the time the medical examiner has established Warren Beaver was being shot to death some fifteen miles away?"

Hogg smirked. "I was sitting up reading."

"Thank you, Mr. Hogg. I have no further questions."

As she returned to the defense table, Rosalind couldn't help but feel vindicated. All that effort Graham had gone to to implicate Hogg in Beaver's death had been for nothing.

"A couple of questions on recross," Graham said.

Uh, oh, Rosalind thought.

"Go ahead, Mr. Knight," Judge Shotz said.

"Did anybody see you arrive at your home, Mr. Hogg?"

"My wife was asleep. I didn't want to wake her up."

"So no one can verify that you went directly home?"

"It was after one in the morning. It's not like I thought I needed to have a brass band waiting to establish an alibi."

"So you could have come in at two-thirty in the morning and no one would have been the wiser, isn't that right?"

Hogg sat silent. Graham pushed. "Well, isn't that right?"

"How the hell would I know!" Hogg snapped. "I came in at 1:20 like I said. You can't prove otherwise."

As soon as Judge Shotz called for the noon recess, Rosalind turned to Max. "Did you know about Hogg's campaign contribution to Beaver or the lumber contracts he was awarded?"

Max shook his head. "Didn't come out in the investigation."

Rosalind bit her lip.

Max gave her arm a shake. "Look, I don't care how Hogg felt about the victim or whether he gave the guy a million in campaign contributions. All the evidence I have says it was Morebug who killed Beaver. You're not starting to doubt, are you?"

Rosalind inhaled deeply, letting out her breath slowly. "No, not really. It's just that I don't like surprises and this case keeps giving them to me. If I had just been in on it from the first, maybe I'd feel on firmer footing. Where did Knight find out all these personal things regarding Hogg anyway?"

"Why don't you ask me?" his voice said suddenly from behind Rosalind.

Rosalind turned and looked up at Graham warily. "Eavesdropping, Counselor? Is that the secret to your inside information?"

He smiled. "Have lunch with me and maybe you'll get a confession."

She looked up into the humor in his eyes and the warm glitter behind it. That glitter brought back memories of his lips hungrily seeking hers, his hands pressing her to him. Despite her cold dismissal of him the day before, he had come back to challenge her, refusing to admit defeat or take offense.

She couldn't help but like him for that, in spite of her past wounds at his hands. And now the idea that she might be able to wrangle some information out of her suave, sophisticated opponent was just too enticing to pass up. At least that's the reason she gave herself for taking him up on his offer. She rose. "All right, you're on."

She barely had the presence of mind to say goodbye to Max Hill as Graham took her arm.

Graham drove them to Maximilien, a French restaurant-café overlooking a rain-swept Elliott Bay. When they were seated and had given their order, she leaned back and looked out at the muddy water beneath the dark, heavy sky.

His next words echoed her thoughts once more. "After two and a half weeks of steady rain, you'd think we'd get a respite."

She sighed. "It's getting depressing. About now I'd give anything for a couple of days of sunshine."

"Anything?" Graham repeated. "I'll have to remember that."

She looked over to find him smiling at her, the warm glitter alight in his gray eyes. Once again the clash of inconsistencies mounted in her own feelings. While her pulse raced, memories of her hurt pride dragged an anchor. In confusion and indecision, she looked away.

"Who is your deep throat?"

Graham grinned at her terminology, twirling the ice in his glass of water. He had known she'd accept his invitation for lunch as long as he made the invitation tantalizing enough. But now, watching how the lamplight caught the fire in her hair, he realized it was he who was tantalized. He took a steadying breath. "No big secret, Rosalind. You met her the other night."

Rosalind turned back to face Graham. "I met her? You're not talking about your great-aunt Fran?"

Graham's grin broadened. "I'm not? I could have sworn I was."

"But she's a sweet little old lady!"

Graham nodded. "Without a doubt. I think that's what makes her so very good at finding out things. People feel comfortable talking with her. Before they know it, she's extracted a life history they didn't even know they possessed."

Rosalind laughed at the lighthearted way in which Graham had said it, but when she remembered how much she herself had opened up under Fran's gentle questioning earlier that week, she could see how effective his great-aunt's technique really was.

She shook her head in amazement. "So you sent your own great-aunt snooping for you?"

"Fran really enjoys it, Rosalind. She and my uncle Jack were well entrenched in Seattle's social and political circles and his death opened up a hole that she fills by chairing a very important environmental committee. She and two of her widowed friends are unbeatable when it comes to moving in the right financial circles to get backing for the much needed preservation of our strip of the planet."

Pride and fondness for his great-aunt shone through easily in his manner. It suddenly struck Rosalind that there was much she didn't understand about Graham Knight. A curiosity she didn't know she had fueled her next question.

"Are you involved in this environmental group?"

"I'm proud to say I am. Ever since I began to practice law I've devoted at least half of my practice to representing local groups who are trying to preserve what little we have left of our natural resources."

He looked up at her then, his eyes such a clear, warm gray that a tiny jolt registered in her heart, like a jump on the Richter scale portending the coming of a major quake. She fought down a flash of excited alarm.

"You didn't approve of Warren Beaver, did you?"

"No, I didn't, Rosalind. His time in the office of commissioner of public lands was a black time for us all. Because of him we've lost much of our old-growth forests."

"Is that why you're representing his murderer?"

Graham watched her steadily for a minute, an unreadable expression in his eyes. "I'm not representing his murderer," he said deliberately.

Their food arrived and they both drew silent as they went about its consumption. But Rosalind's mind was rapidly turning over what Graham had just told her about himself.

This same man who had so heartlessly dismissed her work those many years ago cared about the environment so much that he devoted half of his practice to its issues. And he spoke of his great-aunt Fran with such tenderness and love. How could a man have so many different and opposing traits to his character?

He continually confused her with his inconsistencies. The battle over trying to reconcile them was getting emotionally exhausting. A part of her wished he had just remained the insensitive lout she'd always thought him to be. But another part, the part that could feel the force of his presence even with a table between, thrilled to this new knowledge.

You're not that dopey little twenty-two-year-old, dummy. Get a grip. But despite all her brave talk, she couldn't will away the skipping beat of her heart.

JUDGE SHOTZ FIXED her dark eyes on Rosalind after court was resumed. "Ms. Hart, call your next witness."

Rosalind rose. "The People call Brian Wreckter."

Wreckter was a tall, middle-aged man with thin arms and legs and a prominent pouch. He walked with a slight bend to his back, which sent his thick salt-and-pepper hair slightly askew onto his forehead. After he was sworn in, he told the court at Rosalind's prompting that he was a land developer and had been a player at the card game at Morebug's home on the night of Warren Beaver's death. His testimony mirrored that of Raymond Hogg's quite closely right down to the "cheating bastard" remark made by Morebug.

"Mr. Wreckter, when did you leave Mr. Morebug's home that night?"

"At about ten after one in the morning."

"And where were you at two o'clock in the morning?"

"I was in bed with my wife in Beaux Arts."

"Thank you, Mr. Wreckter. I have no more questions."

Graham had been watching Wreckter as the man answered Rosalind's questions. He had brought his right fist to his mouth in a nervous cough after certain questions.

Graham got up and circled the defense table. "Mr. Wreckter, are you familiar with Mr. Morebug's gun collection?"

Wreckter nodded. "I've seen the displayed pieces in his library many times."

"Did you see them on the night of Warren Beaver's death?"

"I probably did. I walked through the library several times that night on the way to the lavatory."

"Were any missing?"

"To tell you the truth, I really didn't notice."

"Mr. Wreckter, how long had you known the deceased, Warren Beaver?"

"I'm not exactly sure. Maybe three or four years. Raymond Hogg introduced us."

"And what was your relationship to the deceased?"

Wreckter brought his fist up for his nervous cough. "We were acquaintances."

"Personal? Business?"

"Personal."

"You never did business with Warren Beaver?"

Another nervous cough. "No."

Graham circled back to his table and picked up a folder. He opened it and scanned a page, giving Wreckter time to get uncomfortable wondering what he was looking at. "Are you acquainted with Linda Dodge?" he asked finally.

Wreckter's cough sounded more like a gag this time.
"Yes."

"Please tell the court what position Ms. Dodge holds."

"She's a lobbyist for DNR."

Graham shook his head. "Seems strange that the tax-
payers are being made to pay for a lobbyist to represent the
interests of a government department like the DNR, doesn't
it?"

Rosalind rose. "Your Honor, I object to this line of
questioning. It has nothing to do with this case."

"Mr. Knight," Judge Shotz said, "I'm inclined to agree
with Ms. Hart."

Graham turned toward the judge. "I beg the court's indulgence. This testimony is germane to the issue at hand and
I promise to show how with just a few more questions of this
witness."

"All right. But make good on that promise, Mr. Knight.
Objection overruled."

Graham turned back to Brian Wreckter. "What is your
relationship to Linda Dodge?"

"We're friends."

"Don't you mean brother and sister?"

Wreckter's cough had definitely turned into a hack. When
it was finished, he choked out his reply. "Yes."

"And isn't it true that last year you gave your sister,
Linda Dodge, two-hundred thousand dollars in personal
checks to pass on to her boss, Warren Beaver, in exchange
for his selling you a choice state property for a housing
project?"

Wreckter's bent back miraculously disappeared as he
straightened as stiff as a scarecrow. His voice was a croak.
"Linda would never have told you!"

Graham's voice rose in threatening volume as he raised
some canceled checks in his hand accusingly. "Isn't it true?"

Wreckter's back bent again as his head went down.
"Yes."

Judge Shotz rapped for order at the new murmur traveling through the courtroom. Graham took the time to pace

in front of the jury so that Wreckter would have to look that way to respond.

"And did Warren Beaver deliver what he promised?"

Wreckter exhaled heavily. "No."

"What did he say when you confronted him about it?"

"He told me he couldn't sell off the state land because the environmentalists were breathing down his back. He said that if they found out, they would yell so loud it would ruin his aspirations for becoming senator."

"So he had political aspirations to become senator?"

"Yes."

"What about the money you paid him? Did he give it back to you?"

"No. He said he'd already spent it to grease the wheels for getting the land to me."

"Did you accept his explanation?"

"At first."

"What about later?"

Wreckter's head came up. "Later I found he'd sold the land to another developer. It was then I knew he had looked me right in the eye and lied."

"Made you pretty mad, didn't it?"

Wreckter's face flushed. "I could have killed him."

"Didn't you?" Graham asked very calmly.

"No. He was already dead by then."

"By then? When did you find out about the sale of state land to another developer?"

"In February. I just happened to drive by the property and see the other land developer's sign."

Graham took a newspaper article out of the folder he still held. "You just happened to drive by? Mr. Wreckter, what if I told you I had a newspaper article dated January fifth, four days *before* Warren Beaver's death, that tells of that state land parcel being sold for development?"

"I don't care if you do. I didn't see it. I told you I found out in February about the double cross."

"You also told this court that on the night of Warren Beaver's death, you drove to your home in Beaux Arts, isn't that right?"

The nervous cough came back. "Yes."

"How long does it normally take you to drive from Hunt's Point to Beaux Arts?"

"About fifteen minutes."

"And how long did it take you on that night?"

"The streets were covered in ice and snow. About thirty minutes I'd say."

"From Hunt's Point, Beaux Arts is on the way to Mercer Island, isn't it?"

"Yes. But I don't know what that's supposed to prove."

"And did anyone see you arrive home?"

Wreckter leaned back, looking safe. "Yeah. My wife, my mother-in-law, my son and his wife. They were all up late, sitting in the den, watching home movies of my grandson."

"Did you stay up with your family members watching those movies of your grandson?"

"No, they were just finishing. I went up to bed."

"Did you? Or did you drive home to establish an alibi and then leave again by the back door to kill Warren Beaver?"

"Objection, Your Honor," Rosalind said. "The defense attorney is engaging in argumentative badgering of this witness."

Graham turned toward Judge Shotz. "Your Honor, I think the witness's shady business dealings with Warren Beaver makes examining his later actions important."

"I'll allow the question, Ms. Hart."

"I didn't leave the house again!" Wreckter shouted, a raw note in his voice.

Graham watched him silently for a minute. "A moment ago you told the prosecution that at two o'clock you were in bed with your wife, is that right?"

The nervous cough. "Yes."

"But isn't it true, Mr. Wreckter, that you and your wife have separate bedrooms?"

Desperation constricted Wreckter's reply. "I . . . we—"

"Isn't that true, Mr. Wreckter?"

"Yes, damn it! But I didn't kill Warren Beaver! I'm telling the truth!"

Chapter Nine

Rosalind needed the judge's ten-minute afternoon recess to recover from the new revelations of Wreckter's testimony. She was beginning to think that the county prosecutor's office should start seriously considering hiring Fran Tulip to supplement their criminal investigation division.

She walked out into the hall and located her next witness. She liked Mrs. Pauline Park's firmness of manner and clean, no-nonsense business suit instantly. She was that kind of middle-aged woman who looked and sounded like the pillar of the community. But however reassured Rosalind was about her next witness, she knew from watching Graham in action against her previous ones that there were no guarantees.

Court resumed on schedule and Mrs. Park took the stand.

"Where do you live in relation to the defendant, Mrs. Park?" Rosalind asked, after her full name and address had been entered into the record.

"Directly opposite Milton Morebug on Hunt's Point Road."

"And can you tell us what you remember about the events of January ninth of this year?"

"Yes. It was twelve minutes after one in the morning and I was out walking my West Highland white terrier. Mr. Morebug's private gate to his driveway opened and two cars left through it. One was a black Bentley belonging to Raymond Hogg. I recognized both it and his personal license plate *Hogg Log*. The Bentley turned left and headed farther up Hunt's Point Road. The second car was a blue Lincoln. I'd seen it before, but I don't know the owner. The Lincoln turned right onto Hunt's Point Road and drove away from the point toward Highway 520.''

"Did you notice anything else, Mrs. Park?"

"Yes. At one-fifteen, Milton Morebug's gold 911 Turbo Porsche came through the gate and turned right onto Hunt's Point Road toward Highway 520, the same direction as the Lincoln."

A perceptible murmur traveled throughout the courtroom. Rosalind was pleased that the implication in Mrs. Park's testimony was being felt, but she wanted to be sure the jury understood its impact.

She picked up a picture of Morebug's car from the exhibit table. "Let me be sure I understand, Mrs. Park. At one-fifteen you saw Milton Morebug's gold Porsche, this car, leave his home and head in the direction of Mercer Island?"

"Objection," Graham called. "Move to strike 'in the direction of Mercer Island.' The deputy prosecutor is putting words in the witness's mouth."

"So ordered."

"All right," Rosalind said. "Let me rephrase. At one-fifteen you saw Milton Morebug's Porsche leave his home. What direction did it take?"

Mrs. Park's answer did not let Rosalind down. "It headed toward Highway 520. There's only one road to Hunt's Point and that's Hunt's Point Road. And there's only one direction you can go on it that will take you toward Mercer Island and that's south, the direction Milton Morebug's gold Porsche took. The car in this picture."

Rosalind smiled internally at the jury's rapt attention. "How long were you in view of Mr. Morebug's security gates?"

"Until one-thirty. That's when I warned Clarence, that's my Westy's name, that if he didn't hurry up and do his business, I was going to leave him out in the snow. He promptly obliged.''

A small chuckle drifted through the courtroom. Rosalind silently blessed Mrs. Park. She was coming across as very likable, and appealing witnesses were believed by juries.

''And during the time you were walking Clarence, did you have a clear view of Hunt's Point Road?''

''Yes.''

''Did Raymond Hogg's Bentley pass by you again?''

''No.''

''Thank you, Mrs. Park. Those are all the questions I have.''

WHEN GRAHAM GOT UP to interview Mrs. Park he knew he was facing his most damaging witness to date. Up until this point, all the jury had heard was that Milton Morebug had gotten upset over being cheated at cards. But now, this woman was describing his car leaving the scene and heading in the direction the victim had taken. He had to try to discredit her testimony.

''Mrs. Park, do you wear glasses?''

''Yes. I have them on now, Counselor, in case you hadn't noticed.''

Graham smiled. ''Yes, I had. Were you wearing your glasses that night you saw the cars?''

''Yes. I only take them off to go to bed.''

Graham paced at a decorous distance from the witness box. ''One o'clock in the morning seems to be a strange time to be walking your dog, Mrs. Park. Particularly when it was so cold out and there was snow on the ground. Is this normal behavior?''

''For me or my dog?''

Another rumble of chuckles drifted throughout the courtroom. Graham smiled. ''I assumed it involved you both.''

Mrs. Park looked for a moment like she was going to smile back at Graham but thought better of it. ''No, our being out after one in the morning was not usual. But

Clarence had been at the vet's a couple of times before undergoing some intestinal surgery and he was still off his daily routine, if you know what I mean. I was trying to be understanding.''

"Were you already awake when Clarence communicated his need to you?"

"Yes."

"What were you doing?"

"I was reading a good book."

"How is it that you remember the time so precisely?"

"I kept looking at my watch. It was cold and I was eager to get back inside the house and to my book."

Graham didn't smile this time. "You mentioned that you knew Mr. Hogg's Bentley, Mr. Morebug's Porsche and recognized the blue Lincoln that all left through the gate that night. Do you spend a lot of your time minding your neighbors' business?"

Graham had hoped to upset Mrs. Park, but she didn't look upset at all and her tone remained crisp and confident. "I try to be observant and make myself aware of who does and who doesn't belong in our little community at Hunt's Point. We had two robberies last year. They stopped when several of us got together and formed a neighborhood watch. On several occasions, we've reported suspicious-looking people to the police."

"But Mr. Morebug has an extensive antitheft system, which includes an electrified fence around his fifteen acres and an entrance barred by security gates and an intercom system. Why would you think him at risk?"

Mrs. Park remained calm. "Most of us have such security precautions. Nevertheless, thieves were able to get past them in two of my neighbors' homes. However, I've found nothing can get past a watchful eye."

Graham went on with his questions for Mrs. Park, but in the end he realized he had done nothing but reinforce the solidness of her testimony with the jury. He finally ended the painful examination with as much grace as he could.

When Judge Shotz adjourned court until the next day, he pulled his client away from his wife and son into a side meeting office in the courthouse and closed the door.

With difficulty he kept the anger from his voice. "Why didn't you tell me you left your house after the card game?"

Morebug's olive green eyes grew wide. "I didn't know anyone had seen me."

"That wasn't the question I asked, Mr. Morebug."

Milton Morebug took a seat in a nearby chair and beckoned Graham into the one opposite. When Graham obliged, Morebug leaned across the table separating them. "My wife and I haven't had a real marriage for nearly ten years. She goes her way, mostly traveling around the world, and I go mine. She doesn't want to know what I do as long as I'm discreet."

Graham had a glimmer of what was coming. "So where did you go on the night of Beaver's murder?"

"I drove to the home of a woman friend."

"Who is she?"

"I can't tell you, Knight. If this gets public, my wife will divorce me to save face with her friends. You don't know what a demanding woman she can be. She'll rake me over the community property coals."

Graham took hold of Morebug's sleeve. "Right now that jury thinks you drove off after Warren Beaver and blew him away. This is your life we're talking about. Believe me, money you can lose in a divorce settlement is a secondary consideration. Now who is this woman?"

Morebug reluctantly exhaled her name. "Linda Dodge."

Graham sat back stunned. "Beaver's chief lobbyist at the DNR? Brian Wreckter's sister?"

"Yes."

Graham got to his feet and rubbed his forehead, as though there was something there he was trying to erase. "But I've already impeached her veracity when I tied her into Brian Wreckter's attempt to buy Beaver's support in selling him state lands. If I put her on the stand as a defense witness, the prosecution is going to tear her apart."

LEROY PONCE WAS LATE for his Thursday evening appointment with Mrs. Ryan, the head of security at Western State Hospital, located south of Tacoma in Steilacoom. It had been a long wet ride south from Seattle and he'd had to stop at the post office box first to check for messages from his employer.

It was the only way they communicated since the anonymous letter that had been left in his mailbox three weekends before. The letter included basic instructions, a thousand-dollar "retainer" and the post office box number and key. Each night he'd stop by the box to see if there were additional messages. There hadn't been any since that first one.

The box had been empty again today. As he hurried to make the appointment at the hospital, Leroy was irritated at the time he'd lost for nothing. It was almost seven when he arrived. His appointment had been for six-thirty. He'd figured Mrs. Ryan wouldn't understand. He'd figured right.

"You think I don't have anything better to do than wait around for you," she had announced in her loud, gritty voice, backed by a two-hundred-pound bulk. "I should just wash my hands of you and let your old man see some of the female attendants and go berserk. The doctors would be sure to see he's tied up in a straitjacket then. All nice and cozy."

Leroy wanted to hit her. Real bad. *Never let a woman give you any lip,* his father's voice echoed in his brain. He'd held himself back just barely, easing the tension snapping through his nerves by fingering the cold steel in his pocket.

"Well, Ponce? Where's my money?"

"Next week I'll be getting real money. I'll give you what I owe you and another twenty thousand like we agreed to look the other way when I spring him."

Mrs. Ryan wrapped her large arms around her even larger bosom. Her light eyes were slits in the ample folds of her face. "Promises are cheap, Ponce."

Leroy's hand gripped the gun in his pocket. He let the action steady him. "I'm willing to pay a late charge. Say another thousand."

He watched her large lips chew on the information greedily. "The late charge will be five thousand," she announced. "But only if you're ready to get your old man out by next Thursday. They're going to move me to another section after next week." Then she rose as a signal that their business was concluded.

Leroy got to his feet. "I want to see my father now."

"So go see him," Mrs. Ryan said. "No one is stopping you."

Leroy walked down the dingy hallway to his father's cell on the end. He realized Ryan must have called ahead to the burly male orderly because the man opened the security door to his father's cell without a blink. He closed and locked it behind Leroy as soon as he was inside.

Leroy found Harold Ponce hunched in his bed staring at a blank wall. He didn't even turn as Leroy entered. Leroy sat on the bed next to his father and stared at the blank wall, too. He and his old man had never said much to each other. Didn't seem any reason to start now.

His old man had been all he had since he was eight and his mother had taken off. He didn't remember her much. But he remembered the drunken nights his father had cursed her and all women.

Except his old man's senility had robbed him of any restraint over the last few years. Now, even seeing a woman enraged him to violence. That's why he was locked in this hole.

He'd get him out. And he'd get that Ryan broad. Tonight she'd made a mistake trying to cheat him out of more than their original deal. It was a mistake she'd pay for with her life. People who tried to cheat Leroy Ponce never got a second chance.

As soon as Leroy got his money, he'd get him and his old man a place of their own. Have a male nurse in each day to bathe his old man, dress him and feed him.

But when that money was gone?

Leroy was forty-five and there were a lot of younger trig-germen out there with no records competing for the jobs. He had that one lousy conviction on his rap sheet because of that damn female prosecutor. Even with his fifty sound hits, the offerings just weren't there like they used to be.

Leroy stole a look at his father, appalled at the empty eyes, slack jaw and drooling mouth. He dropped to his knees in front of Harold Ponce, throwing his arms around his father's legs. The sudden movement caught the old man's vacuous eyes. Something flashed in their depths. "Stop crawling on your knees! Didn't I teach you to be a man!"

Leroy's arms dropped. "I—"

"Shut up or you'll get the back of my hand. Now get out of here! You make me sick!"

Leroy got stiffly to his feet and banged on the cell door. When the male orderly let him out, he trudged out to his old beat-up Honda in the parking lot. He sank behind the wheel, staring through his windshield at the suffocating blanket of heavy rain.

Anger swelled in his gut, poking for focus. Rosalind Hart's image circled through his brain like a target. He never would have been sent up if it hadn't been for her. And if he hadn't been sent up, his old man wouldn't be in this rotten place.

His hand found the gun in his pocket, fingering it in agitation. What he would give to be able to blow Rosalind Hart away this very moment.

No. The little surprises he had left for her were better. The fear had to come first. Lots of it. Unending, unrelenting fear. She would die a thousand times before he finally pulled the trigger. He'd see to it.

ROSALIND ARRIVED home to her new apartment Thursday night in high spirits. Thanks to Mrs. Park's testimony, court had ended on a very good note. She put down her briefcase on the counter and headed to the refrigerator for the open container of milk.

Living alone for nine years had fostered a certain laziness in food selection and preparation, but the one thing Rosalind had always refused to descend to was drinking directly out of containers. She reached for her favorite ceramic mug.

But as she poured the remaining milk from its cardboard container, she frowned at an uncharacteristic pinging sound as it splashed against the sides of the mug. What would cause that?

A logical explanation immediately sprung to mind. Ice crystals must have formed in the milk because the refrigerator had malfunctioned and begun to freeze its contents. It was irritating, but her old refrigerator had acted up before.

Maybe something came loose during the recent move. Rosalind put the mug and milk container on the counter and opened the refrigerator door. After checking the yogurt and orange juice she was frowning.

They hadn't iced up. Why had the milk?

With an uneasy curiosity, she picked up a spoon and dunked it into the mug, scooping out some of the tiny sparkling grains within the white liquid. She laid them on the counter and tried to smash them back into liquid form. They scratched the back of the spoon.

A whirlpool of fear began swirling in the pit of her stomach. These weren't ice crystals. They were too hard. She reached out a finger to touch one. Its sharp edge drew blood.

And then she knew what the crystal grains were—small, jagged chunks of glass! The whirlpool of sickness grew and swarmed throughout her body, leaving incapacitating weakness in its wake. Rosalind grabbed at the edge of the counter to support herself, battling both sudden vertigo and queasiness as images of swallowed glass cut through her mind.

Chapter Ten

Graham was up early Friday morning, preparing his percolated coffee and switching on the small television in the kitchen corner as he went about scrambling a couple of eggs. He rarely watched television, but it was company of a sort. And this morning he was curiously aware of being alone. Coffee for one. Toast for one. Eggs for one. Sharing his breakfast with the shapes and sounds from a local news broadcast he hoped would ease an uncharacteristic emptiness visiting him.

Two early-morning newspeople blared away at him from behind paperless desks. Graham's mind wandered to the problem of introducing Linda Dodge as Morebug's alibi on the night of the murder. He knew he'd have to approach the woman and get her statement before he made any final determination as to what would be best for his client.

He really wanted to wring Morebug's neck for lying to him and putting both of them in this position. It was all so unnecessary. If he had just known what the facts were, he could have kept Linda Dodge's name out of his cross-examination of her brother, Brian Wreckter.

As far as Graham was concerned, that was the thing that made being a defense lawyer so difficult. Clients were always inclined to lie, even when they were innocent. It seemed they all thought that if they admitted doing anything wrong anywhere else in their life, their attorney wouldn't believe their innocence of the crime for which they were charged.

Fortunately, he had a few days left to make a decision about Linda Dodge while Rosalind finished presenting the prosecution's case. As always, thoughts of Rosalind made him smile.

Her name vibrated in the air and for a moment, he thought he'd spoken aloud. Then with a shock, he realized it hadn't been him. He quickly put down his fork and leaned over the counter to turn up the TV's volume.

"The deputy prosecutor for King County has reported several such terrorist-type acts over the last week," the reporter said. "When asked earlier whether she connected the start of this personal vendetta to the start of her prosecution of County Assessor Milton Morebug for the murder of former State Commissioner of Public Lands, Warren Beaver, Ms. Hart refused to comment.

"Recapping again this bulletin just into us. Deputy Prosecutor Rosalind Hart has again been the victim of a personal terrorist act, this time at her high-security apartment in the city. No details are available as to whether Ms. Hart has been injured or whether she will be able to appear in court today to continue with her prosecution of Milton Morebug. We'll bring you more on this story just as soon as it becomes available."

Graham switched off the television and grabbed for the telephone. He had to see if Rosalind was all right, but realized instantly that he didn't have her home number. It was too early for her to be in her office. Then he remembered she had told Fran that her parents lived in Seabeck along the Hood Canal. He took a chance she might be there and dialed information.

The operator had two Harts listed. Graham jotted both numbers down then dialed the first and asked for Rosalind. When he was told he had a wrong number he tried the second and repeated his inquiry.

"May I ask who's calling?" a cautious male voice said.

Graham couldn't believe his luck that he not only had reached her parents but also that she was there. "Graham Knight," he answered immediately.

After a few muffled voices in the background, Graham heard Rosalind's voice give a tentative hello.

He felt an enormous relief to hear her voice. "Rosalind, it's Graham. I heard about your apartment. Are you all right?"

"Yes, but how on earth did you find me?"

"Have you forgotten how thorough Fran's questioning was the other night?"

Graham heard a sigh. "I should have known."

"Are you planning on being in court today?"

"Of course. You know what Judge Shotz is like to no-shows."

The knot in Graham's stomach untied a bit. If Rosalind could still be worried about Judge Shotz's reaction, she must be feeling all right. "Rosalind, what happened? I turned on the television and found you were headline news."

Her hesitation was brief, but her choice of words made Graham understand she didn't want to say some things in front of her parents. "They must have gotten the story from the police. Perhaps we could discuss that matter at another time."

He decided that would be a good bargaining tool and seized it. "All right, give me directions, and I'll pick you up and you can tell me on our way into court."

"That's not necessary. My parents will drive me."

So she didn't have her car with her, Graham thought. Good. Aloud he said, "You must be aware the press is trying to tie my client to whoever is doing this to you. That kind of prejudicial news reporting can do irreparable harm to Milton Morebug's chances for a fair trial."

She hesitated. "But I assure you I had nothing to do—"

"I know that. But I also know that you and I need to talk at length if we're going to prevent a mistrial. You are interested in seeing this case through to the end, aren't you?"

"Of course."

"Well then give me directions and let's get together so we can talk. Go ahead. I've got a pencil and paper handy."

As Rosalind gave him directions on how to get to her parents' place, Graham smiled. He knew she wouldn't have accepted the protection he was really offering, but she rose to the professional implications without hesitation.

Slightly disconcerted at his real motives as he drove through the heavy rain toward Seabeck, he reminded himself that what he had told Rosalind about the news reports was true. They were suggestive that his client had a part in these terrorist activities against her. He was determined to stop those insinuations about his client.

But Graham was much more interested in getting them stopped because of the harm they were doing to Rosalind. His normal single-mindedness that relegated everything but his client's acquittal to the back burner was being replaced by his growing feelings for the deputy prosecutor. He recognized that truth on some level, and tried to dismiss it.

But on no level could he dismiss the exciting memory of the feel of her in his arms. He nudged the pedal farther to the floor.

GRAHAM INSISTED on dashing through the heavy rain to meet Rosalind's parents even though she was ready at the door with briefcase in hand, reminding him that they only had a short time to make it to the ferry.

Still, it was hard for her to be cross with him after seeing how pleased her parents were at the old-fashioned charm of his manners. When her dad winked at her as they left, she felt sure he thought Graham and she were an item. She had a lot of explaining to do when she next spoke to her parents.

"Tell me what happened at your apartment," he asked as soon as they were under way.

Briefly, Rosalind described her episode with the cut glass in her milk. As she finished and turned to him, she saw the muscle twitching in his jaw. "You realize, of course, he's trying to tell you you're not safe anywhere. Smartest thing you did was having your parents come pick you up."

Rosalind shook her head. "I wonder. Last night it seemed like the logical thing to do, what with the police searching through everything including my car for more booby traps, but now I'm afraid I might have put my parents in jeopardy. What if he followed me to their home?"

Graham shook his head. "He seems pretty focused on scaring you, not your parents. We'll have to keep you out of his reach until the police can get a lead on him."

Rosalind's heart beat faster. At that moment she couldn't decide if it was from anger or excitement because of his presumption he had a right to involve himself in her business. "We?" she repeated.

Graham glanced at her. "Of course, we. You don't think I'm going to let this guy keep threatening you and give the news media a field day speculating that Morebug's in back of it, do you?"

Rosalind exhaled. "Oh."

Graham smiled internally at the meaning behind her new tone. He was glad he could still keep her guessing and off balance. Despite the steady harassment she'd received, she was far from folding.

But when he glanced at her now silent profile, he could see the new faint lines of fear around her lips and the way her hands shifted back and forth across the car seat. She was holding together all right, but she'd received some pretty severe jolts. And the distress they'd brought her he found increasingly intolerable.

He'd like to get his hands on the creep threatening her for just five minutes. The depth of his rage surprised him. Disconcerted, he kept his eyes on the road as he asked his next question. "Did Max Hill ever arrange for a bodyguard?"

"He offered one, but I told him to forget it. Whoever is doing this may be following me around, but he does his stuff while I'm away. I don't see how a bodyguard could protect me from that."

Graham nodded. "Still no leads as to who it could be?"

Graham saw Rosalind's head shake from the corner of his eye. "All the murderers I've put away are still away."

"Perhaps it's someone who's decided to move up to murder. Maybe you should be looking at anyone you prosecuted."

Rosalind shrugged. "That's a lot of people."

"You've got a lot of life to lose, Rosalind. Don't let Hill get away with not turning over every stone."

Rosalind appreciated the sincerity in Graham's tone, but she felt the necessity to come to Max's defense. "Hill is the best investigator in King County."

Graham tasted a lick of unwelcome jealousy. Before he could swallow it, his next comment slipped out. "Is he? Then I wonder how he missed so much on this case we're arguing."

Rosalind turned in her seat. "I don't see he's missed much, at least not much as it pertains to Morebug's guilt."

"No, just a whole bunch that pertains to Morebug's innocence," Graham said more bitterly than he had intended to.

"What are you talking about?"

"I'm talking about the land deal Warren Beaver had going with Hogg and Wreckter. You heard their testimony. Beaver was clear-cutting state forest land and selling the lumber to Hogg as a payback for the campaign contribution. Then he reneged on his deal to sell the land to Wreckter for development into housing and shopping centers. The man was a cheat and a liar. How is it Hill's investigation didn't expose that fact?"

Rosalind's voice rose. "Why should that have anything to do with Beaver's death? And why would you expect Hill to go digging up all that unrelated stuff about Beaver when he was killed less than an hour after Morebug fought with him with Morebug's gun and a witness saw Morebug going after him?"

"So you're admitting Hill made up his mind Morebug did it right away and that's why he stopped investigating?"

Rosalind snorted. "I'm admitting nothing of the sort! Hill did talk to Beaver's family and associates. At length. I have stacks of depositions. But you know what? Not one of them contains a scrap of evidence that anyone but Milton Morebug had the motive, means and opportunity to kill Warren Beaver."

Graham gripped the steering wheel in mounting frustration. "I gave you motive, means and opportunity for both Hogg and Wreckter."

"Oh sure. You made a big deal about how both Hogg and Wreckter could have taken the murder weapon during the card game that night, but what you didn't explain is how they got the gun back into its display case without Milton Morebug even knowing it was gone."

"One of them must have gone back the next day."

Rosalind shook her head. "Hill was out there with his search warrant by eleven that next morning. He'd just come from questioning Hogg and Wreckter. Morebug wasn't home. Hill put a man in the street on watch. When Morebug came home at three that afternoon, Hill got word from his lookout and drove to Morebug's place to serve the warrant. That Hunt's Point home is like a security fortress. Neither Hogg nor Wreckter could have gotten back into it to replace the gun if Morebug hadn't let them in. So how did the cleaned murder weapon get back in the display case if Morebug didn't put it there?"

Damn. That's a good question, Graham thought. Aloud he said, "Do you know for a fact that Hogg or Wreckter didn't steal one of Morebug's electronic card keys to release the front security gates to gain access?"

"And do you know for a fact that one of them did?" Rosalind countered, "And that he somehow also learned the secret door code to let himself into the house?"

Graham was far from giving up. "Your own witness, Mrs. Park, said there had been two burglaries in the Hunt's Point homes that had circumvented all security precautions. That proves there are ways to get inside."

Rosalind shook her head. "You're trying to make this case far more complicated than it is."

"Am I, Rosalind? Or are you trying to make it far more simple than it should be?"

She crossed her arms over her chest. "Clearly, we're not going to agree so why are we even discussing this?"

Graham looked over at the lift of her chin and decided he enjoyed the strength of her inherent stubbornness. A small smile circled his lips. "Do you only discuss subjects you expect agreement on?"

She gave him an irritated sidelong glance. "I doubt I'd find any subject we could discuss if that were true."

Graham's smile got bigger. "Rosalind, have you already forgotten that moment we shared embracing the same subject...so agreeably?"

Rosalind's thoughts immediately flew to the memory of Graham's kiss and the way she had crushed him to her, hungry and demanding. She tried to concentrate on the rhythmic swishing noises being made by the windshield wipers. "I have no idea what subject you're talking about."

Rosalind's hands traced up and down her arms nervously, telling Graham he'd elicited the memories he'd intended. Naturally, he had no intention of admitting it. "Why, I was talking about our agreeing on how nice it would be to have a couple of days of sunshine, of course. Don't you remember?"

Rosalind's forehead puckered into a frown. "Oh. That."

"So you see, Rosalind, even if we were to run out of trials or terrorists, we could always talk about the weather."

She exhaled wearily as she glared at the pounding rain. "Maybe when this trial is over, I can take some time off and go someplace warm and sunny where I can forget..."

As Rosalind's voice trailed off and her frown deepened, Graham knew she was thinking about cut glass in her milk. He decided the best thing he could do was distract her.

"Speaking of weather," he said, "I once brought a case against a television weatherman on behalf of a client who had lost some expensive boat charter contracts because the weatherman had read a week-old report on the air by mistake."

Rosalind turned in her seat. "You sued a weatherman?"

Graham gave her a smile. "Want to hear how?"

"I can't wait."

Graham went into a long dissertation about the unusual case, rewarded by her frequent smiles. She was visibly more relaxed as they got on the ferry for Seattle. He started on another story about a man suing his neighbor because his neighbor's cat was attacking his dog, making the rottweiler a nervous wreck.

"Your client's dog was a rottweiler?" Rosalind repeated, not believing her ears.

"Yes. It seems the cat would hide at the top of the common wooden fence separating the properties and when the dog would amble by, the cat would drop onto its neck, rip it with its claws, and then scramble up the fence. After about two weeks of these attacks, my client couldn't even get his dog to go into the backyard. The judge called it the case of the commando cat."

Rosalind started to laugh so hard, other travelers in the ferry's cabin turned to stare. Graham led her outside onto the covered deck, enjoying her merriment. When she had regained her composure, she managed to ask how the case came out.

"We won, of course," Graham said with a smile.

She began to giggle. "You actually won a case representing a rottweiler against a cat?"

Graham nodded. "It was a Manx, trained by its owner to attack dogs in this unusual manner since it was a kitten. When I got one of the attacks on videotape with the owner on the other side of the fence egging the cat on, we proved malicious intent and the jury gave my client an award for pain and suffering plus damages to cover the dog's treatment therapy."

"Treatment therapy?" Rosalind echoed.

"Doggy behavior modification so it wouldn't run at the sight of any more cats."

The image of a fierce rottweiler running at the sight of cats caused Rosalind to laugh until her sides began to hurt.

"And then there was the case of the man's pet bullfrog that croaked so loudly when it rained that it interfered with the glee-club practice at the local church."

"No," Rosalind said, one hand raised in surrender as the other clutched at her side. "I can't take any more."

Graham laughed with her as he took her hand and led them to a couple of the outside chairs. They sank into them as gradually their laughter ceased. Then they quietly drew closer as the rain-swept wind bustled around them. Rosalind settled within the warmth of Graham's circling arm, tasting the salt of the sea on her tongue and enjoying both the smell and feel of its pungent odor clear through to her sinuses.

All sorts of caution lights flickered in her head as an inner voice told her to draw away from Graham, but she ignored both the lights and the voice. For nearly an hour, he'd brought laughter back into her life. She didn't want to question why. She was just grateful to have gotten free from the dark emotional cloud of fear that had been suspended over her spirit. At least for a little while.

She knew when the ferry arrived in Seattle, neither their past nor their adversarial role could be denied. But for this moment, this quiet full moment, they were just two people who had laughed together and now huddled close in comfort against the force of the elements.

"Ms. HART, your first witness?"

Rosalind rose from behind the prosecution table in the courtroom of Judge Gloria Shotz. "The People call Emilio Fortuno."

Emilio Fortuno was a slim, sixtyish man with a full mane of hair, still as black as night, and a bland, honest face. He testified he owned a small all-night grocery store just outside of Bellevue. Step-by-step, Rosalind took him through the events on the night of January eighth.

Warren Beaver, a frequent customer, had come in some time after one in the morning—Fortuno couldn't be sure exactly when. Beaver had bought a gallon of homemade and hand-packed double-chocolate ice cream. Fortuno explained his wife, Maria, made the ice cream herself. Many customers made a special trip to his store just to get some.

"Did you wait on Mr. Beaver personally?"

"Yes. I don't let my Maria work at night even though we are in good neighborhood and our store is right next to police station. It's because of police I stay open all night. Lotsa cops stop by store on way home from shifts."

"How long was Warren Beaver in your store?"

"Maybe two, three minutes. He pay me cash, he tell me say hello to Maria, and he leave."

Rosalind had no further questions of Fortuno. Graham didn't cross-examine.

Rosalind's next witness was a forensic examiner who had had the job of going over the contents of Warren Beaver's car at the scene of the murder. He testified that he found a gallon of Maria Fortuno's homemade ice cream on the passenger seat. Due to the freezing temperatures and open car door, the ice cream had not melted.

Again, Graham had no questions on cross-examination.

Rosalind next called Amanda Lewis, an official from the state's department of transportation. She was a tall, plain, dark-haired woman with a large beak of a nose and quick, birdlike movements. After a lengthy read of the woman's credentials, the court accepted her status as knowledgeable on road conditions.

Ms. Lewis described icy and hazardous road conditions on January eighth. Rosalind entered various enlarged maps of the Seattle area and vicinity into evidence and proceeded to mark three specific areas with the alphabetical letters A, B and C.

"Ms. Lewis, based on the hazardous road conditions that you testified existed on the night of January eighth, how long would you say it would take a driver to get from point A, identified as Milton Morebug's home at Hunt's Point, to point B, the family-owned store of Emilio and Maria Fortuno just east of the city of Bellevue?''

Ms. Lewis cocked her head as though she had to see the exhibit sideways in order for it to make sense. "Providing the driver took the most direct route, I'd say fifteen minutes."

"So if Warren Beaver left point A, Milton Morebug's home, at one in the morning, then he would have been at point B, the Fortuno grocery, at one-fifteen?"

"Yes."

"And how long would it take for a driver selecting the most direct route from point B, the grocery store, to point C shown here on this map and identified as the site of the car crash, and murder of Warren Beaver?"

"Approximately forty-five minutes."

"So if the driver left point B at one-fifteen in the morning, he'd reach Point C about two o'clock, is that right?"

Ms. Lewis nodded. "Give or take a couple of minutes."

"And if someone left point A, Milton Morebug's home, and drove directly to point C, the site of Warren Beaver's death, approximately how long would that take under these same hazardous road conditions?"

"About forty-five minutes."

"Just a couple of further questions for clarification, Ms. Lewis. If Warren Beaver left Milton Morebug's home at one in the morning and stopped at the grocery store shown as point B, what time would he have been at point C?"

"Two o'clock. An hour later."

"And at what time would someone have had to leave point A, Milton Morebug's home, in order to arrive at point C, the site of Warren Beaver's murder, at the same time as the victim?"

Ms. Lewis leaned her head sideways again. "I'd say one-fifteen, since it would have taken approximately forty-five minutes to go from point A directly to point C."

"Thank you, Ms. Lewis. I have no more questions."

Graham got up to cross-examine the witness. "Ms. Lewis, were chains required on these roads January eighth?"

"No. The roads had been cleared of snow and sanded."

"Under those conditions, how long would it have taken someone at this point here on the map, just about where the home of Brian Wreckter would be in Beaux Arts, to have driven to point C, the scene of the murder?"

"Maybe thirty minutes. I haven't tested it out."

"But you did test out the other times from points A, B and C under conditions similar to the night of January eighth?"

"Yes. At the direction of the investigating detective, Mr. Hill."

"What day did you check out the roads, Ms. Lewis?"

"May I consult my notes?"

"Of course."

Ms. Lewis reached into her suit pocket and drew out a small blue notebook. She flipped through the pages until she found the right one. "On January twentieth."

"And were the road conditions identical on January twentieth to those on January eighth?"

A hesitation. "Well, not exactly."

"Not exactly? How different were they, Ms. Lewis?"

"Well, it was a few degrees warmer by then and most of the ice had melted."

"So the road conditions were actually quite different when you did these time tests than they would have been on the night of the murder?"

"Yes. But I made corrections to allow for the changes."

"But those corrections were only your best guess since the road conditions were so different?"

"Yes, but—"

"Ms. Lewis, how long did it take you on January twentieth to drive from point A, Mr. Morebug's home, to point C, the site of Warren Beaver's murder?"

Reluctant. "Twenty minutes."

"So you guessed the time would be more than doubled?"

"With the increased ice—"

"Ms. Lewis, please answer just yes or no. Did your guess of the time it would take to drive from point A to point C double the actual time it took you to drive there?"

"Yes."

"Could you be wrong? Just yes or no."

Very reluctant. "Yes."

"Could you be as far off as ten or fifteen minutes or even more? Again, please just yes or no."

Her birdlike hands fluttered in frustration. "Yes."

"And would it be possible for someone to have driven from point A, Mr. Morebug's home, to point C, the site of the murder, on the night of the murder in less than thirty minutes?"

"Driving so fast over icy surfaces—"

"Please, Ms. Lewis. Just answer yes or no. Is it possible?"

"Yes."

Graham smiled. With that yes he had just reintroduced Raymond Hogg as another possible murderer of Warren Beaver, despite the fact that Mrs. Park hadn't even seen him take off after Warren Beaver by one-thirty. Even if he passed her a moment later, he still could have had time to drive to Mercer Island and kill Beaver. "Thank you, Ms. Lewis. I have no further questions."

ROSALIND ROSE. "Your Honor, as it is already 11:50, I wonder if we might adjourn for lunch early so that my examination of the next witness will not be interrupted by the noon recess?"

Judge Shotz pursed her lips. "I'll do better than that, Ms. Hart. I intend to adjourn court for the rest of the day and resume with your next witness Monday morning."

Rosalind just stared in surprise. Could the infamous Gloria Shotz really have said *she* was adjourning court early?

Judge Shotz turned to face the jury.

"Due to the extensive media speculation affecting certain principals in this case over the last twelve hours, I am forced to sequester you, ladies and gentlemen of the jury, for the remainder of this trial."

A murmur rose throughout the crowded courtroom, loud enough for Judge Shotz to rap her gavel for order. Rosalind felt somehow guilty when the judge's glance swept in her direction.

"A bailiff will take you to lunch as soon as I adjourn court for today. Then court personnel will accompany each of you to your homes to pack a suitcase or arrange with family members to have a suitcase packed for you. You will be comfortably housed in a nearby hotel for the remainder of this trial."

Rosalind watched various members of the jury exchanging uneasy glances. Judge Shotz went on in her booming voice. "Please remember, ladies and gentlemen of the jury. You are not to discuss this case with anyone, not even your fellow jurors, until all the evidence has been presented in this court and the case is given to you for deliberation. As of now you will be prohibited from watching news programs on television, from listening to the radio and reading the newspaper. And you are not to speculate on the reasons for this sequestering."

Judge Shotz straightened and turned toward the room. "Court stands adjourned until ten o'clock Monday morning."

Max Hill turned to Rosalind as the jury started to file out under the bailiff's direction. "Did you expect this?"

Rosalind shook her head. "Maybe I should have. The press has been pretty circumspect on what it reported on the trial until they got wind of this harassment against me. Too much of a temptation to sensationalize, I suppose."

Max shook his head. "I wish I could tell you my crime-scene investigators found some evidence last night, but they didn't. They did find a shoe box full of poisonous spiders waiting for you to open it. Whoever is doing this, he's determined."

Rosalind took a steadying breath as she heard the ominous tone in Max's voice. "Have you had any luck in your investigation on the friends of the murderers I've put away?"

Max shook his head. "A bunch of dead ends."

Rosalind found herself thinking of Graham's suggestion. "Max, it might be someone I put away for a lesser crime."

Max shook his head. "I'm willing to look into it, but I think it's a reach, Roz. Guys who commit burglaries and such don't go in for this harassment scene."

"But you'll check?" Rosalind asked.

"Sure. Still, you realize this guy could just be some psycho who tries to terrorize women in positions of power or something? This morning I faxed the particulars to the FBI's psychological profiling unit to see what they might be able to come up with. It could be they have records of similar types of terrorism."

"You mean he might have come in from another state and that's why you don't have such a record?"

Max nodded. "It's a possibility. Frankly, the way he's gotten into your apartments, I think he's too smooth to be inexperienced. But if I'm wrong, then catching him may be almost impossible."

Cold icy slivers were shooting their way up Rosalind's spine at Max's words.

Rosalind was thankful for the warm intrusion of Graham's voice just over her shoulder. "Rosalind, can I speak with you?"

At Rosalind's signal, Max got up reluctantly from the prosecution table in the now deserted courtroom and gave her shoulder a pat before strolling toward the exit. Graham immediately took his vacated chair and leaned toward her.

"There's something I want you to see. Will you take a ride with me?"

"Now?"

"We have the afternoon off."

"My witness is waiting outside. I'll have to tell her I need her for Monday."

Graham got to his feet and picked up her briefcase. "Come on, we can do it on the way."

"What about lunch?" Rosalind asked.

"If you can wait awhile, I know a place I think you'll enjoy," Graham said as he led the way out of the courtroom.

LEROY PONCE WATCHED Rosalind leave the courtroom with the defense attorney and followed them to the parking garage. It irritated him that the two of them were so friendly.

Could that have been why he got convicted? Could his defense attorney have been in league with Rosalind Hart to put him away? New anger arose in Leroy as he started his old Honda and followed them out of the garage.

GRAHAM GOT ON I-90 and headed the Mercedes east. The morning's loud icy rain was now being buffeted by a strong wind. When Rosalind recognized where they were going, she turned to Graham. "I know this route. When I was young my parents and I used to drive out to Cle Elum during the winter just to see all the beautiful trees covered in snow from the highway. It was like a Courier and Ives Christmas card."

Graham's profile turned grim. "These days it might remind you more of a Salvador Dali painting."

Rosalind was perplexed by Graham's remark until the miles kept passing and icy rain kept crusting on the vast expanse of barren, desertlike land. When she finally saw the highway sign for Cle Elum, she shook her head. "What happened to the forest?"

Graham exhaled a heavy breath. "Greedy corporations with highly paid lobbyists got to the officials in charge and they clear-cut the trees."

"But that was national forest land!" Rosalind protested.

"It still is. But that doesn't mean the government can't award contracts to loggers to take the trees. You see the results—nothing left but a barren desert. And state-owned forests are falling to the ax just as rapidly. Under Warren Beaver's term in office, he approved the logging of more than two-thirds of the state's old-growth forests."

Rosalind shook her head. "This is dreadful. We're doing the very same thing to our trees that Brazil is doing to its rain forest. And we're throwing stones at them! Is it the local saw mills that are to blame?"

"No. Most of the raw logs never get to local sawmills. They're sold to Korea, Taiwan and Japan because of the high stumpage prices those countries offer. When they get the logs they process them into plywood and other finished goods and then sell them back to us at a huge profit."

Rosalind frowned. "Just like England used to do when we were one of its colonies."

Graham nodded. "Except now we're a colony of the Pacific Rim countries, selling off our natural resources to the highest bidder until one day Washington will be a desert."

Rosalind grew silent as Graham circumnavigated several tricky turns off I-90 until he drew up in front of a structure that looked more like a wood cabin than a restaurant. Only the sign Gumbo in neon letters, blinking through the heavy sleet, gave it away.

"Come on. It's time I bought you lunch," Graham said.

Rosalind shook her head. "I've lost my appetite."

Graham gave her a smile. "Well, this is the perfect place to get it back."

He got out of the car and opened the door for her. Then they both made a dash for the restaurant door as an icy wind-filled rain whirled about them.

Rosalind was assailed by heavenly smells as soon as she stepped inside the cozy and warm room, which looked more like someone's home than a restaurant. They shed their coats and a short, middle-aged woman with a golden bun and cherub cheeks showed them to one of the six tables. Rosalind noticed four of the remaining five tables were already occupied.

The round woman reappeared a moment later with a small carafe of white wine and two glasses. She set them before Graham and Rosalind without a word and disappeared again.

Rosalind looked at the white wine in confusion. "Did you call the order ahead?"

Graham smiled as he poured the wine into their glasses. "No. This isn't a normal kind of restaurant. The man and woman who own it prepare only one dish and offer only one beverage."

Rosalind took a sip of her wine and found it excellent. "What is the dish?"

"Gumbo. Just like the sign outside says. They do it northwest style, a little lighter than the Louisiana version."

"I don't think I've ever had gumbo. What's in it?"

"See for yourself," Graham said as a large fragrant bowl was set in the middle of their table and two more small wide bowls of white steaming rice were set in front of them.

Rosalind picked up the ladle and dipped into the gumbo, coming out with crab, shrimp, oysters, vegetables of every description and something that looked like sausage in a thick brown sauce. After depositing it over her hot rice, she handed the ladle to Graham. Their quiet waitress delivered a loaf of hot, sliced corn bread to their table and Rosalind dug in.

It was a heavenly meal. Rich, toasty, spicy. The bowl emptied like magic before her as did the wine and corn bread.

When Rosalind finally sat back, she looked up to see Graham watching her with a smile on his lips. "More wine?"

She shook her head. "No. Thank you. That was great."

Graham leaned back. "I've been coming here to Gumbo's since I was in law school at UW." He looked around appreciatively. Then his voice descended as a small frown appeared on his forehead. "At least this is one thing that hasn't changed."

Rosalind understood Graham was thinking about the cut trees. "Did you bring me out here because you wanted me to sympathize with your client for having killed a man like Warren Beaver?"

Graham shook his head. "Only a deranged fanatic would think killing people is the way to stop the carnage of the forests. This has nothing to do with Morebug. I showed you the devastation because I know you're the kind of person who will do something about what you believe in. We need fighters."

Rosalind leaned forward. "How long have you and Fran been fighting the tree cutters?"

"Not long enough, Rosalind. The state owns eleven million acres of forest and aquatic lands and wealthy businessmen are constantly buying their way into exploiting it for their own use. That prime piece of state property Beaver let go for development he 'exchanged' for useless sunken land from the developer a few miles away. For a kickback."

"I don't understand. How could he get away with that?"

"He got away with it because we're all so busy with our own small worlds, we're not paying attention to what's happening in the one that sustains us. Until one day when we wake up and find out it's too late."

Rosalind took a deep breath. "Like driving through a forest we haven't seen in a while only to find it gone."

"Yes," Graham said. "Exactly." He put a chunk of money on the table. "We should get back while the roads are still passable. Ready?"

Rosalind nodded quietly and they left. The driving sleet had become a thick windy snow. They walked carefully to the car so as not to slip on the icy surface.

They inched back to Seattle. Wailing winds gathered the clumps of snow and slammed them against the Mercedes. Rosalind was silent as she thought of rapidly dwindling natural resources instead of her personal fears. She began to suspect that may have been why Graham had suggested the drive.

She looked over at his profile, full of concentration as he battled to keep the car on the slippery highway. Strength, determination, gentleness—they were all there in the finely chiseled planes. *This is what a friend would do,* she said to herself. *Laugh you out of your problems, distract you from them.*

Friend? You would call this man friend? He threw your work in the trash! He stomped on your hopes and dreams!

Rosalind turned her head away from Graham, her eyes staring into the punches of swirling white belting the passenger window, and sighed. Rejection in those vulnerable years was so hard to overcome. It had taken her a long time to battle her way out of its yoke, to reclaim her confidence, to regain her trust. To risk it all again, with the same man—

Rosalind never had time to finish the thought. Suddenly her shoulder belt was digging into her chest, the breath squeezed out of her lungs as she was thrown sideways. Her ears clogged with a hideous roar and her eyes widened in terror as the Mercedes careened off the highway, crashed through the guardrails, and skidded toward the sheer drop off the highway's edge.

Chapter Eleven

Graham desperately fought with the skidding car, yanking the steering wheel with all his willpower in order to stay away from the steep embankment.

Blinding snow battered the windshield as the car twirled on the ice like an out-of-control skater. But the seconds stretched by and still the road remained level beneath the sliding wheels. Graham longed to hit the brakes, but he knew braking would send them into a spin and increase the likelihood of flipping the car. He had just one option. He concentrated with every ounce of his strength on keeping the wheel straight and hung on.

For what seemed like an eternity, the car skidded through the blinding snow. All the while a voice inside told him this couldn't be happening. How could the tires have completely lost traction? Then, just as though it had run out of gas, the Mercedes finally came to a halt with a deep, metallic groan.

Graham was breathing hard enough to feel his lungs labor. He wiped the perspiration from his brow with the sleeve of his suit jacket and gradually coaxed his fingers into relaxing sufficiently to unwind from the steering wheel. He switched off the engine. Then he turned to Rosalind.

She was flat against the seat, as pale as a ghost, staring at him with enormous fear-filled eyes. With shaky hands he unbuckled his safety belt and leaned over to gather her in his arms. Her head came down on his shoulder with an audible shudder.

He realized they both were trembling. He rocked her gently, getting comfort as well as giving it and feeling thankful to be alive. Gradually the scent of her perfume and the feel of her soft yielding body so close to his started other feelings. When he raised a hand to stroke her hair, she drew away.

"What happened?"

Graham exhaled, a little disappointed, but gave her a small smile. "Haven't got the faintest. Let's see if I can find out."

He slipped out of the car into the driving snow. When he saw they had been traveling on a narrow embankment parallel to the highway and were less than six inches from the edge of the thirty-foot drop, he swallowed hard. Trying to put their close brush with disaster out of his mind, he concentrated on checking each of the tires. When he got back into the driver's seat and closed the door, he wore a new expression.

Rosalind stared at his face. "My God, what is it?"

He gripped the steering wheel and looked at the snow-caked windshield. "Someone sprayed the tires with a clear, thick material that apparently hardened as we started to drive."

Rosalind shook her head. "The tires were sprayed? I don't understand."

Graham's voice remained tight and strained. "I can't say I do either, but someone deliberately filled the crevices in my tires with something that hardened, and when it did, it made the tire surface as smooth as glass. It appears our losing control was no accident. Someone wanted us to crash."

ROSALIND FELT NUMB as Graham used his car phone to contact the police. Even when they arrived and towed the Mercedes away to go over it for evidence, she had a hard time fighting off the feeling of unreality. She answered their questions with stoic brevity.

An officer gave Graham and her a lift to the impound lot in Seattle where her Chrysler LeBaron had been cleared for release. She signed for it and trudged through a heavy downpour of snow to find it at the end of the lot.

Wind whistled through the bending trees as the heavy snowfall pelted the car in its slow pace across the busy streets of Seattle. It was close to eight o'clock when she drove onto the Winslow ferry and switched off the engine, with Graham in the passenger seat.

When she just sat there for a moment, Graham raised his hand to touch her cheek with a featherlike stroke. "Come on, let's get something hot to drink."

They took their cups of hot chocolate over to the window to watch the snow fall as the ferry slipped through the icy waters of Puget Sound. Rosalind hadn't sailed on the ferry before during a snowstorm. Overlaid on the night's blackness was a thin knobby veil of white that sank into the sea. It had an unreal feeling that matched the wake of her emotions after the car crash.

"It was the same man who's been after me, of course."

Graham heard the deadpan of her voice and was not reassured after her hours of quiet. "Yes. He must have tampered with the tires while we were eating."

"You're putting yourself at risk by being with me."

Graham crunched his empty paper cup. "It doesn't matter."

Rosalind turned to him, appalled at the sudden flow of tears from her eyes, but not knowing what to do about them. "I must stay away from you. I must stay away from everyone."

Graham's heart twisted inside his chest. He reached for her, but she stepped back. In desperation, he sent his words where his touch could not reach. "You mustn't do this, Rosalind. Don't you see? This is exactly what he's trying to accomplish. He wants you to feel cut off and afraid. Don't give in. You're a fighter. Fight back."

Rosalind flipped the errant tears away with the back of her hand as anger grew in her voice. "I want to. God, how

I want to! But how can I fight back against someone who never shows himself? Someone who never comes at me directly but leaves booby traps into which he waits for me to step?"

"Then fight him by frustrating him, Rosalind. By refusing to show the fear he craves. By refusing to let his reign of terror intimidate you. Don't give him the satisfaction of knowing he's succeeding. Thwart him at every turn."

Graham watched his words penetrate and light a new gleam in Rosalind's eyes. "You're right. I've been going about this the wrong way. Every time the reporters have lunged at me with questions, "I've given them nothing but a string of no comments that must have made me seem cowering and afraid. But now that Judge Shotz has sequestered the jury, I don't have to worry about what I say to the press."

Graham stepped forward. "What is it, Rosalind? What are you thinking?"

She looked up at him and smiled. "I'm thinking that what I really need to do is hold a press conference and send a new message to this creep."

Her fire was back in full force. He basked in its returning light and heat, taking another step toward her. "Now that's the Rosalind Hart I know."

Rosalind felt overly warmed by his words and the steady gleam in his gray eyes. She could feel her heartbeat increase as she suddenly became aware of how closely he was standing next to her and the lean, exciting energy that pulsated around him. Too aware. With a discipline she felt slipping the more she was around him, she stepped away and deliberately stared into the ship's lights catching the edges of the rapidly falling snow.

When the ferry pulled into Winslow, the ground was a foot deep in snow and the wind was plowing more into them every second. Graham tuned in to a local radio station and found the news report advising them they were in a full-scale blizzard.

"As if we couldn't have figured that one out ourselves by now," he said with a tolerant grin. "Why don't you let me drive to my place? I know these roads well."

Knowing it would be safer, Rosalind relinquished the wheel. Even so, they had to proceed at a snail's pace and they passed several vehicles abandoned in the snow because their drivers hadn't slowed down. The wind howled fearfully now, buffeting the car back and forth. When he finally pulled under a carport and announced they were there, Rosalind couldn't even see the house in the direction he was pointing.

"Come on in and we'll check the local television station's weather report."

Rosalind followed him through the snow to the front door of the house, deafened by the roaring wind and feeling chilled to the bone as it cut through her light raincoat. When the door closed behind him, she was relieved to be out of its gusts and in the quiet, if cold, air of the house. Now if there was just some light...

But when Graham tried the light switch, nothing happened.

"Electricity's out. I should have expected this. All it takes is a wind and some tree falls over a power line. Puget Power refuses to put their cable underground. Keep saying it's too expensive. They'd rather put people out of heat and light during every windstorm and pay hundreds of thousands of dollars in overtime every year to repair crews. Crazy, huh?"

"It's freezing," Rosalind said as a shiver ran through her. "What are you going to do?"

"Here, take my hand and I'll lead the way into the living room. It won't take a moment to get the wood stove going."

"I should be starting for my parents' home in Seabeck—" Rosalind began.

She felt Graham's hand clasp hers in the dark. "You'd never make it, Rosalind. We just barely made it here. The roads are pretty near impassable. Come on, let's at least get warm."

There was no point in arguing. She knew he was right and she was cold. She followed his lead into the living room.

When the fire from the wood stove struck up almost instantly, Rosalind sank down on her knees in front of it on the soft thick carpet and reached her hands out to the warmth.

"The telephone is right next to the couch if you want to call your parents and let them know you're all right," Graham said as he turned on a battery-operated fluorescent lamp. "You should do that quickly. When the power is out for several hours, the telephone fails, too, since it also depends on electricity to keep it going. I'll be back in a few minutes."

Rosalind made her call brief, thankful that her parents placed such confidence and trust in her that they didn't question her closely when she said she was safe. But was she safe? She watched shadows of blowing trees across the dark windows and got up to draw the drapes.

Graham returned a few minutes later with a couple of covered dishes and a pot of water. He placed them on top of the wood stove.

"What's that?" Rosalind asked, taking off her coat as the room began to heat quickly from the blaze of the wood stove.

"Dinner," Graham answered. "It's been a lot of hours since lunch and I don't know about you, but I'm hungry."

Rosalind uncovered one of the dishes to get a preview. She frowned. "I can't seem to make it out."

Graham's hand covered hers as he gently replaced the top. "Let it be a surprise, then. You like surprises, don't you?"

She felt the warm caress of his touch march through her like an invading army. She stepped back.

He smiled and let her retreat—for now. But a need inside him protested almost painfully.

"While we're waiting for dinner to cook, let's have some refreshment. I don't have any wine in the house, but I do have a bottle of champagne in the refrigerator. Be back in a minute."

When he returned, he placed a long-stemmed goblet in front of her and poured the fizzing liquid. Rosalind couldn't remember the last time she had champagne—must have been at somebody's wedding. When they clicked their glasses in front of the roaring heat stove, the moment seemed suddenly very festive.

"It would have been difficult for him to have followed us here, wouldn't it?"

Her question reminded Graham that the terror that stalked her was never very far from her mind. For this one night at least, he wanted very much to take it away. Watching the creaminess of her skin near the firelight brought other wants tugging at his insides. He leaned forward.

"Why have you never married, Rosalind?"

She took another sip of her champagne, enjoying its cool sweetness as she looked away from the melting heat in his eyes. "No time to think about it, I suppose. Things never stopped being hectic since law school. You must know how it is, not having married yourself."

"But I have married."

Rosalind looked up, a bit surprised. Then she chastised herself. Of course he married. Why shouldn't he? It wasn't like he was waiting for her to come back into his life.

Like she had been waiting for him to come back into hers?

She tried to wash away the angry embarrassment over her own foolish thoughts with another gulp of champagne. She hadn't been waiting for Graham. She'd been busy making a career for herself. For God's sake, she hadn't even liked him for nine years! And now? Graham immediately refilled her empty glass.

"Of course, I'm not married anymore," he said. "Marriage was the biggest mistake of my life. Shows you what a fool a man makes of himself when he falls in love. I was divorced before the first year passed. That's when I moved out of Seattle and bought this place here on the island. It was a physical and symbolic retreat from what my life had become."

Rosalind was surprised at the disappointment underlying his words. "Was it really so unpleasant being married?"

"Only a single person could be naive enough to ask that question. But enough about my mistakes. Tell me about you. Any serious heartbreaks?"

Rosalind desperately searched for a subject change. He had been her only heartbreak and that was not something she ever wanted to discuss. She squinted in the dim light looking toward the bookcase. "Are those your parents in that picture?"

Graham's voice dropped as he looked in the direction of her pointing finger. "Yes."

Rosalind got up and went over to the bookcase, picking up the picture frame and bringing it back to the better light of the wood stove. It was a smiling family scene. Husband and wife—both tall, blond, slim—each with an arm around their son, a smaller copy. "No brothers or sisters?"

"No."

She leaned forward. "You said once that Fran and your great-uncle Jack raised you. What happened to your parents?"

Even in the dim light, Rosalind didn't miss the sad lines that etched themselves in Graham's jaw. For several moments he just looked into his glass of champagne.

Graham had manufactured a lie about his parents years before that he'd learned to tell to his inquisitive acquaintances without undue conscience problems. But something in the sound of her voice made him suddenly uncomfortable with any kind of a lie.

His head came up and he looked directly into her eyes. "My father went to prison for killing the man who murdered my mother."

Rosalind watched a cold pain blow into his warm gray eyes and battled a small constriction in her chest. She hadn't the faintest idea what she could possibly say. Silently she placed a hand on his arm.

He gave her a faint smile as his hand closed over hers. Her touch seemed to make the telling of his story much easier.

"My mother and father were coming out of a restaurant when a man with a gun approached and demanded their money. When my mother had difficulty removing her wedding rings, he shot her and then my father. Then he tore the wedding rings off her finger and ran."

Graham looked away for a moment before resuming. Rosalind realized that he was carefully controlling his voice, trying not to let the emotion come through. "My mother died before she reached a hospital. My father pulled through. He identified the man who had shot them from a mug book. The police went to the man's apartment, searched it and found my mother's wedding rings. They arrested him and brought him to trial.

"Unfortunately, the police made a clerical error that invalidated their search warrant. The wedding rings were ruled inadmissible evidence and the case against the man rested with my father's eyewitness testimony. My mother's murderer had a couple of friends swear he was with them at the time of the robbery and murder. It was three against one and the jury came back with an acquittal."

Rosalind's grip tightened on his arm.

"My father had been warned by the prosecuting attorney that the man might get off. He waited until the man walked out of the courtroom. He shot him twice in the head. Then he surrendered himself and pleaded guilty to premeditated murder. A year later he was killed by another inmate."

Rosalind swallowed a hard, painful lump in her throat.

Graham's carefully controlled voice went on. "Fran and Jack took me to live with them. Fran was my mother's aunt. She and Jack never had any kids of their own and yet they welcomed me into their adult life without reservation. They were a real family to me."

Rosalind leaned forward. "Did your parents' deaths have anything to do with your deciding to become a lawyer?"

"As a matter of fact, they did. I went through a lot of soul-searching in my life then. What my father did brought home to me the futility of personal revenge. His vendetta had only resulted in our being separated. I lost not just one parent but two. For the first time I began to understand the importance of life under the law. Laws aren't just made to punish the guilty. They're there to try to prevent the grief stricken from giving in to impulse and ruining the rest of their lives."

Rosalind studied his strong, sensitive profile, which filled before her eyes with a heartrending vulnerability. Then some memory jumped out of her mind and she pulled the rip cord before it plunged away.

Her voice ballooned in excitement. "Wait a minute. I know your father's case. The man who shot his wife's freed murderer and then just quietly turned himself over to the police. But I can't quite remember where I read about it."

Graham shrugged. "The People versus Peter Sterling? I'm surprised you know it. It happened nearly twenty years ago."

Rosalind's throat went dry as the name clearly registered and slipped snugly into a waiting memory cell. It all came back to her then. She hardly recognized her own voice. "Dear God, that was it. But how could Peter Sterling be your father? Your last name is Knight."

"Now it is, but I was born Graham Sterling. Knight was my mother's maiden name. Fran and Jack had my name changed to protect me from the sensationalism surrounding the trial. It also helped my anonymity at the new school I transferred to when I went to live with them."

Rosalind stared unseeing into the fire. The People versus Peter Sterling. How unbelievable that it had been that case—the trial of his own father—that she had researched so carefully those nine years ago and innocently brought to Graham seeking his approval of her work! How could she have known that it would be the one case Graham could not have borne to include in a *Law Review* article?

His words came tumbling back to her. *Lousy case selection. There's nothing there that I find even remotely appealing.* And then she knew. Graham hadn't rejected her or her work. He had rejected being made to relive the tragedy of his mother's and father's deaths.

"Rosalind?"

She turned to look into the warm melting gray of his eyes.

For nine long years she had carted around foolish hurt and anger against him for nothing. What a waste. What a fool she'd been. Tears stung her eyes.

Graham couldn't bear to see Rosalind sad. He had no idea what had brought it on but worried that he had spoken too openly about his parents and their tragic deaths. Some madman stalked her and she was in constant fear for her life. What she needed was a healthy dose of laughter, not disaster.

Putting down his champagne glass, he quickly moved to her side, leaning over to gently kiss her cheeks where the tears fell. He wrapped her inside his arms, luxuriating in her feel. "Did I ever tell you about the case where I defended a woman photographer who was being sued by an animal trainer because he claimed her flashbulbs had made his iguana impotent?"

Rosalind's lips broke into a smile as she looked deeply into the tenderness in his eyes and knew that the real Graham Knight was there—had been there all the time—she had just been too blind to see.

With a deep rumbling sigh, her lips went to his with all the chaotic longing she'd denied for so long. She felt his lightning response, the thunder of his groan as he crushed her to him, his fingers raking desperately through her hair, releasing it from its tight braid to flow free about her shoulders as she tore the shirt from his back.

Once again, Graham recognized all his scrupulously made plans for seduction were turning out to be hers. She moaned as her hands roamed his bare flesh, driving him wild. Her lips were hot and restless, tasting his and then moving on to savor every inch of his face. She yielded to his searching hands eagerly, molding her body to his. She was irresistible—a blend of demand and submission that pounded the blood in his veins and answered so many questions he didn't even realize he had needed to ask.

She was fire—an all-consuming flame that scorched him with her heat. And even when the raw urgency of their lovemaking had been satisfied, he still clutched her to him, knowing he had not had enough—that he'd never have enough of this woman.

Rosalind felt a release and contentment she hadn't thought possible. Now that she lay in his arms, she could admit to herself that she had wanted this man, needed this man since she'd first met him in law school. For her this was the culmination of a dream she had not been bold enough to even entertain. She felt she had lost him and then found him again, and it was all the sweeter because of the longing of the intervening years.

And then suddenly his words of only a short while ago flashed through her mind. *Marriage was the biggest mistake of my life. Shows you what a fool a man makes of himself when he falls in love.*

He was quiet beside her, holding her closely, but saying nothing. Because he felt nothing beyond the physical attraction? More than likely. Rosalind slowed her galloping emotions. *Take this lightly. Don't expect too much. Enjoy what he can give.*

"Graham?"

It was the first time she'd called him by his first name. Hearing it on her lips sent a contented little ripple around his heart. He nuzzled up to her ear. "Yes, Rosalind?"

"Is dinner ready yet?"

He drew back in feigned surprise. "Dinner? At a time like this? Women. Whoever said they were the romantic sex?"

Rosalind laughed as she rolled away, Graham relinquishing his hold on her very reluctantly as the smooth curves of her body stretched in front of the firelight. He felt transfixed as he watched her get to her feet, her shoulders back, her head held high, and all that glorious, indignant red hair bouncing down her bare arms and breasts like smoldering fire.

"Hungry?" she asked as she lifted a pot cover.

"For a lot of things," he said.

She smiled as her eyes traveled over his strong, naked body that visibly proclaimed at least what one of those things was. Pretending not to notice, she turned back to the wood stove. "This smells good. Do we eat it out of the bowls?"

Graham rose, reaching both of his hands around her, drawing her back to him. Rosalind luxuriated in the hot excitement of his body. What need she had for food fled in the presence of the deeper need she had for this man. She could barely believe how strong, thorough and yet tender their lovemaking was. He left no inch of her unexplored, left no doubt in her mind as to the depth of his physical feelings.

And his other feelings?

She already knew them. He thought a man who fell in love was a fool. He thought only a single person was naive enough to ask how bad marriage could be. He'd proclaimed his feelings all right. What she had now was all she was going to get.

She sighed as she swallowed the longing deep in her heart. Only time would be able to tell her if what he offered would be enough.

LEROY PONCE SHOUTED curses at the driving snow as he waited for the tow truck to pull his old Honda out of the snowbank. After an hour he recognized his wait was futile. Nothing but a snowplow could navigate these roads. The guy from the towing place must have given up and turned back. Nothing to do but go back to the Bainbridge Island gas station about five blocks away where he had made his call. He leaned over to get the flashlight out of the glove compartment and opened the door.

Freezing snow blew into his eyes and nose. But not it, nor the Honda getting stuck, nor the absent tow truck was at the base of his anger. He was really mad because he had lost them.

He hadn't lost a car he'd been tailing for twenty years. But somehow after he'd followed them off the Winslow ferry, he'd lost them in the driving snow, and they had gotten away. And it didn't look like he was going to find them. At least not tonight. He shouted more curses into the full air and got snow in his mouth for his trouble.

By the time he reached the gas station, he was freezing as well as angry. When he found the owner had not only closed up the station over the past hour but had also boarded it up against the blizzard, the anger turned to fury.

Without a thought, he pulled the compact Walther 9 mm automatic pistol from his pocket and shot the lock off. Let the police try to get through on these roads, he thought. But no burglar alarms came on. When he stepped inside and the light switch refused to work, he realized it was because the electricity was off. He slammed the door closed against the wind and snow and shone his flashlight around the room.

He yanked a crowbar off the mechanics pegboard in the back and pried open the soft drink and candy machine doors. Then he sat down and propped his feet up on the desk, ate the candy bars and guzzled the pop. It would be a long night, but he didn't mind. He'd found a phone book. He'd spend his time looking for the address of Graham Knight.

ROSALIND DEVOURED her dinner ravenously, finding it to be a delicious homemade stew with tender chunks of beef and fresh-tasting vegetables. While they ate, they listened to worsening reports about the widespread blizzard hitting Seattle and the Puget Sound area on Graham's battery-operated radio.

"Looks like I'm going to be your guest for the weekend," she announced after the report was finished.

Graham thought she looked right at home in his white cotton robe, sitting in front of the wood stove with her beautiful long legs extending toward the fire. Right at home. He smiled. "You won't find me complaining."

She smiled back. "Dinner was great."

He knew her compliment pleased him far more than it should. He felt a vague sense of being out of control and then shrugged it off as a momentary aberration. "Stews are my specialty. They're easy to make and once I opened up my practice after law school and found myself working sixteen-hour days, I needed something easy."

Rosalind laid back on the carpet, cupping her hot tea in her hands, leaning her shoulders and head against the base of the couch for support. Graham had put on an old pair of jeans and a soft gold sweater when he'd gone to get his robe for her. Propped up on his elbow as he stretched out on the carpet, he looked long, lean and incredibly sexy with the matching gold stubble on his chin.

Just looking at him sent her heart skipping happily. Once again she tried to remind herself to keep cool. She busied her mind with questions. "Why did you select private practice?"

Graham took a sip of tea and placed his cup in the saucer on the carpet. "The groups fighting for reform were weak and scattered. They needed cohesiveness and legal advice. For the first year, that's all I did. Then I started to pick up criminal cases. Practice is about half-and-half now."

"You don't have a partner?"

"I've been thinking of adding one. But frankly for the first eight years, the practice has barely supported me. As I'm sure you realize, it's tough going into private practice without a lot of cash."

"But I thought that Fran—"

Graham shook his head. "She's well off, but she knows I won't take her money. She held my parents' life insurance in trust for me and used it to help me through law school. But after that we had an agreement that I'd do it on my own. And I have, but it's been a battle."

Rosalind liked the fact that he had made his practice on his own. She decided she had been wrong about a lot of things regarding him. She normally hated being wrong, but this time it made her glad. "You never thought about joining the prosecutor's office?"

Graham shrugged. "It's more of a challenge to fight for the accused."

Rosalind shook her head. "But how can you represent a murderer?"

Graham's look never wavered. "I can't and I don't."

"But you're defending Morebug."

"That's because he's innocent, Rosalind."

She studied the clean lines of his face and knew he believed every word he was saying. It made her a little angry to think Morebug had been such an effective liar to have gotten Graham on his side. More than ever she was determined to see the man behind bars. "You'll never convince me."

Graham smiled as he watched the straightening of her back, the gleam of battle in her eye. He loved to see the fight in her. He rolled over to where she rested against the couch and kissed her defiant chin as his hand sought the soft, yielding flesh beneath her robe. "It's okay, Ms. Deputy Prosecutor. I don't need to convince you. I only need to beat you."

Her lips traveled up to his ear, deliberately blowing her words soft and sexy as her hands expertly attacked the zipper on his jeans, reached inside and dragged an appreciative moan from him. "We'll see who beats who, Counselor."

Chapter Twelve

Although the electricity was still off on Bainbridge Island, Monday morning's radio broadcast advised Graham and Rosalind that most Seattle businesses were up and running as usual. The winds had died down Sunday night and the new heavy rains had already washed away a lot of the snow. They took a chance and headed for Seattle. A call to the courthouse once they arrived confirmed that the court of Judge Gloria Shotz would convene at ten-thirty.

As far as Rosalind was concerned, that was perfect. First she got hold of her boss and then she spoke at length with Max Hill. Next she called around to the television, radio and newspapers. Representatives flocked to the courthouse within the hour.

They set up the lights and cameras, and Graham gave her a smile from the sidelines just before she began.

"Ladies and gentlemen of the press, there has been much speculation about reported acts of terrorism against me over the last week and a half. I've called this press conference to clear the air of speculation and assure you that these attacks have nothing to do with my prosecution of Milton Morebug for the murder of Warren Beaver."

"Ms. Hart, how can you be so sure?"

"Because there is absolutely no way the defendant or anyone associated with him could benefit by such attacks."

A young male reporter shouted his question from the back. "Ms. Hart, do you know who your tormentor is?"

Rosalind rose to her full height and smiled. "Some little, insignificant twirp who's afraid of showing his face."

"What's his name?" blurted out several reporters at once.

Rosalind shrugged. "I have no idea, and frankly I don't care to. He's not worth my time."

"But, Ms. Hart. Aren't you scared—"

Rosalind's eyebrows went up. "Scared? Of what? A shadow who's afraid to come out in the open? You must be joking. I face flesh-and-blood murderers in courtrooms every day. This man is nothing but a fly who will be swatted when the time comes. I don't waste my time even thinking about him."

There were more questions but Rosalind cut them short, advising the press that she had to prepare for the upcoming court session. When she rejoined Graham in the wings, he gave her a quick hug. "Well done. When will it air?"

"By noon. And again this evening. If that doesn't incense the creep to show his face, I don't know what will."

"Is Hill on board about the bodyguard?"

"Yes. He's plainclothes. That man over there." Rosalind pointed discreetly to a stocky man in dark blue slacks and shirt who leaned against the wall, ostensibly reading a magazine. "He has the day watch. He'll drive me to a different hotel every night where I'll have adjoining rooms with the night-watch detective."

Graham frowned. "Wait a minute. You'll have adjoining rooms with a night-watch detective?"

Rosalind smiled as she slipped her arm around his hard lean waist. "Yes, *she* will be already situated in the room next to me and will have stocked my room with clothes for the next day."

Graham looked somewhat placated, but not much. His arm tightened around her. "I don't like being away from you, Rosalind. I don't like it a lot. You were safe at my place all weekend. Why don't you come back there with me tonight?"

She gave her head a reluctant shake. "This weekend we tempted fate, and we won, probably courtesy of the blizzard. But, Graham, I'm not going to risk us both again. Not after what he did to your tires. I need to be his single focus. That's how we can get him."

Graham hated the idea that she was setting herself up as a target, while at the same time he realized that probably was the only way to find out who the creep was. He told himself he should be glad for this evidence of her strength. After all, it was he who had encouraged her fight. Still, there was a part of him that wished he'd kept his mouth shut.

ROSALIND AND GRAHAM were at their respective tables when Roger Horn emerged from the judge's chambers to call everyone to order at ten-thirty.

Rosalind brought her witness, Mrs. Faith Fox, to the stand. Mrs. Fox was fifty with dyed black hair, a nose two sizes smaller than her face, and plump, nervous hands.

"Where do you live, Mrs. Fox?" Rosalind asked.

Mrs. Fox's very small voice described her residence on Mercer Island Road as being directly opposite the turnout that Beaver's car had gone over on the night of the murder.

"And did you have occasion to look out your window in the early-morning hours of January ninth of this year?"

"Yes. I had just come out of the shower. I thought the hot water would help to soothe me. You see, I don't sleep too well. I have these terrible migraines that—"

"I understand, Mrs. Fox. A migraine headache kept you awake," Rosalind said, cutting her off. "And what, if anything, precipitated your looking out your window?"

"Nothing special. I turned off the lamp and was on my way to bed when I thought I saw a flash of something and looked out the window."

"Do you know what the flash was?"

"No. Maybe headlights."

"And what time was it that you looked out your window?"

"Around two o'clock in the morning."

"What did you see when you looked out your window?"

"Well, I saw tracks in the snow where a car had driven over the shoulder."

"Did you see anything else?"

"Well, yes, I saw another car pulling over to the shoulder. It stopped and a man got out."

"Mrs. Fox, where exactly did you see this car?"

"On the shoulder, just past the tracks going over the edge."

"Can you describe this car you saw?"

"All I could see by the lamplight was an outline. It was one of those Porsche bodies—low and sleek-looking."

Rosalind made a quick trip to the evidence table. "Your Honor, may I approach the witness?"

"Yes," Judge Shotz said.

Rosalind walked up to Mrs. Fox and handed her the picture of Milton Morebug's 911 Turbo Porsche. "Is this the body shape of the car you saw on the night of Warren Beaver's death?"

Mrs. Fox took a long, hard look and returned the picture. Her plump hands grasped the arms of her chair. "Yes."

"Can you describe the man you saw who got out of this car?"

"No. It was dark and he was too far away."

"Can you tell us what he did?"

"Well, he got out of the car and walked in the direction of the tire tracks that went over the embankment."

"And then what if anything did he do?"

"He went down the embankment."

"Did he come up again?"

"I don't know. My head was hurting so bad, I turned away from the window and went to lie down. After a few minutes, I mercifully drifted off to sleep."

"Thank you, Mrs. Fox. Those are all the questions I have."

Graham approached Mrs. Fox from a circumspect distance and gave her a smile. His voice was solicitous. "I understand migraines are dreadful. I hope you don't have one now?"

Mrs. Fox shook her head, the tension easing in her hands grasping the arms of the witness chair as she responded to the tone of Graham's voice. "No. Not now."

Graham smiled. "Glad to hear it. They affect your vision?"

"Yes. Sometimes."

"How?"

"Well, things can get fuzzy and shadowy."

"To the point that shapes can be difficult to see?"

"Well, yes."

"Did the migraine you were suffering from affect your vision on the night of Warren Beaver's death?"

"Objection, Your Honor."

"Overruled. You may answer the question, Mrs. Fox."

Mrs. Fox's hands were back to grasping the arms of the chair. "I saw the car and the man, just like I said."

"Mrs. Fox," Graham said gently. "Your head was bothering you quite a bit that night, wasn't it?"

She bit her lip. "Yes."

Again, very gently. "Were your eyes affected?"

Reluctant. "Yes. Some."

"And when you looked out the window and saw that car parking on the shoulder, could you really see its shape clearly in the dark of the night through that blinding migraine?"

Rosalind stood. "Objection, Your Honor. Defense is characterizing the witness's migraine."

"Sustained. Strike blinding. Jury will disregard."

Graham hadn't looked at either Rosalind or the judge. He acted as though they didn't exist at all. He kept his eyes on Mrs. Fox with that same solicitous, patient look. "Tell them what it's like to endure the pain of one of those migraines, Mrs. Fox."

Rosalind's voice rose. "Objection! Irrelevant."

Graham was still watching the witness. "Ms. Hart thinks your migraine pain is irrelevant."

Judge Shotz's voice boomed. "Mr. Kni—"

She was too late. Mrs. Fox lurched forward, her right hand grasping the front of the witness box. "No one understands! It's a nightmare! You can't think. You can't see. The world becomes a pulsating blur of pain that just won't go away!"

Shotz's lips strung tight. Her words shot out like arrows. "Approach. Both of you."

When they got there, she struck out at Graham. "Mr. Knight, I'm warning you to stop these intemperate and prejudicial remarks about Ms. Hart in front of the jury. If I hear any more, I promise you I will hold you in contempt of this court. Now is that understood?"

Graham nodded as though properly chastised, but as they stood side-by-side he had swiftly grabbed and squeezed Rosalind's hand. Excitement shot through her veins as she held her own private irreverent smile in check.

When they returned to open court, Judge Shotz looked over at Rosalind. "I believe, Ms. Hart, that you raised an objection as to the relevance of Mr. Knight's question to Mrs. Fox concerning her migraine pain. I'm going to allow it. Objection overruled."

Graham turned back to Mrs. Fox. "A moment ago you told this court how your migraines were so painful that you couldn't see. Is that correct?"

Mrs. Fox looked down at her hands in her lap. Now that her outburst was over, her voice was even smaller than before. "Yes."

"Mrs. Fox, I'm not trying to impugn your testimony. I just want you to be absolutely sure that what you tell the jury is an accurate depiction of the facts as they occurred. Do you understand?"

"Yes."

"Then is it possible that when you looked out your window under that dreadful pain you only thought the car was rounded like a Porsche?"

"It's possible."

"Could it have actually been a Bentley or a Lincoln?"

"I guess."

"So now you're really not sure what shape the car was?"

"No."

"Thank you, Mrs. Fox. I have no more questions."

ROSALIND GAVE Graham credit. He didn't miss an angle. He'd turned Mrs. Fox's identification around so smoothly it looked effortless. Whatever she did, she couldn't have her last witness's testimony end so damagingly.

"Ms. Hart?"

"One or two questions on redirect, Your Honor."

Rosalind rose and smiled at Mrs. Fox. "I know it's hard to come into a courtroom and sit in that witness chair while people badger you with questions. I know if it were me, I'd be having difficulty keeping my thoughts straight. Are you finding it hard to think clearly?"

Mrs. Fox looked grateful that Rosalind didn't seem mad at her. She exhaled a yes.

Rosalind nodded in understanding as she paced a few steps toward her witness. "After all, it's been eleven months since the night of Warren Beaver's murder. Most of us would have a hard time recalling everything we saw or thought eleven months ago. Are you having a hard time doing that?"

Mrs. Fox's voice gained some volume. "Yes."

"But on the morning of January ninth when a detective came to your door and asked you what you had seen literally just hours before, do you believe that the events of that previous night were clear in your mind?"

"Yes."

"And what were those events?"

Mrs. Fox straightened slightly. "A car shaped like a Porsche parked on the shoulder and a man got out of it and walked toward the tire tracks in the snow going over the embankment."

Rosalind smiled. "Thank you, Mrs. Fox. Those are all the questions I have. Your Honor, the People rest."

IN THE INTERVENING ten-minute recess, Graham pulled Milton Morebug aside. "I'm going to put Linda Dodge on the stand, Mr. Morebug. I've got to. The jury has heard evidence that you left your home right after fighting with Beaver and a car resembling yours was at the scene of the crime."

Morebug looked anything but pleased. "But you got that Mrs. Fox to back down from her identification of my car."

Graham shook his head. "Don't forget Ms. Hart's redirect. At this moment I'd say the jury is not sure whether your car was there. I need to make them certain you were somewhere else. If we can do that, then we've got a good chance of acquittal."

Morebug wiped his palms across his slacks. "You already implicated Linda in that shady business between Beaver and her brother. I thought you said the prosecution will tear her apart?"

"Ms. Hart will try. But I can defuse the prosecution's ammunition by getting Ms. Dodge to admit to her wrongdoing under my examination. Since I brought it up in the first place, the jury can't think that we're trying to suppress her part in the land deal scheme. It will make her testimony about you seem more credible."

Morebug shivered as though he'd just gotten a chill. Graham grasped his shoulder. "Both you and Ms. Dodge have assured me your affair was just that with no complications or strings on either side. Isn't that right?"

"Yes. So what?"

"So if you got together occasionally over the last five years for company, it doesn't sound so bad."

Morebug didn't look convinced. "There's got to be another way. If Linda testifies about our relationship, my wife will throw a fit."

Graham scratched his chin. "Can you get your wife to leave the courtroom before Mrs. Dodge's testimony?"

Morebug shook his head. "From the beginning I told her her presence in the courtroom was imperative to show her support. I can't think of any good excuse to tell her it's not required today. Can you?''

''She doesn't suspect?''

Morebug exhaled heavily. ''Probably. But suspecting and having the particulars announced in court for all her friends to hear and read about isn't exactly the same thing. I tell you, Knight, financially she'll crucify me in the divorce courts.''

Graham rubbed the back of his neck. ''We can only concentrate on one case at a time. If we don't win this one, I think an expensive divorce will be the least of your worries. Come on. The court recess is just about up. Let's go do it.''

JUDGE SHOTZ TURNED to Graham. ''Is the defense ready to present its case?''

Graham rose. ''Yes, Your Honor. As its first witness, the defense calls Linda Dodge.''

Linda Dodge was in her late thirties—a tall, attractive brunette with an olive complexion and dark, somewhat recessed eyes. Rosalind was surprised Graham had called her as a witness, despite the fact that she was on the defense list. After Max Hill's investigation of her background, Rosalind could have sworn Graham wouldn't want her crossexamined.

She watched Linda Dodge take the witness box as though it was the dentist chair and she was about to have all her teeth drilled. She was obviously here against her preferences.

Graham took a few steps toward the witness then stopped. ''Ms. Dodge, what is your marital status?''

''I'm divorced.''

''And what is your current position?''

''I'm chief lobbyist for the department of natural resources under the state commissioner of public lands.''

''Did you know the deceased, Warren Beaver?''

''Yes. He was my boss.''

''When you worked for Warren Beaver, did you pass payoffs to your boss from your brother?''

"Objection," Rosalind said. "Mr. Knight is leading his own witness."

"Sustained."

Graham shifted to another foot. "Let me rephrase my question. What if anything did your brother, Brian Wreckter, ask you to do involving your boss, Warren Beaver?"

"Brian asked me to take checks to Beaver."

"How many times?"

"I don't remember exactly. Maybe five or six."

"Can you tell this court exactly how that worked?"

"My brother asked me to put his personal checks in a white envelope and slip them into Warren Beaver's middle desk drawer when he stepped out of his office."

"Did your brother tell you what these checks were for?"

Linda Dodge gulped nervously. "He said he and Beaver had made a land deal and that the less I knew about it the better."

"You didn't ask for particulars?"

"I didn't."

"Why was that?"

Linda Dodge shifted uncomfortably in her seat. "Warren Beaver had a lot of shady things going on. He was always telling me to leave the room when certain people called or dropped in."

"Couldn't he have just wanted some privacy?"

"No."

"Why are you so sure?"

"Because he told me straight out that it would be better for me to know only the clean stuff if I was going to do my job at DNR."

"Those were his words? It would be better for you to know only the clean stuff?"

"Yes."

"What was the clean stuff?"

"He made some improvements in public land management."

"Was that all you publicized?"

"Yes."

Graham paced slowly into the center of the room signaling his next subject change.

"Ms. Dodge, do you know the defendant, Milton Morebug?"

"Yes."

"In what capacity?"

A stiffening of her back. "He's my lover."

A loud gasp erupted behind Graham as Milton Morebug's wife jumped to her feet. With large, startled eyes she looked from the woman on the stand to her husband and then back again before turning and fleeing the courtroom, her son at her heels.

A loud buzz of voices followed their departure, bringing Shotz's gavel into instant play. After pounding it twice, her voice boomed over the continuing disturbance. "Order, or I'll clear this courtroom!"

The ruckus died down instantly, several reporters filing out of the courtroom after the disappearing wife and son.

"Mr. Knight, you may resume."

Graham deliberately walked in the direction of the jury. He wanted them to see the calmness on the full face of his witness. He imagined her hands and knew they would be steady on her lap, just as they had been when he had questioned her privately.

"Ms. Dodge, how long have you been Milton Morebug's lover?"

"We've been getting together for mutual comfort and sharing for five years now. Nothing heavy or complicated."

"And where were you on the night of January eighth of this year, the night your boss, Warren Beaver, was murdered?"

"I was at my condo in the city."

"Were you alone?"

"I was until about two in the morning."

"Who joined you at that time."

"Milty, I mean Mr. Morebug."

The ensuing low murmur was instantly silenced by Judge Shotz's gavel. Graham remained standing where he was by the jury. "Ms. Dodge, why are you so sure of the time Milton Morebug arrived at your place that night?"

"I was waiting up for him."

"You were expecting Mr. Morebug to come by?"

"Yes. He'd called me earlier that evening before the players arrived for his weekly card game. He told me that as soon as the game was over, he'd come by."

"And he arrived at two in the morning?"

"Yes."

"And how long did Mr. Morebug stay at your place?"

"The rest of the night."

"Thank you, Ms. Dodge. I have no further questions."

ROSALIND ROSE, trying to decide with each step she took toward Linda Dodge what would be the woman's weakest point. She seemed to have so many of them, it was hard to choose. Rosalind circled in front of her while she let the tension mount.

"Ms. Dodge, you've testified that you knew your boss had 'shady' deals going on, is that correct?"

"Yes."

"But you only publicized the 'clean stuff.' Is that right?"

"Yes."

"But isn't that lying to the voters, Ms. Dodge?"

Linda squirmed in her chair. "My job was to promote Warren Beaver and his land policies, not to denigrate them."

"You mean your job was not to tell the whole truth?"

"Objection," Graham called.

"Sustained."

Rosalind paced away from her. "So what you're saying is that if you get paid to perform a job, you're loyal to the person paying you. Is that right?"

"It was my job to be discreet about . . . Mr. Beaver. I did my job."

"You did your job," Rosalind repeated. "Ms. Dodge, who paid for the condominium you own overlooking Lake Washington?"

Graham was on his feet, a sharp alarm going off inside him. "Objection, Your Honor. Irrelevant."

"Your Honor, if the court will bear with me, I'm sure I can establish the relevance," Rosalind countered.

"Overruled. Go ahead, Ms. Hart."

Rosalind cast Linda Dodge a hard look. "Well? Who bought it, Ms. Dodge?"

The witness's eyes began to water. "Milton Morebug."

Rosalind watched the jury as Linda said the words. Some of them seemed to have anticipated the answer. The others didn't look like they appreciated the surprise.

Rosalind turned to Linda. "Is it in Mr. Morebug's name?"

"No. The condo's in my name."

"You testified that you and Mr. Morebug got together for 'mutual comfort and sharing.' But what really seems to have happened is that Mr. Morebug bought the condominium for you for services rendered, isn't that right, Ms. Dodge?"

Linda shook her head vehemently. "No! That's not true! You're trying to make me out to be some kind of..."

When Linda failed to find the right word, Graham rose to assist. "Objection, Your Honor. Prosecution is badgering this witness."

"Only if you consider the truth to be badgering, Counsel," Rosalind retorted.

"That will be enough, Ms. Hart!" Judge Shotz boomed. "Objection overruled. Get on with it."

Rosalind circled closer. "Ms. Dodge, did the defendant buy the condominium you live in for you, yes or no?"

"Yes."

"And the new BMW you drive. Yes or no?"

"Yes."

"So you were employed as Milton Morebug's mistress, isn't that correct?"

Tears stung Linda's eyes. "You make it sound so cheap!"

"Cheap? A two-hundred-thousand-dollar condominium? A forty-five-thousand-dollar BMW? Doesn't sound too cheap to me. You've already testified how loyal an employee you were to Warren Beaver, Ms. Dodge. Loyal enough to hide the truth of his shady dealings. And I think you're at it again. I think you're lying now for your other employer, Milton Morebug, pretending he was at your condominium at two in the morning. Providing him with an alibi like a good loyal little employee. Aren't you?"

Linda Dodge rose to her feet, her hands flapping wildly. "No! No! Stop! Somebody, please make her stop!"

"Your Honor—" Graham began.

"Overruled," Gloria Shotz said before Graham could get the objection out. "Ms. Dodge, sit down. Ms. Hart isn't through with her cross-examination."

"Oh but I am, Your Honor," Rosalind said in a deadly calm voice, her face clearly expressing what she thought of Ms. Dodge and her testimony. "I'm sure the jury has heard enough from this witness."

GRAHAM LEFT the courtroom with his client through the judge's chambers when the noon recess was called. At the moment he didn't even want to speculate what questions the media would shout. All in all, it hadn't been a good morning in court.

"You didn't tell me you were keeping the woman," Graham said to Morebug as they made their way out the back toward the parking lot.

"I didn't think it mattered," Morebug said subdued.

Graham ground his teeth. "Well you can see it did."

Morebug's voice rose. "I told you you shouldn't have put Linda on the stand. Damn it, you should have listened!"

"No, damn it, you should have told me the truth—the whole truth!" Graham shouted back.

For a moment Morebug's fists clenched and he looked like he was ready to fight. Then suddenly his hands unclenched and he fell back against his car in the lot. "Oh hell, you're right. Damn it, I just didn't want any of this to come

out. I didn't kill the slob! Why is my life being turned up
side down?''

Graham took a deep breath of the rain-filled air befor
gesturing Morebug into the driver's seat of his Porsche
When he was inside, Graham closed the door and leaned in
through the open window. "I know what you're going
through isn't easy, Mr. Morebug. I can sympathize. But
can't take any more surprises. You understand?'' Morebu
nodded and then turned the ignition and took off in a sub
dued roar, his hands clenched on the wheel.

Graham frowned. There was something about that hand
clenching he didn't like. He had a sudden urge to see Rosa
lind, to sweep her off to some romantic place for lunch
where they both could forget everything but each other. O
course, it was impossible. She had a bodyguard now and he
had some thinking to do before court resumed for the af
ternoon. He exhaled a frustrated breath as he sloshed
through the rain toward a small coffee shop down the street
He found a back table.

Three character witnesses waited to be put on the stand
that afternoon to testify that Morebug was an honorable
nonviolent man who paid his taxes and contributed to
charities. Somehow, he didn't think they were going to go
far in convincing the jury of Morebug's innocence.

Maybe one of Linda Dodge's neighbors had seen More
bug's car drive up to her condominium on that night. The
thought brought renewed hope to Graham as he dug into hi
briefcase to check on Ms. Dodge's address. If he could ge
a private investigator out there this afternoon talking to he
neighbors—

The single sheet fell into his lap like manna from the gods
It was page five of the police report, and right there on the
page he'd read at least twenty times before he finally no
ticed the one piece of evidence he and everybody else had
previously overlooked. Graham smiled.

"Mr. Knight, are you ready to proceed with the de
fense?'' Judge Shotz asked at the beginning of the after-

noon session. Graham rose, legal maneuvering coursing through his brain. "Your Honor, may I approach the bench?"

Judge Shotz motioned both him and Rosalind forward.

Rosalind brushed up against him deliberately. He smiled as he tried to keep his voice low and unhurried, fighting down the excitement of possibilities churning through both his mind and body. "Your Honor, I wonder if I could have your indulgence in recalling one of the prosecution's witnesses at this time."

Judge Shotz looked perturbed. "You've already had an opportunity to cross-examine all the witnesses, Mr. Knight."

"Yes, Your Honor. But I've just discovered what may be an irregularity in the physical evidence from the crime scene. I believe it is imperative that I clear up this discrepancy. With the court's indulgence?" Graham gave her his most winning smile.

"Who is it you want to recross?"

"Detective Max Hill."

Shotz's lips twisted. "As long as he's in court I suppose we won't be unduly delaying matters. All right, Mr. Knight. I'll allow Mr. Hill to retake the stand."

Hill took the witness chair. Graham picked up his official report, a copy of which he had just reviewed over lunch.

"Your Honor, may I approach the witness?"

Judge Shotz nodded.

Graham advanced. "Detective Hill, I'm holding here the Mercer Island PD report that lists the items taken into evidence from the crime scene. Will you take it please?"

Hill obliged, although he looked perplexed.

"Now, Detective Hill, will you please turn to page five of the report."

Graham waited while Hill paged through. "Directing your attention to the third paragraph on that page, Detective, would you read for this court what has been entered there?"

"'A cast of the tire marks going over the embankment was taken as well as two casts of tire tracks on the shoulder.'"

Graham handed Hill another report, already turned to the proper page. "And will you now read the first paragraph of this page on the crime-scene evidence?"

Hill obliged, still looking perplexed. "'The cast of the tire marks going over the embankment was matched to the victim's car. The cast from the shoulder was matched to Stephanie Pond's car.'" He looked up from the page. "Counselor, I don't see—"

"Don't you? The first report clearly shows that there were *two* casts of tire tracks taken from the *shoulder* at the crime scene. But this report only refers to *one* cast from the shoulder being included in the list of evidence. Where did the other cast from the shoulder go, Detective Hill?"

Hill stared at him hard but was quiet.

"Detective?"

Uncomfortable. "I don't know."

Graham's tone held just the right amount of sarcasm. "Well, since a cast of those tire tracks might very well reveal who drove the murder vehicle, don't you think you should find out?"

Chapter Thirteen

A murmur rose from the gallery and Graham felt the jury's satisfying stir. He turned toward the bench. "Your Honor, a vital piece of evidence is missing from this trial. It was in the hands of the prosecution and now it has mysteriously disappeared. An explanation—"

Rosalind was on her feet. "Your Honor, Mr. Knight is implying the prosecution is attempting to conceal evidence on this case and that is completely untrue and untenable. I would ask Your Honor to make it clear to the jury that no such impropriety—"

Graham turned to her, deliberately interrupting. "Ms. Hart, the most generous interpretation of the absence of that crime-scene cast the defense can imagine is that the prosecution on this case is so incompetent that it has lost or misplaced valuable evidence."

Rosalind turned to Judge Shotz. "Your Honor—"

"All right, Mr. Knight. Please save your prosecution bashing until your closing arguments." She turned to Max Hill who still sat in the witness box. "Detective, you reviewed all the evidence on these reports. Did the Mercer Island PD make an error when they wrote that two tire casts had been made from the shoulder at the scene of the crime?"

Max Hill sat there in the witness box sweating into his expensive and well-tailored suit, looking as though he had no idea how to answer. In all the years she'd known him,

Rosalind had never seen him so flustered. It was as though he didn't know what to say. Then he looked over at Graham and seemed to come to a decision. His jaw tightened. "No. They were not in error."

"So there were two casts?" Judge Shotz asked.

"Yes. I'm sure of it."

"Do you have any idea where the second cast from the shoulder is?"

His spine straightened. "It has to be still in the evidence room. Everything was taken there before evaluation."

"Do you think you can find the second shoulder cast in the evidence room, Detective Hill?"

"I certainly intend to try, Your Honor."

Judge Shotz turned back to the courtroom. "Court is recessed until tomorrow morning, at which time Detective Hill will retake the witness stand and fill us in on the success or failure of his search." Shotz rapped her gavel.

Outside the courtroom, the hallway was strewn with television lights and reporters, shouting questions at both Graham and Rosalind.

Rosalind got the brunt of them as she was the first to exit. She no commented as she scurried to the elevator that would take her down to her office on the fifth floor.

Graham watched her until he was sure that her plainclothes bodyguard was close behind. Then he gave his attention to the media. After a devastating morning, his redeeming afternoon performance made him inclined to talk.

"Milton Morebug has been unjustly accused of this crime," Graham said smiling. "We've said that from the first. It isn't surprising to me that the prosecution's case is falling apart."

Falling apart was a gross overstatement, but Graham felt light and just a bit reckless.

A young reporter shoved a microphone in his face. "Mr. Knight, is it true that the prosecution was deliberately withholding evidence favorable to your client?"

"It would be inappropriate for me to comment on that," Graham said, still smiling. "Now if you'll excuse us, Mr. Morebug has had a trying day. I'm sure you understand."

LEROY PONCE FELT good to have Rosalind Hart in his sites again. Particularly after that hell of a weekend hoarded up in that lousy gas station. At least he'd gotten out before the owner had returned. And now he knew where both Graham Knight's office and home were. That was important for future reference.

But after that beating the defense attorney had just given her in court, he didn't think the deputy prosecutor would be spending much more time with Knight. Still, he wanted to be able to find her anywhere, anytime, for anything.

He knew the prosecutor had already given her a new office at the other end of the hallway from her old one. And they had a security guard patrolling that hallway during business hours. He also spotted the personal bodyguard loitering around. None of those things bothered him.

No doubt they'd have her in some hotel room tonight with an adjoining suite to another cop. Amateur stuff. He knew he could always get to her wherever and whenever he wanted. He'd been proving he could hit anybody for more than twenty years.

He'd caught her pitiful performance on the television's noon news as he sat in a bar grabbing something to eat. Her obvious ploy of trying to bait him into showing himself was laughable. Only an idiot relinquished his cover. And he was no idiot.

Actually, when he thought about it, he knew he should be grateful to Rosalind Hart. Without her to distract him, he would have gone crazy just sitting in that lousy courtroom day after day with still no word from his employer. At least his plans for her were helping him to pass the time.

He'd follow her again tonight, find that hotel room, sneak in, and see what it felt like to put his hands around her throat. Maybe even hold her head under water for a few minutes. It was a satisfying image.

Rosalind dropped her briefcase to the floor next to her desk, fell into her chair and sank her head in her hands. She was furious.

How could she have possibly missed the discrepancy of the three tire casts being taken at the crime scene and only two of them evaluated?

Graham had made her look like an amateur. And damn it, she felt like one. And the worse part about it was she didn't know what else she may have missed. She looked at her watch. Well, she had a few hours now before going to her hotel. No better way to spend it than to go over the evidence again.

When the knock came a few minutes later, she opened the door and found herself face-to-face with a man.

"What can I do for you?"

He was young, dark, well built, and somehow familiar. Finally she recognized him from the courtroom as Daniel Morebug, Milton Morebug's son. He looked angry and nervous. "The man outside said I could see you. It's about my father."

Knowing he'd been passed by the hall security guard reassured Rosalind. She sat down, gesturing Daniel Morebug to a side chair. He took it and came straight to the point. "My father is as guilty as sin, and I can prove it."

Rosalind didn't know what she'd been expecting from Milton Morebug's son, but that certainly wasn't it. "What proof?"

Daniel Morebug got up to pace. "He and Beaver had an arrangement. My old man introduced Beaver to contacts who'd deal under the table and Beaver gave my old man a forty-percent cut of the profits. It's been going on for years. I can give you all the names. You'd be surprised who's on it."

"How does that tie in to Beaver's murder?"

Danny sat down. "That night that Beaver died. I heard him and my old man talking in the library before the card game. My old man was really mad. Beaver was reneging on his deal. My old man said if Beaver didn't give him his cut, he'd kill him.''

"You were in the house?"

"Nobody knew. Not even the old man. I needed some cash and I didn't want to broadcast my presence if you know what I mean. I hid when my old man and Beaver walked into the room. I've learned a lot listening in on his conversations."

"And you're willing to testify to what you know about your father's dealings with Beaver and what you heard that night?"

"That's why I'm here."

Rosalind didn't like looking a gift horse in the mouth, but this was sounding too good to be true. "Why didn't you come forward sooner?"

Daniel Morebug's eyes turned hard as jade. "Because I didn't know about that Dodge woman my old man had on the side. My mother's been sobbing her eyes out all day. The bastard is going to pay for hurting her! After I testify, that jury will convict him for sure!"

THE FIRST THING Rosalind did when she got to her hotel that night was to call Graham at home. Disappointed when she got his answering machine, she left her number. She said good-night to her bodyguard in the adjoining suite and settled comfortably in a chair, working on the sequence of questions she planned to ask Daniel Morebug in the morning and waiting for Graham's call.

Of course she knew Graham would fight her putting a surprise witness on the stand, but she was sure that with a lot of persistence she'd eventually get the court to accept him. At least it was something to combat the nearly mortal wound Graham had been able to give her case that afternoon.

Despite the effects, he was wonderful to watch—like a magician the way he could make evidence appear and disappear.

When the phone rang, Rosalind grabbed it eagerly, hoping to hear his strong, deep voice.

"It's Max, Roz. I've got good news."

Rosalind put down the pad in her hand, fighting her disappointment. "Don't keep me in suspense, Max. What is it?"

"I found the third tire cast."

Rosalind sighed in relief. "Thank God!"

"Give me some credit, too, Roz. And listen to this. Even though it's too late to match the cast with Morebug's tires since they've gone through an additional eleven months' wear, I was able to establish that the tire that made the track was the special size that fits his Porsche."

Rosalind felt her enthusiasm bubble. "We've got him, Max! You've virtually placed him at the scene and I've got his son ready to testify in court tomorrow about his father's shady dealings with Beaver and Beaver's tie-in to others."

Max sounded surprised. "Daniel Morebug is going to testify?"

"Yes. He came to my office this afternoon. He's out for revenge because Morebug's affair has hurt his mother. I hope he stays mad enough to get through his testimony."

"So do I. Get some beauty sleep."

Rosalind hung up the phone, switched on the radio and headed for the shower. She shed her clothes and stepped into the wet spray, feeling pleasantly invigorated as the warm water pelted her body and drowned out the sound of the music.

Would Danny Morebug be angry enough to confront his father tonight? Would Milton Morebug attempt to dissuade his son from testifying? She sighed. No point trying to second-guess what a witness was going to do.

She closed her eyes and lifted her face to the warm, pulsating stream from the shower head. Weird noises pounded in her ears as they always did when she was in a shower. Imagined sounds of a door opening. A voice. Footsteps. Tonight she refused to let them torment her. She was locked in. A policewoman was next door. She was safe. She opened her mouth and sang a watery line from the song that had begun on the radio.

Suddenly, the shower floor reverberated with the weight of a second body and a strong hand looped around her neck. Rosalind's song died in a choking gasp of instant fear.

She'd imagined many times what she would do if attacked—what evasive moves she would make. But now that it was actually happening, Rosalind found she was frozen and numb! She couldn't even move to defend herself!

"Rosalind? Rosalind?"

She heard her name being called as though from a long way off. Then the hand around her neck moved to her shoulder and turned her slowly around. When it finally penetrated that it was Graham in the shower with her, Rosalind disintegrated into his arms like jelly.

Graham reached over to turn off the water. "Rosalind? What's wrong?"

Her voice sounded breathless, unreal. "I didn't know it was you."

Graham wrapped her in his arms, tightly. "I'm so sorry. I called out saying I was here, that I'd been passed by your bodyguard. I asked if I could join you in the shower. I thought you called out that it would be wonderful."

Despite the aftermath of her shock, Graham's words still made her giggle when she realized what it was he had heard. "I was singing a song."

He took a deep breath and let it out. "I thought your voice sounded a little funny. Stupid of me not to realize the shower would drown out my arrival. Forgive me, love. I must have scared the pants off you."

She leaned her head back, recovered now, and with a twinkle in her eye. "As you might have been able to discern by now, they were already off."

He feigned a puzzled look and sent down an exploratory hand. "Why yes. Umm, nice. Can we, uh, get on with this shower?"

She wrapped her arms around his neck, her voice liquid and low, her body rubbing against him, wreaking havoc with his attempts to reach for the faucets. "Be sure to make it hot."

LEROY PONCE was surprised to find an envelope in the post office box late Monday night. He quickly tore it open. Twenty one-hundred-dollar bills fell out. The note was brief. "Kill Daniel Morebug tonight. Come by tomorrow morning after noon for the remaining forty-seven thousand."

Leroy smiled. Finally the word had come. Soon he'd have the money he needed to spring his old man. And as soon as the old battle-ax let him out, Leroy would kill her and take the money back. That would teach her to try to cheat him.

But first he'd find Daniel Morebug and kill him. These little business affairs would delay what he had planned for Rosalind Hart. But only temporarily. As soon as he got his money, she was next on his list.

FOR THE FOURTH MORNING in a row, Rosalind woke up to feel Graham's warm body beside her and a happiness deep in her soul. Being with him this way made her feel drunk with love. As she looked at his strong handsome face in sleep, she knew that the love she felt for him she could have given to no one else.

His eyes flickered open and a dazzling spray of warm gray shone her way. A sweet burst of pleasure rumbled deep inside her as she brought her lips to his. "Good morning."

He returned her kiss heartily, gazing into the sleepy warm brown of her eyes. "Good morning. And how is the second-best attorney in this bed?"

She sat up so her hands could find her hips. "My, aren't we cocky this morning. I wonder if your tune will be changing after I pull my surprise witness on you."

A small frown creased Graham's forehead. "Surprise witness?"

"I see that got your attention."

Graham watched that lovely light of challenge sparkling in her eyes and felt for a moment as though his own destiny had just been snatched from his hands. He caught his disappearing breath and shook the sensation aside. "And what's this surprise witness going to say?"

She kissed the end of his nose. "That your client is up to his muddy boots in Warren Beaver's dirty deals and that it was because Beaver reneged on Morebug's cut that Morebug killed him. As I've told you all along, Knight, you're backing a killer."

Graham gave her shoulder a squeeze. "You can't spring a surprise witness this late in the trial."

Rosalind's eyes sparkled back. "Watch me."

But as she swung her legs to the side of the bed, Graham caught them and held on tight.

"Not so fast, my limber lawyer. Who is this surprise witness, some disgruntled property owner?"

"You'll find out soon enough."

Graham took a bite out of her toe, looking delighted at her immediate and loud "Ow!"

"Why you underhanded—"

He grinned as he grabbed for her waist and held her tightly. "Could lawyer be the word you were searching for, my love?"

She smiled at the indefatigable good humor radiating out of his eyes. That was twice he had called her his love. Was he aware of what he was saying? Could it be that she would be able to convince him falling in love was not so foolish after all? Why not? She wasn't a fighter for nothing. She licked her lips. "Counselor, it's time to rise and shine."

Graham took a quick glance at the clock as he nuzzled her ear. "It's only seven. Why are you so eager to get out of bed?"

Rosalind's eyes shone mischievously into his. "What makes you think I have any intention of getting out of bed?"

Graham grinned as he shifted her body on top of him. "Come here, you wanton. I'll give you rise and shine."

Rosalind laughed happily as she wrapped her arms around him and all thoughts evaporated in the steam of their passion.

GRAHAM'S SMILE of contentment from his night and morning with Rosalind was quickly wiped off as Rosalind called a confident-looking Max Hill back to the stand as court resumed. Step-by-step Rosalind took Max Hill through his investigation into the missing tire cast and the subsequent identification of it as the same type used on his client's model of Porsche.

Graham got up reluctantly when it was time to cross-examine. "Detective Hill, how is it that this third tire cast has remained missing for nearly eleven months and all of a sudden turns up after a few hours' search?"

Max shrugged. "Simple. We didn't know it was missing all those months. But once I knew it was, thanks to Counselor's careful reading of the reports, it wasn't difficult to find it. It had slipped off a counter and was wedged against the counter and the wall in the evidence room at headquarters. When the attendant and I looked behind the counter, there it was."

Graham continued to ask questions designed to make Detective Hill's procedures look sloppy and disorganized, but Max Hill's refusal to become flustered helped to make him seem creditable to the jury. Graham finally let up. Judge Shotz called a fifteen-minute recess.

Trying to appear confident as he no commented through another throng of reporters, Graham herded Morebug into a small meeting room at the end of the hallway. He closed the door and rested against it as he looked long and hard at his client.

"Did you go after Beaver?" he asked.

Morebug's eyes darted nervously around the room. "No."

"Neither Hogg nor Wreckter were driving a Porsche that night."

"I tell you, I didn't go after Beaver. It wasn't me!" Morebug paced the floor angrily, but his hands were steady at his sides.

Graham didn't move. "Answer me yes or no. Were you in on the dirty deals that Beaver was orchestrating?"

Morebug stopped pacing. "Where did that question come from?"

"It came from me. I want to know."

Morebug's hand slashed through the air as though it was a cutting knife. "That has nothing to do with his murder!"

"Your son is ready to testify that it does. The prosecution filed a motion this morning to have him accepted as a witness. What does he know that I don't?"

At the mention of his son, Morebug's sunken cheeks billowed. "Damn! It's all because of his mother!"

Graham's voice was very quiet. "So it's true."

Morebug turned on him. "So what if we had a few deals going? I've never pretended to be a saint. Hell, he was the devil. Always talking out of both sides of his face. You'd do your part—set up the deals for him and introduce him to the right people—and then the bastard would refuse to pay up. I've never been surprised somebody killed him. I'm just surprised it took so long."

Graham sat down and motioned for Morebug to sit opposite. His client did so reluctantly. "I've never understood why you invited Beaver to sit in on the card game that night. Was it because he really was there to pay you off?"

Morebug exhaled heavily. "Yes. When Hogg arrived and saw Beaver there, I made up the excuse that he was replacing Sanders in the game. I'd arranged for Beaver to make direct contact with an Asian conglomerate that would take all the trees he could cut out of the Olympic forest. They had money to burn and Beaver had trees to sell. The official paperwork would only show half of what they were really paying and only half of the trees they were really taking. It was a multimillion-dollar deal."

"And Beaver refused to give you your share that night?"

Morebug sneered. "He tried to double-cross me just like he did everybody else. But I warned him I'd tell the Asian conglomerate he couldn't be trusted if he didn't pay me and they would have walked away from the deal. By the time I got through with Beaver, he knew he'd have to pay. That's why the bastard tried cheating me in the card game. He just had to try to grab whatever he could."

"What happened to the Asian conglomerate deal?"

"When Beaver got killed that night, the whole deal fell through. I lost a chunk of cash."

Graham sat in thought for several minutes. Then he rose slowly from his chair. "I'm putting on your character witnesses as soon as we reconvene. They should take us to lunch. After lunch I'm going to put you on the stand."

"And what in the hell am I supposed to say?"

"The truth."

Morebug's green eyes widened. "You can't be serious."

"I'm deadly serious. I want you to tell the jury all about the lumber deal with the Asian conglomerate. All about how Beaver threatened to shortchange you and what you told him. Once they know Beaver would have lost the whole deal if he didn't pay you, that will remove any motivation for you to kill Beaver. And if you get up there and say it first, then nothing your son can later say will have any effect."

Morebug exhaled heavily. "I'll be ruined."

Graham stared at his client frowning. "Would you rather be convicted of murder?"

DURING THE FIFTEEN-MINUTE recess Judge Shotz called after Detective Hill's cross-examination, Rosalind once again went out to the hallway to look for her surprise witness. Daniel Morebug was nowhere to be found. She went to the pay phones and dialed his home number. Mrs. Morebug advised her in a voice of the martyred that neither Daniel nor his father had come home the previous evening. Rosalind thanked her and hung up. She dialed her own office two floors below. The receptionist assured her no messages had come in from the younger Morebug.

Rosalind shook her head as she hung up the phone. Damn. Where was Daniel Morebug?

LEROY PONCE WAS madder than hell. Not only was his forty-seven-thousand dollars not in the post office box, but he'd also received an insulting note from his employer saying he wasn't getting it. He had killed Daniel Morebug and now his employer was trying to weasel out of giving him his money!

Leroy's hand grasped his gun. He wasn't taking this lying down. His employer thought he could get away with cheating him because he was anonymous. But he'd made a mistake. The note he'd written Leroy was on embossed stationery—very identifiable paper.

Now Leroy Ponce knew who his mysterious employer was, and he had no intention of letting him get away with stiffing him. It had all come to him on his short drive from the post office to the courthouse. He knew exactly what to do.

He was going to kill the bastard and then he was going to kill Rosalind Hart. Then he'd drive to that damn nut hospital, spring his old man and kill that damn battle-ax Ryan.

He'd kill them all.

"YOUR HONOR, the defense calls Milton Morebug to the stand," Graham said after the luncheon recess.

Rosalind's head jerked in his direction. Then she leaned toward Max Hill at her side and whispered, "I think Graham Knight just made his first mistake."

Max Hill didn't comment. He looked restless.

"What's wrong?" she asked.

Hill gestured back to the gallery. "There's not even standing room back there anymore. I don't like it. Must be the policeman in me that keeps wanting to disperse a crowd."

Rosalind turned to get a look. The courtroom spectators were indeed rubbing shoulders. And now that they had testified, Hogg and Wreckter were right there among the press and the curious.

She turned back as Milton Morebug was sworn in and her attention shifted to the witness box.

Graham approached his client with a straight step. "Mr. Morebug, did you like the deceased, Warren Beaver?"

Morebug's look and hands were steady. "No."

"Why was that?"

"Warren Beaver approached me as he had many people asking for my cooperation and promising easy money in return. He never intended to live up to his end of the deal. Later I found out that was the way the man worked."

"Then you have personal knowledge of others Beaver treated this same way?"

Morebug nodded. "You've heard the testimony of Hogg and Wreckter. There were lots more where they came from. Beaver once bragged to me that he operated on the rule that there wasn't a man he couldn't buy with the promise of easy money. Told me he'd bribed his way out of tight spots and even brushes with the law because his 'rule' continued to hold up."

Graham stepped from in front of Morebug and circled toward the jury box. "Mr. Morebug, I want to take you back to the night of January eighth of this year—"

Rosalind felt Max Hill's body turning even before she was conscious of the sense of commotion behind her. She jerked around just in time to see a short man with a full dark beard raising his hand. A flash of light shot from his hand and a roar exploded in the courtroom. Then another. Her hands grabbed for her ears. Then the next thing she knew some shadowy force from behind her knocked her down to the floor and covered her.

She couldn't see. She couldn't think. She couldn't catch her breath. She felt buried under the bulk on top of her. People screamed. More thunder roared in her ears. Blinded and deafened, Rosalind stiffened in dread and abject horror.

Chapter Fourteen

Just as the roaring echoes began to die down in her ears, Rosalind detected the wonderful, unmistakable smell of cologne as Graham's voice whispered in her ear.

"It's all right. It's all over."

As he rolled off her, for the first time Rosalind realized he had been the shadow that decked her and was now helping her get to her feet. The first thing she noticed was the smoking gun in the hand of Max Hill, his body turned toward the back of the courtroom.

She followed Hill's eyes to see the small, bearded man lying on the floor of the courtroom, a Walther 9 mm clasped in his still hand, his surprised eyes open and staring. On some level she was beginning to understand that Max had killed the man, but on another level the thought was being rejected as just too incredible.

A commotion behind her whipped her around toward the witness stand where Bailiff Roger Horn was noisily approaching with the court clerk. Milton Morebug was slumped over the edge, two holes turning red on the front of his white shirt. "He's dead," Horn screeched. A wave of unreality swarmed over Rosalind.

Graham's warm arms instantly wrapped around her and helped her into her chair. Even after she was seated, he didn't withdraw his arms but remained kneeling next to her, holding her close. When she looked over at him, he smiled; but she was taken aback by the unusual pallor of his face.

Judge Shotz began yelling orders. Things were still a bit hazy for Rosalind but she heard the small woman's voice calling to the court clerk to get the police and an ambulance and to the photographers to halt the flashes that signaled their busy picture-taking.

Max Hill walked to the back of the court and barked his own orders for the reporters and gawkers to follow the jury into the jury deliberation room until summoned for questioning. Bailiff Roger Horn helped in herding them into the room while Hill knelt over the body.

Rosalind looked up at Graham, still feeling disoriented. Time stretched and balled like bread dough. "What happened?"

Graham exhaled a trapped breath. "That bearded man Hill is leaning over suddenly stood up and began shooting. His first two shots were aimed directly at Milton Morebug. Then his gun began to arc and . . ."

When Graham didn't finish, Max Hill did so as he strode up behind them. ". . . and then Knight pushed you to the floor and covered you with his body, taking the next shot and giving me a chance to get a bead on the guy. Where are you hit, Knight?"

Rosalind's whole body jumped in reaction. "Graham! You're shot!"

Graham's arms tightened around her in reassurance as his eyes smiled into hers. "It's just a graze. Really. No cause to worry."

Graham looked up at the detective. "Who is he, Hill?"

Hill wore an interesting expression, like a light had just been turned on in his brain. He pulled his left hand from behind his back and held out a fake black beard and hairpiece. "Come over here, Rosalind. I want you to take a look."

With Graham still by her side, Rosalind approached the body. When she got close enough to see the face, recognition dawned. "It's Leroy Ponce! Must be three years ago when he was caught carrying a loaded, unregistered gun and no permit. Remember, Max? Nothing in your report turned up a legitimate means of support. I always felt in my bones that he was into far worse, but we could only get a conviction on the possession charge."

"He got out nearly six months ago," Max said. "Looks like I owe you an apology, Roz. When you suggested I look into all the guys you put away, you were right on target."

Rosalind licked dry lips. "You mean you think it was Ponce who's been waging the systematic attempt to terrorize me?"

Hill nodded. "As soon as he popped Morebug, he deliberately turned his gun on you. Bit too coincidental for another explanation, don't you think?"

A new wave of weakness washed through Rosalind's legs as she became aware of how close to death she had come. She leaned into Graham's warm body thankfully, feeling the strong, steady beat of his heart. "But why did he kill Morebug?"

Hill went down on his knee beside Ponce's body. He reached into his suit jacket for a pair of tweezers, then gently removed a folded, buff-colored paper peeking out of Ponce's pocket. Carefully he unfolded it with his metal tweezers. After a brief scrutiny, he shoved it their way. "This might explain it."

Rosalind and Graham both leaned down to read the note.

Rosalind could barely believe her eyes. "According to this letter Ponce was hired to kill Daniel Morebug. Dear God, that must be why Daniel didn't show up to testify this morning! He's been murdered. At someone's direction!"

"And I think we can be pretty sure who that someone was," Max Hill said. "Notice that this stationery is from the office of the county assessor. Remember you told me Daniel Morebug was about to give testimony that would have virtually convicted his old man? Well, it doesn't take too much detective work to figure out that Milton Morebug must have gotten wind of it and arranged to have his own son killed.''

Rosalind shook her head in disbelief. "His own son. Incredible! And then when Morebug told Ponce he wasn't getting paid, he made Ponce mad enough to kill him."

Hill carefully refolded the letter with his tweezers and slipped it back into the dead man's pocket. "Looks like hiring Ponce was just a desperate attempt Morebug used to try to keep out of the hangman's noose." He looked back over his shoulder at the dead body of Morebug, still slumped over the witness box. "I don't like closing murder investigations this way, but maybe in this case, it's better all around."

The courtroom exploded at that moment as several uniformed officers and a couple of detectives pounded through the doorway. Hill, Graham and Rosalind each gave their statements, and just as Rosalind was finishing up, a paramedic crew barged in and headed toward the body of Leroy Ponce.

Rosalind and Graham stepped to the back of the courtroom, his arms circling her again, as the medical group examined Ponce and pronounced him dead. Then they headed en masse toward the body of Milton Morebug. When Graham's voice came from beside her, Rosalind realized it had a new note to it.

"This isn't right. Morebug was about to admit to his illegal dealings with Beaver. Why would he have needed to keep his son from testifying?"

Rosalind turned to see him frowning. "But you saw the stationery. Morebug hired Ponce. Everything fits."

"No, it doesn't. Milton Morebug didn't kill Warren Beaver. And that makes the rest of this all wrong."

Rosalind shook her head. "Graham, I know Morebug was your client and I realize that you honestly believed in his innocence, but you've got to reconsider your stand on this. All the evidence points to his guilt."

Graham's shoulder had been throbbing for the last several minutes. The graze wound hurt like hell. His fear over Rosalind's close call with death wouldn't let him leave her despite the pain, so he had just gritted his teeth. But now the pain and his frustration over watching his client shot to death had begun to take their toll. His teeth were clenched when he answered her. "Then all the evidence isn't in."

Rosalind frowned as she stepped out of the warm circle of his arms. "Judge Shotz will call a mistrial. It's over."

Graham looked into her eyes and saw the gleam of a gathering fight. More than ever he delighted in finding it there, but as he fought through his pain his voice became edged in irritation. "It's not over. And you'd be able to see that too if you haven't always been so conveniently blind to the facts that—"

"I've been conveniently blind?" Rosalind almost shouted as she felt the blood rushing into her face. "A dozen Seeing-Eye dogs couldn't have dragged you to the truth!" And with that exit line, Rosalind tramped over to the investigating detective, told him she'd be in her office if needed, and then grabbed her shoulder bag and briefcase and stomped out of the courtroom without a backward glance in Graham's direction.

Graham took a step forward to follow, but the paramedics descended on him. Deciding he'd probably just make things worse if he persisted in talking to Rosalind while she was angry and he was still in pain, he gave up and removed his bloodied clothing on command, submitting to the paramedics' ministrations. If only the damn throbbing hadn't interfered with his thoughts, he wouldn't have had such an edge to his voice when he'd talked to Rosalind. And he wouldn't feel that something just out of his awareness was poking to be acknowledged.

ROSALIND FUMED all the way to her office. She knew she shouldn't have given in to her anger, but she really did want this case settled and she resented Graham's pigheaded persistence. When she reached her office, she plopped down dejectedly in her chair and rested her head back, trying to find a calm spot in her thoughts. But all she could think about was the irritable tone of Graham's voice when he accused her once more of being wrong.

Damn. She and Graham had disagreed before. Hell, they had disagreed from the first about this case. So why was she so upset over his unwillingness to just let it go now?

Because in her own mind something didn't feel right?

No. She refused to even entertain such a thought. Morebug had killed Beaver because Beaver had refused to give him his payoff and Morebug had hired Leroy Ponce to kill his own son rather than allow him to testify against him. Everything fit.

All the evidence. Graham's words came back to haunt her thoughts. Yes, the evidence pointed to that conclusion, but maybe Graham thought something was missing? How Morebug had come to know Leroy Ponce, maybe? Perhaps if she could find the tie that bound the two men together, she'd be able to convince her doubting love.

That he was her love she didn't doubt. She had always thought the idea that there was just one person you could completely and wholeheartedly give yourself to during a lifetime was just romantic wishing. But she recognized a part of her had loved Graham Knight since she first saw him in law school. And now her whole being was his for the asking. But would he ask?

A sigh as deep as her soul escaped her lips. She didn't like this uncomfortable estrangement that had so quickly walled up between them. Anything to knock it down was worth a try. She got up from her desk and threaded her way to the elevators. The receptionist, busy at the switchboard, didn't even look up when she passed.

As soon as the paramedics had cleansed and bandaged his wound, Graham thanked them and began to put his shirt and suit coat back on. With every movement he acutely felt

he missing chunk of flesh out of his shoulder. He wondered how those macho men on TV could get shot in an arm
and leg and still manage to battle the bad guys through the
final ten minutes of the film. Someone had a good imagi-
nation.

"You'll be okay but you'll need to ride with us to the
hospital so a doctor can write you a prescription for pain
pills," one of the paramedics said. "Believe me, the pain is
going to get worse before it gets better."

Graham grimaced through the act of sliding his arm into
his suit coat. Despite the promise of relief, he didn't want to
cloud his mind with pills. "No, thanks. I've got things to
do."

"You'll be sorry," a paramedic warned.

Graham admitted he probably would be and thanked the
paramedics for their ministrations. Then he dismissed them
from his mind. He felt an unfinished urgency revolving
around the very shocking and unsatisfactory events bringing the trial of Milton Morebug to an end. But first and
foremost, he wanted to find Rosalind.

They were both fighters—he knew that. But Rosalind had
never retreated before from one of their battles. That she
had this time, left him with a very uneasy feeling.

That wasn't his only uneasy feeling. The sharp and sudden terror he'd experienced when he saw the gun arcing toward her had broken down an emotional wall inside him.
He'd felt every piece crumbling as he jumped in to protect
her. Now, pouring out from behind it was all his love he'd
been bottling up, trying to deny. And all his doubts that it
might not be returned.

He was an impatient man. He had to know where he
stood with her. Now. He pushed open the courtroom door
and headed toward her office.

ROSALIND WALKED OUT of the courthouse elevators to the
first-floor homicide/assault unit. She ran into Susan Mast
just coming out of her office. The crime-scene investigator

was holding a file and appeared to be headed toward her boss's door.

"Is Max Hill around?" Rosalind asked.

Susan thumbed toward a closed door. "He's being interviewed by Internal Affairs regarding the shooting. Purely routine," Susan assured her as she brought her hand to Rosalind's shoulder. "How are you, Roz?"

Rosalind answered distractedly. "I'm okay."

Susan didn't look completely convinced. "You sure?"

Rosalind gave her a smile. "Sure."

Susan relaxed her scrutiny. "The whole office is buzzing about the courtroom thing. Word is Ponce was the guy after you?"

"Looks like it. Will you do me a favor?"

"If I can."

"I want to see if I can find any previous connection between Ponce and Milton Morebug. Max found a letter in Ponce's pocket that had been typed on Morebug's stationery at the county assessor's office. The letter talked about Morebug hiring Ponce to kill his own son."

Susan nodded. "So you think Morebug might have been supporting Ponce's harassment of you after all?"

Rosalind shrugged. "Maybe. Can we look for a connection between the two men?"

Susan nodded as she beckoned Rosalind into her office and closed the door. She put the file down on her desk and sat in front of her computer. "We'll call up Ponce's file and see what we've got."

Susan's fingers flew over the keys and Leroy Ponce's information flashed across the screen. Rosalind leaned over Susan's shoulder as Susan read the information in the file aloud.

"Mother ran off after repeated beatings by her husband when the kid was eight. Father ended up in a county facility for the criminally insane because of a vicious attack that killed a woman attendant in a rest home. No other family. No evidence of past or current means of support. That's it."

"What about Milton Morebug's file?"

Susan gave her a questioning look. "All of that should ave been in the court documents Max Hill provided along ith all the rest of his investigative materials. You must have ad through it sixty times by now."

Rosalind nodded. "So let's make it sixty-one."

Susan shrugged and pulled up the file. After several min-tes of silent reading, Rosalind straightened and shook her ead. "Nothing new. So we're at a dead end."

"On Ponce's and Morebug's file," Susan agreed. "Shall e go for Beaver's, too? Maybe Morebug met Ponce rough him."

"Good idea," Rosalind agreed.

Susan's fingers were busy with the keys when her inter-om buzzed. She finished the final strokes and leaned over press the key. Her clerk's excited voice squawked rough. "The boss says you better get your tail in his of-ce with that file right away or you'll be working both the hristmas and New Year's holidays—for the next five ears."

"I'm on my way," Susan said as she picked up the pre-iously discarded file and jumped out of her chair. She eckoned Rosalind to take her seat. "Afraid you're on your wn for a while. I'll be back as soon as I can."

Rosalind waved goodbye as Susan headed toward her oss's door. She slipped into Susan's chair and started to ead through the just emerged file of Warren Beaver.

She was surprised to learn that Beaver had been brought for questioning just two months before his death. It eemed a neighbor had seen a car hit a Mercer Island man te one night and then speed away. A description of the car nd partial license plate had matched Beaver's vehicle.

But the only item of evidence, the paint-flecked bloodied lothing of the man, had somehow gotten lost from the ev-ience room before the paint could be matched to anyone's ar. Beaver had not been detained.

Rosalind sat back in Susan's chair, feeling very uneasy. Vhy hadn't Beaver's questioning on this hit-and-run case appeared in Judson Fry's notes? Surely this information must have come up in the investigation of the case. What i Beaver had been guilty of the hit-and-run murder of tha man? Wouldn't that have opened up new suspects in his own death? Maybe the detective on the hit-and-run case could help her decide.

Rosalind paged down through the file. The investigating officer was listed as Bob West at the Mercer Island PD. She picked up the phone.

"Yeah, I remember the case real well," Bob West said. " sure thought Beaver was guilty. Shame that evidence ended up getting lost. Max Hill was pretty mad about it, too, when he took over the case."

Rosalind felt an uncomfortable jolt. "Wait a minute. Max Hill took over the case?"

"Yeah. Called and asked for it. Said he wanted to come down on Beaver hard to make a stand against drunk drivers. We were sort of busy so I said sure. Max and I go back aways. We do each other favors from time to time. Not tha that case proved much of a favor when the evidence got lost but those are the breaks."

Rosalind wasn't sure why she asked the next question. "Bob, did you have anything to do with the case of Beaver's death?"

"Sure. It was my guys who investigated the crime scene until Max pulled the strings to get it in his hands."

Rosalind swallowed uneasily. "Are you saying you didn' ask for the sheriff's help?"

"Hell, no, I didn't ask. Oh, we're always happy for all the lab and forensics stuff. But we don't get that many homicides that I'm willing to give one up—particularly one as ho as the Beaver killing. Hill owes me for stealing that."

Rosalind thanked Bob West and hung up the phone as a icy unrest slithered down her spine. This coincidence was too strong. Max Hill had been the investigator on the case of the hit-and-run murder where Warren Beaver had been the chief suspect and somehow the only piece of evidence that migh ave tied Beaver to the crime was "lost." And then Max Hill makes sure he's the detective assigned to the case of Beaver's own death where not only isn't Beaver's past record included but another piece of important evidence is "lost."

Something was very wrong. Police procedures were so tight, disappearing evidence was a very rare thing. The odds of it happening to the same detective on two cases involving the same man were just too astronomical to compute.

"Don't tell me you've decided to take a job on this side of the old legal fence," Max Hill's voice called from the door, breaking in on her thoughts.

Rosalind's eyes shot up to the man who had just become the focus of her suspicions and doubts. Too late, she tried to collect herself and control her expression. "You startled me."

Hill's eyes narrowed as he quickly closed the distance between them. "I did more than that, apparently. What have you been sticking your nose into, Roz?"

Rosalind's heartbeat raced as Hill came closer to look at the computer screen. She tried to hit the clear button, but his hand shot out and grabbed hers before she could.

A nasty quality she'd never heard before lined his words. "So, you decided to do a little investigating on your own I see? That's a real shame, Roz. A real shame."

Rosalind tried to push away, but he held her tightly.

He leaned over to flip off the screen with his other hand, his body shielding the expression on both their faces from anyone who might be looking their way, as his fingers dug painfully into her arm. "If you don't come with me now, very naturally and very quietly, I will take the gun out of my holster and shoot you and anybody else whose attention you draw. You got that straight?"

Icy daggers of fear stabbed through Rosalind's brain. She nodded numbly, unable to speak.

BUT YOU MUST have seen her," Graham protested to the le receptionist for the prosecutor's offices.

"She went into her office," the patient woman answered.

"But she's not there now. And her shoulder bag is gone. She must have come past you again. Are you sure she didn't say where she was going?"

"Mr. Knight, I handle a switchboard that is lighting up like a Christmas tree while I keep repeating this same information over and over to you. I didn't see Ms. Hart leave. I must have been otherwise occupied. Now, if you'll excuse me."

The receptionist turned to answer her calls. Graham exhaled a frustrated breath. His shoulder felt like it was on fire. But there was another urgent fire that overshadowed the pain. He must find Rosalind. Had she taken a taxi home?

ROSALIND FELT disembodied, like she was in a nightmare—space and time distorted. Her body moved through the crowded office without her even being aware of the instructions she was giving it. All she was clearly conscious of was Hill's grip on her arm and his harsh voice commanding her.

"We'll take the stairs up," he decided, opening the door with his shoulder and shoving her into the stairwell as the door slammed behind them.

Rosalind plunged forward into the railing, the bite of the metal knocking the breath from her lungs. Curiously it was the sudden pain that helped to clear the daze from her mind. She turned around to face Hill, the handsome features of his face so at odds with the man beneath.

"What's happening to you, Max? I've got to understand. Why are you doing this?"

The question was a sincere one, and Hill appeared to read it that way. "Okay. Guess it won't hurt to tell you. Start up the stairs and don't get any ideas. I'll be right behind you."

Rosalind turned and placed her hand on the cold metal banister as Hill's equally cold voice followed her slow ascent.

"Hell, you know the paltry salary we take home. It's no secret I like to live well. So sometimes I help the wealthy out of a jam. When I heard Beaver was being questioned in a hit-and-run, I got the case assigned to me and made sure the press was locked out. I told Beaver I'd get rid of the evidence for a hundred-thousand. He jumped at the offer. So the evidence disappeared. Trouble was, so did Beaver's memory."

"He refused to pay you?"

"Yeah. If I had known what the bastard was like, I would have let him take the hit-and-run rap. But it was too late. I had destroyed the evidence and the bastard knew it. Only thing left was to destroy Beaver."

Rosalind was having trouble catching her breath despite the slowness of her ascent. "Destroy Beaver?"

"It wasn't hard. I waited for him to come home that night. I ran his car off the road. I thought I might get lucky and that would finish him off. But when I got out of my car and went to look, he was staggering out of his, waving that stupid gun at me. I took it away from him. That's when he got scared and told me it wasn't his or even loaded. He swore he'd just stolen it from Morebug's place where he'd been playing cards. He said he liked to steal things. Did it all the time.

"That's when I got the idea. I slipped a few bullets in and unloaded them into his double-crossing chest. Then I convinced the brass that the sheriff's office should handle the case because it would overlap several cities.

"They weren't hard to convince. They knew it would bring headlines and they wanted them. So I got the case. It was easy to pretend to find the gun in the display case in Morebug's place the next day. After hearing about his argument with Beaver, I knew I could pin it on him. It fit in perfectly."

Rosalind began to picture Hill's words in her mind. Things were starting to make sense. "Except for that second tire cast from the shoulder?"

"That's right. I slipped up letting the information about the cast from my own tires on the report."

"It was a cast of your Porsche's tires?"

"Of course. Read right over the damn thing. When Knight called me on it, I can tell you it gave me a few bad minutes. Until I realized there wouldn't be any problem 'finding' it again. It could no longer be matched to the tread on my tire any more than it could be matched to the tread on Morebug's."

Rosalind climbed even more slowly now, playing for time and information. "Was it you who brought Leroy Ponce into all this?"

"Yeah, sorry, Roz. But you have to understand, Ponce was insurance. While doing my investigation into the Beaver case, I found out the guy had a big mouth. If he had said something to one of his cronies about me, I wanted to have Ponce around to shut them up. Ever since I had done my background check on Ponce when we got him on the possession charge, I knew he had to be a hit man. So I contacted him and kept him around just in case. Ponce never knew who he was working for."

"Then you sent him that letter on Milton Morebug's stationery to make everyone think it was Morebug who hired him?"

"Clever, huh? After you told me Daniel Morebug was going to testify about his father's deal with Beaver and how he knew a lot about Beaver's other deals, I couldn't take the chance that the father and the son might not only know but also talk about my arrangement with Beaver. I had to get rid of them both. What better way than to have Ponce do it for me?"

"By making Ponce think it was Milton Morebug who had hired him and refused to pay him. But how did you know

Ponce wouldn't just go to Morebug and demand his money?"

"Because I knew about Ponce's quirk. One of my stoolies did time with Ponce. He heard Ponce brag about how he'd killed an employer for trying to short him a thousand dollars on his payoff. Didn't say a word to the guy. Just brought out his gun and shot him through the heart. Ponce told my stoolie that cheats never got a second chance with him. I was counting on his using killing as a way to solve his problem."

Just as killing was the way you saw to resolve yours, Rosalind thought. She was having a hard time accepting the utter evil of Max's plan and how unaffected he seemed to be by the wrong he had done. She knew it would be purposeless to point it out to him. Purposeless and probably dangerous.

They had ascended to the third floor and Rosalind paused in front of the closed door leading to the ramp that joined the administration building to the courthouse. She turned back to Hill. "So you knew it was Ponce harassing me the whole time?"

Hill shook his head. "Funny thing was, I didn't. I really never connected the two. I had no idea that Ponce bore you a grudge. It wasn't until Ponce pointed that gun at you in the courtroom that I realized he had to be the one."

Hill took a step closer. "You know, I saved both Knight's and your life when I shot him."

Hill's look told Rosalind that her thanks wouldn't be inappropriate. She could feel his hot breath on her cheek.

"I've always had a thing for you, Roz. You know that. Let's see if we can't salvage something out of this. I don't want to hurt you. Oh, I killed Beaver and Ponce all right. But they were both real scum, you know that. After all, isn't that what a cop is paid to do? Rid society of its scum?"

His face was close to hers and Rosalind tried with all her discipline not to back away from this cold-blooded murderer who didn't even recognize what he was. She had to pretend to go along. She had to play for time.

"Maybe what you're saying makes sense, Max. Maybe we could reach an... understanding."

His arm went around her waist and he drew her roughly to him. Rosalind had no time to prepare her reaction. Her hands pushed him away as every inch of her recoiled in loathing. He couldn't help but feel her revulsion. The arm that had circled her in a loverlike embrace a second before, smashed her up against the door to the ramp. Her chin hit the ungiving surface, sending a shock wave of pain through her jaw. She gasped.

His voice spat hard and harsh in her ear. "You just made yourself a bed of thorns, Roz. Now you're going to lie in it."

Her voice was ragged with a fear she couldn't control. "What are you going to do?"

He grabbed her arm and twisted it behind her back. "What I have to do to keep your mouth shut."

Rosalind gasped from the pain. "If you kill me, they'll catch you."

"No they won't. You're going to die from one of Ponce's undiscovered little booby traps. A real tragedy. After I'm through planting the evidence, it will be open and shut."

Max shoved her through the doorway into the hallway. "Just remember if you draw anybody's attention, they're dead too. Now we're going to take the ramp over to the administration building and then down the stairs and across the street to the county parking lot where my car is. Now, go!"

Somehow Rosalind got her body to respond. She was walking through a living nightmare, more frightened than she'd ever been in her life. When they finally exited the administration building, she was stiff as a board. They stepped out into the pouring rain and navigated across the street to the county parking lot. With each step away from buildings and people, she knew she was coming closer to death. She came to a halt.

"I'd like to do this without pain to you, Roz, but that decision is yours. Now move it!"

Desperately Rosalind looked for something, anything she could grab to defend herself. There wasn't anything. Only a rain-drenched parking lot in front of her and a murderer behind her.

She willed her feet to move, but they refused. Then she felt him punch her in the back. She fell to the wet, oil-slicked cement, scraping her palms and knees, the breath knocked from her lungs. "Get up!" Max yelled.

Tears of pain and anger welled in her eyes. She concentrated on the anger, letting it fuel her strength. She was not going to go meekly to her death. She would die fighting.

Rosalind rose to a crouch, noting his exact position from the corner of her eye, swaying in feigned weakness. Then she quickly stretched to her full height and kicked out at him with all her might. Her foot connected in the vicinity of his groin as he let out a surprised grunt, doubling over.

Rosalind spun around and ran for all she was worth. The heavens opened up in a sudden torrent and the slick pavement stretched before her like a river of water. She bolted in a straight line through the parking lot, trying to put distance between herself and Max Hill.

Then another thought formed in her mind and she veered left, away from the parking lot toward the street of fast-moving cars. She would flag one down. She would get help.

Except suddenly her feet gave way on the slick pavement and she landed painfully on her tailbone. A night full of stars flashed before her eyes as a dazed numbing seized her limbs. Seconds passed, how many she couldn't tell. When she finally shook the stars away and gazed up through the pouring rain, Max Hill's angry wet face loomed over hers. His chest heaved as the black hole of his gun pointed at her heart.

She felt the sharp blow of his kick to her side like a knife in her ribs. She yelled in pain, but her feeble cry was drowned in the thunderous downpour. Max grabbed her arm and yanked her to her feet mercilessly as his words came out in an angry wheeze. "Now get in that car and drive or I swear I'll break every bone in your body, one by one."

Rosalind looked up to see Max's Porsche only a few steps away. The irony that she'd been running almost directly toward it in her desperate bid for freedom deepened the oppression of her defeat. She stumbled over to the car as commanded and slumped behind the wheel like a rag doll. He threw the keys onto her lap and pointed the gun at her heart. "Drive."

She was shivering from the rain. Her spine still smarted from her fall. Every breath dragged across her bruised ribs. Through eyes bleary from pain, she located the ignition and started the car. Slowly she maneuvered it across the parking lot, feeling emotionally and physically beaten.

And then she saw Graham's silver Mercedes and a spark of hope stirred in her. He was a block away on her right, traveling toward the parking lot. If he saw her, there was no reason for him to think anything was wrong. He'd probably just wave and drive by. Unless—

She stomped on the gas pedal and the Porsche's engine roared as its tires screeched out of the parking lot. Max let out an oath as he was thrown backward by the sudden acceleration. Rosalind twisted the wheel into a sharp turn onto the street knocking him against the passenger door. Rosalind shoved her foot to the floor. The car leaped forward, squealing and thundering like a hungry beast. As they tore past the silver Mercedes, Rosalind blasted the horn.

"What in the hell—" Max shouted.

Rosalind ignored him. She was looking in the rearview mirror, watching the Mercedes spin to a surprised stop.

"Look out!"

Rosalind's eyes flew back to the road. She swerved just in time to miss barreling into the back of a delivery van. The Porsche jumped the sidewalk, careened into a waste disposal bin then dove back onto the street, cutting in front of a taxi whose driver expressed his sentiments by a loud horn blast.

"Slow down or I'll shoot!" Max threatened, shoving the gun barrel to her right temple.

"Shoot and die!" Rosalind yelled back. As the tires tore over rough sections of the road, she could feel the cold black barrel scrape along her skin. Adrenaline was causing her heart to pound so fast, the beats seemed to be running together. She kept her foot to the floor knowing that speed was her weapon, that with it the man beside her didn't dare shoot.

Max swore ugly, threatening oaths. Rosalind closed her ears to his threats, keeping her focus on the road looming up so quickly in front of her. Sweat poured off her as she swerved again to avoid a car in her path and felt the jarring impact as the Porsche clipped its fender. In and out of traffic she twisted the wheel again and again. Her nerves felt like raw, scraped meat. Buildings, cars, everything she passed blurred like shadows in some nightmare.

Then she caught the flash of silver in the rearview mirror. Graham was back there! He was following!

Her joy died stillborn as she jolted in response to the deafening roar beside her. Her head jerked sideways. Max was leaning out the window. He was shooting at Graham!

"No!" Rosalind screamed. "I won't let you kill Graham!"

Rosalind jerked the wheel, directly into the path of an oncoming truck. A strange almost inhuman sound escaped from Max as he lunged savagely for the wheel.

His hands clawed at her arms. Rosalind yanked the wheel and stamped on the brake. The Porsche spun around in a left-handed skid, knocking Max back into the passenger seat, cracking his head on the window frame. The gun fell to the floor and he crumpled after it.

Rosalind gave him no thought. She had her hands full trying to control the Porsche. It was hydroplaning on the wet road, spinning like a top. She held on, silently screaming as the world spun crazily around her. Then the car smacked into a street lamp, and the steering wheel caught Rosalind in the stomach, knocking the breath from her body.

The Porsche engine heaved the plaintive sigh of a wounded animal as it came to an unsteady stop. Rosalind closed her eyes, blessing the stillness, and laid her head against the steering wheel as her whole body began to shake.

Chapter Fifteen

Graham stood behind Rosalind's chair as she completed her statement to the investigating detective. After following her heroic but horrifying drive through the streets of Seattle, and having to pry her hands off the steering wheel of that crashed Porsche, his hands were still shaking from his fear for her. He steadied them on the warm, safe reality of her shoulders.

"How is Max Hill?" Rosalind asked when her statement was finished.

The detective gave Graham a ghost of a smile before resuming his professional air. "Oh he just got a bump on the head from the accident. But it seems he, er, fell and broke his jaw while the paramedics were seeing to your injuries. He's in surgery now having it wired back in place. Don't worry. He'll be in shape to stand trial."

"Glad to hear it," Rosalind said, her fingers lightly feathering Graham's newly cut knuckles as they rested on her shoulders. "Do you need me for anything else?"

"Not at the moment. Thanks to you, we've got a whole slate of charges. As soon as the investigation is complete, we'll get him indicted. I'll keep you informed."

ROSALIND AND GRAHAM stepped out of the revolving door of the courthouse, into the rain-swept December day. She paused under one of the supporting arches. "I wish I was prosecuting Hill. I'd nail him to the wall."

Graham understood and appreciated the vehemence in her voice. "Yes. When someone sworn to uphold the law begins violating it, they ridicule us all."

Rosalind's eyes sought his face. "You must have a powerful right cross to have broken his jaw. I'm sorry I missed it."

Graham smiled as he brushed back the strands of fiery red hair that flew onto her cheeks. "After trying to kill you, he's lucky that's all I broke."

She sighed as she leaned against Graham's chest, burying her head in the folds of his coat, drinking in his scent, letting it fill her with its heady strength. "You realize of course I would have won that case if it had gone to the jury."

Graham chuckled as he kissed the tip of her obstinate nose, which was getting quite wet from the rain. "Of course I know nothing of the sort."

Rosalind's head went back, the old combative gleam in her lush brown eyes. "I guess the only way we can prove it is by having a rematch, Counselor. You ready to take me on?"

Graham's arms tightened as he felt the irresistible challenge of her. "I'm ready to take you on, Rosalind. More than ready." He leaned down to kiss the rain on her cheek and then her eyes and finally her mouth, hungrily, possessively.

Rosalind thrilled at the unrestrained need in his touch, matching it, demanding more. When they finally drew apart, his voice was low and husky. "I love you, Rosalind. I know now I've loved you since the first day I saw you."

His words showered happiness into her heart, but an enigmatic smile circled her lips as she responded. "No, not the first day, my love. Not until nine long years later."

He looked at her quizzically and she sighed. "I'll tell you all about it one day. But not today. Today I just want to concentrate on being alive and being with you."

He drew her hands into his as his eyes studied her face. 'And have you no other wishes, Rosalind?''

Her eyebrows went up in appraisal at the tentative note in his voice. "What did you have in mind?"

Graham's fingers found the hollow beneath her cheek and traced its line to the fullness of her lips. "You once told me you'd do anything for a few days of sunshine. Marry me, and I promise we'll honeymoon for the entire month of January south of the equator under a bright, hot sun."

She looked into his eyes, thrilling to the clear gray sincerity reflected there, and the hint of worry at what her answer would be.

Rosalind lifted her chin, her tone a new challenge. "I thought you didn't believe in love and marriage, Graham Knight?"

"Meeting you has taught me that it wasn't love and marriage that were wrong for me, it was the person I fell in love with and married. Darling, I can't envision a future without being married to you. We'll be partners in my firm—our firm. We'll stand together, fighting for what we believe in. Darling, say you'll marry me."

"Hart and Knight," Rosalind repeated thoughtfully, as though she was trying out the sounds.

Graham watched the gleam of mischief in her eyes, and began to realize he was being taken for a ride. He grinned as he lifted her up and twirled her around in the rain.

Rosalind hung on, a carefree laugh bubbling from deep within her. "Graham, put me down. We're both going to catch pneumonia."

"Not until you agree the firm's name will be Knight and Knight."

Rosalind laughed again. "All right. But my Knight is first. And our honeymoon will be only two weeks and we'll go to either Texas or Florida. After all, we've got to get back to this beautiful tree-lined state of ours while there are still some trees we can save."

He set her back on her feet in front of him, but didn't release his hold. "I should have realized you'd be demanding in a plea bargain."

She circled her arms around his waist, a new gleam in her eyes. "You don't know what demanding is, Counselor. Wait until the honeymoon."

Graham's gray eyes shone as warm as any sun. "For your information, Ms. Deputy Prosecutor, I don't intend to wait."

His lips sealed hers in a joyful pledge as the rain poured down, soaking them both. But it didn't matter because neither of them was noticing anymore.

Take 4 bestselling love stories FREE

Plus get a FREE surprise gift!

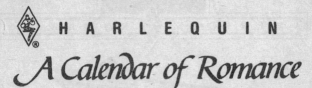

HARLEQUIN

A Calendar of Romance

Our most magical month is here! December—thirty-one days of carolers and snowmen, and thirty-one nights of hot cider and roaring fires. Come in from the cold, get cozy and cuddle with a Christmas cowboy and snuggle with a magic man. Celebrate Christmas and Hanukkah next month with American Romance's four Calendar of Romance titles:

#465
A CHRISTMAS
MARRIAGE
by Dallas Schulze

#466
A COWBOY
FOR CHRISTMAS
by Anne McAllister

#467
SWEET LIGHT
by Judith Arnold

#468
A COUNTRY
CHRISTMAS
by Jackie Weger

Make the most romantic month even more romantic!

COR12

HE CROSSED TIME FOR HER

Captain Richard Colter rode the high seas, brandished a sword and pillaged treasure ships. A swashbuckling privateer, he was a man with voracious appetites and a lust for living. And in the eighteenth century, any woman swooned at his feet for the favor of his wild passion. History had it that Captain Richard Colter went down with his ship, the *Black Cutter,* in a dazzling sea battle off the Florida coast in 1792.

Then what was he doing washed ashore on a Key West beach in 1992—alive?

MARGARET ST. GEORGE brings you an extraspecial love story this month, about an extraordinary man who would do anything for the woman he loved:

#462 THE PIRATE AND HIS LADY
by Margaret St. George

When love is meant to be, nothing can stand in its way . . . not even time.

Don't miss American Romance
#462 THE PIRATE AND HIS LADY.
It's a love story you'll never forget.

PAL-A